There was nothi[ng] say to Joe Rivers.

Talk about misjudging a [...] somebody she might care about; she'd been attracted to him, believed he was a good guy. Wrong, wrong, wrong.

When Joe ran up beside her and caught hold of her arm, she yanked away. 'Don't make me hit you, Joe.'

'What?'

She spun around. 'You heard me. If you don't cease to pester me, I'm going to land a roundhouse right smack in the centre of your sorry face.'

But it wasn't a sorry-looking face, she realized as her dark eyes clashed with his. He was probably the most handsome man she'd ever known. His black hair was mussed. His jaw was tight. And his eyes, oh Lord, his eyes were the deepest, purest blue. They penetrated straight to her soul. She longed to touch him, to collapse against his strong shoulder.

But she couldn't. Not now. Not ever.

Dear Reader,

They're rugged, they're strong and they're *wanted*! Whether sheriff, undercover cop or officer of the court, these men are trained to keep the peace, to uphold the law. But what happens when they meet the one woman who gets to know the real man *behind* the badge?

It's the LAWMAN series and this month you'll meet Joe Rivers, the test pilot turned investigator.

Though this book is about pilots, author Cassie Miles is terrified of flying, and the man in her life worked as an aerial photographer! 'I sat in the cockpit and imagined the wonderfulness of soaring into cloudless blue skies,' Cassie says, 'but then I climbed out of the plane and kissed the earth!'

Be sure you don't miss a single LAWMAN...because there's nothing sexier than the strong arms of the law!

Happy reading!

The Editors

SILHOUETTE™ ▲ Intrigue™

CASSIE MILES

Rule Breaker

All the characters in this book have no existence outside the imagination of the author, and have no relation whatsoever to anyone bearing the same name or names. They are not even distantly inspired by any individual known or unknown to the author, and all the incidents are pure invention.

Silhouette and Colophon are registered trademarks of Harlequin Books S.A., used under licence.

First published in Great Britain 1997
Silhouette Books, Eton House, 18-24 Paradise Road,
Richmond, Surrey TW9 1SR

© Kay Bergstrom 1996

ISBN 0 373 22381 1

46-9706

Printed and bound in Great Britain
by Mackays of Chatham PLC, Chatham

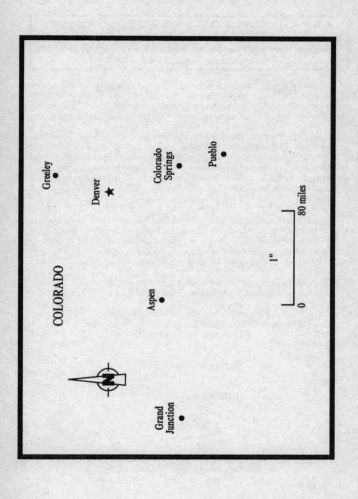

Chapter One

"If the good Lord had meant for man to walk..."

Bailey Fielding stopped herself before she snapped the annoying passenger's head off. Dealing with ignorant people always irritated her, and this young man with his blow-dried hair and three-piece suit was most certainly dumber than a fish in a bucket.

Forcing a cool smile, she looked away from him. Her gaze focused long, wide and far away, beyond the runway, beyond the terminal. She squinted into the distance, seeing the front range of the Rocky Mountains. Then, even farther. To the skies. There was her home, in the air, the only place she'd ever felt truly comfortable.

Bailey leaned proprietarily against the gleaming white body of the twin-engine de Havilland Otter turboprop, folded her arms beneath her breasts and drawled, "My grandpa Mac always used to say, 'If the good Lord had meant for men to walk, he wouldn't have invented wings.'"

"Quite obviously, Miss Fielding, you've missed my point. I don't object to flying, per se—I'm concerned about the credentials of Rocky Mountain Sky Airlines." He cleared his throat. "Are you the pilot on this flight from Denver to Aspen?"

"Copilot," she said.

He looked marginally relieved. "Don't get me wrong, miss, I have no problem with your gender. After all, I work for Congresswoman Jillian Grambling, and her stand on women's issues is quite well-known. But you look awfully young to have such a tremendous responsibility."

Though she could have told him that she was twenty-seven and had been flying airplanes with her grandfather in Mac Augustine's World War II Airshow since she was fifteen, Bailey only nodded. This self-important aide to a congresswoman wasn't worth wasting her breath.

Her glance drifted toward the hangar, where a blond woman, nearly as tall as Bailey's five feet ten inches, stepped out into the fresh April sunlight. The woman, Kate Rivers, seemed to sparkle, catching shimmering highlights in her hair and reflecting gold in her complexion. Though Kate and Bailey were dressed in a similar fashion, Kate filled out her pale blue cotton blouse in a far more eye-catching way.

When Bailey looked at her, she had to fight an unworthy pang of jealousy. Again, she recalled the wisdom of Grandpa Mac. "When the good Lord was passing out beauty," he used to tell her, "he gave you brains instead."

Plain as a prairie chicken, Bailey had straight brown hair that she wore pulled back in a ponytail and brown eyes that turned black as a starless midnight when she was angry. Her nose was stubby, and her chin had a sharp, stubborn edge. She never bothered to wear makeup anymore. What was the point? She'd never really learned to use it effectively, and it would take more than mascara to make her as pretty as Kate Rivers.

And it wasn't only Kate's physical attributes that twisted Bailey's stomach into a knot of envy. Beautiful Kate had a husband. Joe.

Though Bailey hadn't exchanged more than a few minutes' conversation with Joe Rivers, he was a man who made her heart pound as hard and fast as a piston engine. Even now, while she watched him accompany his wife from the hangar, she had to press her lips together to stifle a yearning sigh. Joe Rivers was a rangy six feet four inches tall with Apache black hair and rugged features. He always looked uncomfortable in a suit.

As Bailey watched him, Joe fidgeted with the knot on his flashy Jerry Garcia necktie. She almost laughed out loud. Who'd he think he was kidding? This man wasn't meant to reside behind a desk. Though his hair was dark, his eyes were as blue as the Colorado skies. Those were the eyes of a traveler, an adventurer, a pilot.

Bailey recognized the restless spirit within him, a drive that was similar to her own, and she ignored the ache in her belly as she watched him pull Kate into his arms and kiss her on the lips.

Forget him. Joe Rivers belonged to another woman.

She turned back to the young man who worked for the congresswoman. "There's your pilot," she said.

He beamed with satisfaction. "And what's *his* name?"

"*Her* name is Kate Rivers."

The aide to Congresswoman Grambling made a squeaky noise in the back of his throat.

"It's a good thing," Bailey said, "that you don't have a problem flying with a female pilot and copilot."

"Erk," he said.

"We'll be taking off in about forty-five minutes," she informed him. "And we'll make sure you enjoy your flight."

THOUGH THERE WERE SEATS for twenty on the twin-engine Otter turboprop, there were only eleven passengers on Sky 642 from Denver to Aspen—twelve, including Joe Rivers. Since he worked for the FAA, Joe was able to snag rides whenever there were seats available. Today, Bailey knew, he and Kate were planning a lunch date in Aspen before the return to Denver this evening.

Bailey was trying hard not to be petty and jealous. But it was difficult not to be critical as she watched Kate run through the usual preflight procedures and checks.

The last time she'd flown with Kate, which was about two weeks ago, Bailey had noticed an increasing tendency toward sloppiness in following the safety checklist. As they taxied away from the hangar and terminal, Bailey said, "Aren't you even going to check the rudder?"

"Yeah, sure." Impatiently, Kate pressed on the foot pedals. "It's not like there's going to be anything wrong, Bailey. There's never anything wrong. I've been flying this Otter for years, and she's a good, reliable girl."

"Always a first time," Bailey said.

"I checked, okay?" A frown pinched the corners of her beautiful green eyes. "Don't make such a big deal about this pilot stuff. When you get right down to it, we're nothing more than a couple of glorified taxi drivers."

Except that if they screwed up, they wouldn't get away with a dented fender. Bailey didn't say anything further. It was bad luck to talk about crashing and burning when you were in the cockpit. Instead, she flipped channels on the radio and spoke into the mike on her headset to Galloping Greta, the woman who did scheduling for Rocky Mountain Sky flights when she wasn't pursuing her avocation of marathon running. "We're ready to go, Greta."

"Hang on a sec," Greta said. "I think Claude had a message for the congresswoman."

"Great," Kate muttered. She was careful not to relay her comments through her mike. "Now we'll be late on takeoff."

"Not much choice," Bailey replied. "When the boss man speaks, we have to listen."

"Don't be so sure about that. Claude Whistler acts tough and official, but he's a pussycat."

"Can't prove it by me." Or by anybody else, Bailey thought. In starting up Rocky Mountain Sky Airlines and Charter Service, Claude had done the nearly impossible. Not only had he convinced the FAA to authorize two regular flights per day to Aspen/Grand Junction and to Pueblo/Alamosa, but he'd convinced a mob of local travel agents to use him even though they didn't fly out of Denver International Airport. Bailey thought Claude was a pretty formidable character. And she was endlessly grateful to him for giving her this job.

Into the headset mike, Kate said, "What is it, Greta? We're ready to go."

"Claude's on the phone. He'll be off in a second."

Kate gave a derisive snort. "All right, Bailey. As long as we're just sitting here, why don't you go back and check on the passengers."

"Right," Bailey grinned at her. "Any special message for your husband?"

"Yeah, tell him to prepare for a rough flight."

"Before or after we land in Aspen?"

"Both."

Bailey left her copilot chair in the cockpit to enter the cabin and make sure all the passengers were comfortable and had their seat belts fastened. Though Joe Rivers was sitting in the last row, her gaze went immediately to him. When he winked at her, Bailey pretended for a second that it was more than a friendly greeting, then she pulled herself back to reality. *He's Kate's husband.* She'd have to be some kind of idiot to fall for a man who was already taken.

In the front row was Congresswoman Jillian Grambling, a woman Bailey admired for her passion in defending the poor, the homeless and the disenfranchised. Bailey held out her hand. "I'm pleased to meet you, ma'am."

"Thank you. And how will the weather be in Aspen?"

"Today's clear and sunny with a nip in the air. About sixty-two degrees Fahrenheit. There's a stiff breeze at fourteen knots. The only snow that's left is up on the mountain for the skiers."

"I'm guessing from your accent that you're not originally from Colorado."

"No, ma'am. I was born in New Orleans and raised in Florida." Bailey glanced pointedly at the nervous aide in his three-piece suit. "That's where I learned to fly. About fourteen years ago."

The other person accompanying the congresswoman, a petite older woman, piped up. "That long ago? Sweetie, you don't look that old."

"Mother, please," the congresswoman chided.

"I'm not being insulting," her mother said. "Honestly, Jillian, you don't have to correct me all the time. Ever since your father died, you seem to think it's your job to take up the slack." She turned back to Bailey. "How old were you when you started flying?"

"I did my first solo flight in a single-engine Cessna when I was thirteen."

"My, my, imagine that. Thirteen?"

"I wasn't supposed to, of course. The FAA wouldn't approve. But there was an emergency."

A pregnant tourist had gone into labor on a remote island off the coast of southern Florida, and Grandpa Mac was passed out, dead drunk and unable to stand, much less fly an airplane. Thirteen-year-old Bailey flew into Miami and ordered a helicopter standing by to pick up the woman and shuttle her to a hospital, where she gave birth to a daughter named Sue...which was exactly what the woman did. She sued. That was when Grandpa Mac abandoned passenger charter flights and pursued his dream of the World War II Airshow full-time.

"Thirteen?" the nervous aide questioned. The strangulated "erk" again echoed in his throat. "Only thirteen?"

"Relax," the congresswoman advised. "This young woman has been flying for half her life."

"You got that right," Bailey said. "Ever since I got pushed out of the nest, I took to the wing."

She moved back to talk with the other passengers. Gradually she was working her way down the aisle to Joe. In the back of her mind, she was trying to think of something clever to say to him, and alternately chiding herself for being so foolish.

Bailey stopped beside an older couple who looked prosperous but bone weary. After advising them to fasten their seat belts, Bailey said, "On such a short flight, we don't have a hostess, but I'll be back here from time to time to make sure you have something to nibble on and to drink."

"Vodka?" the man asked.

"You listen to me, Charles Valente, no booze."

"Honey, I've got a lot of sorrows to drown."

His wife placed a gently restraining hand on his forearm. "We're going to Aspen, so you can relax. The doctor said to cut back on alcohol."

"I'm not dead yet, honey." He looked up at Bailey and offered a smile that didn't light his eyes. "I'll be looking forward to a drink later."

She stopped beside Joe and squatted down beside his seat. When she looked into his brilliant blue eyes, she forgot any attempt at wittiness. She felt a totally unwanted shiver racing up and down her spine. Good gracious, he was a handsome devil of a man.

Clearing her throat, Bailey said, "Kate says to prepare yourself for a rough flight."

"Big surprise," he said. "So, Bailey, how've you been? I haven't seen you for a while."

"Not since the hangar party." Why had she mentioned that party? It took place only a month after she had been hired, and she'd gotten in a stew with one of the other pilots who thought he was Mr. Operation Tailhook. "I've been doing well. I like working for Sky Air."

"Hey, I heard you were related to Mac Augustine."

"My grandpa," she said. "How'd you hear about Mac?"

"The man's a national treasure. He's forgotten more about turboprops than most of us will ever know."

His praise warmed her more than if he'd been talking about Bailey herself. She'd always felt that Mac was underappreciated. "I'll tell him you said that."

There was one more person at the rear of flight 642. He sat way in the back of the plane, all by himself, reading a magazine through dark sunglasses. A consciously handsome man, Bailey thought, probably a male model or an actor. Throughout the winter ski season, there had been a lot of celebrity types on the flight to Aspen. She'd never been much impressed. Her heroes were pilots, like the famous test pilot Chuck Yeager and the legendary stunt pilot Jimmy Doolittle. Bailey didn't have much use for these fancy-schmancy glamour boys.

"Excuse me," she said to her last passenger, "I'll have to ask you to buckle up your seat belt now, sir."

"Why?" He took off his sunglasses and flashed a glance that was probably supposed to be smoldering. "Are you planning to crash?"

"No, sir. But there might be turbulence in the mountains."

He spread his arms wide. "Why don't you fasten it for me?"

Bailey didn't allow her disdain to show on her face. It wouldn't do to insult the passengers, and she was willing to put up with some nonsense. Pilot jobs were few and far between, and she didn't want to blow it.

"Come on," he urged. "Buckle me down, baby."

"Oh, my," she said in her best Southern accent. "I just don't think my poor heart could take the thrill. And golly gee, I wouldn't want to be accused of sexually harassing you. Not with a congresswoman on board."

Behind her back, she heard Joe chuckle.

To the actor, she said, "Please fasten your belt."

He shrugged and snapped himself in. He muttered under his breath, and Bailey thought she heard the word *witch* or something worse.

Back in the cockpit, she discovered they had been cleared for takeoff. Kate taxied to position.

"What did Claude want?" Bailey asked.

"He just wanted to remind both of us that Jillian and Ted Grambling are among his nearest and dearest friends, and we should make nice."

Ever since Denver International Airport had gone into business, the smaller fields like this one in the southeast end of town were busier, but there still wasn't a wait of more than a few minutes.

While the nose of the Otter pointed west, Bailey felt the familiar tickle in the back of her stomach. No matter how many times she experienced aerial ascent, she was always exhilarated by leaving the earth and breaking into sky. It was a miracle, like making love, only better. Beyond gravity, she was free.

Neither of the two women talked until they reached their cruising altitude of 18,500 feet above the sea level, high enough to clear the Continental Divide. Leveling off, they swept through the ether blue toward the stunning panorama of the snowcapped Rockies. The twin engines, one on each wing, hummed efficiently.

As they left the plains behind, Kate heaved a deep, heartfelt sigh. "Bailey, what do you think of Joe?"

"I don't know him real well." She gulped. There was no way she'd admit that Joe Rivers was the central hero in a number of her own private fantasies. "He seems like a good man."

"That's what I hate about him," Kate confided.

Though she tossed her blond mane, an aura of sadness weighed heavily upon her. Her usual vivaciousness was subdued, slowed. She lifted her hands above her head and stretched before again wrapping her manicured fingers around the yoke-shaped steering wheel. Again, she sighed. Then shook her head slowly from side to side, as if to clear her mind. It was almost as if she were drugged.

"Are you all right?" Bailey asked. "You're looking a little sick."

"Sometimes," Kate said, "I think Joe's too good for me. He's forgiving and kind. But he's also too stable, too predictable. Do you know what I mean?"

Bailey could guess what she meant, but she didn't want to get involved in a marital squabble. Trying to avoid a situation, she unfastened her belt and said, "I'd better go check on our passengers, make sure they all have peanuts and drinks."

"I need adventure and challenge," Kate said. There was a catch in her voice. "I can't live like this."

Though Bailey wasn't totally unsympathetic, she couldn't understand what Kate was complaining about. She was gorgeous. She had a great job and a husband whom Bailey secretly coveted. What possible reason could Kate Rivers have for being unhappy?

"Forget the passengers for a minute," Kate said. "Talk to me, Bailey. Tell me I'm not crazy."

"Okay, five minutes. You talk. I'll fly the plane."

In her copilot's seat, Bailey took over the simple navigation and held a steady course while she listened.

"Joe's my second husband," Kate said. "We've been married for seven years. I'm turning thirty-four in August, and I probably ought to be thinking about buying a house and raising babies. But I don't want to."

"Is he pressuring you to quit and settle down?"

"Not exactly." She exhaled a genuine moan of distress, leaned back in her seat and closed her eyes. "When we were first married, he was a test pilot, and those guys are so sexy. Top gun, and all that. Now that he's behind a desk at the FAA, he's different."

Being careful not to betray her hopes, Bailey asked, "Are you thinking of dumping him?"

"I don't know. Something's happened. I don't want to, but maybe... maybe a separation."

Deep inside, Bailey groaned. A separation, huh? That way, Joe wasn't really free, but Kate had a chance to play around. Talk about having your cake and eating it, too. "You know, Kate, this is none of my business. I ought to get back there and see that everybody has their honey-roasted peanuts."

"Listen to me." Harsh desperation edged her voice. "Bailey, please. You're a woman. You've got to know what I'm going through."

Bailey shrugged. It was hard to be consoling, even when a sob delicately shuddered across Kate's shoulders.

"What should I do?" Kate demanded.

"Well, now," Bailey drawled. "Much as I hate to stick my nose where it doesn't belong, it seems to me like there's only one really solid reason why a woman and a man stay together. Do you love him?"

"Love. Do I love him?" Kate's voice was low, nearly drowned out by the hum of the twin propeller engines. "I don't want to lose him, but I can't be with him. Not all the time, every day for the rest of my life. God, I don't know what to do."

Neither did Bailey, but Kate's outpouring of emotion was beginning to worry her from a strictly safety angle. Kate's hands were shaking. Her breathing was ragged. When she closed her eyes and leaned back against her seat, Bailey had the impression that Kate shouldn't be piloting a paddleboat today, much less an airplane.

Using the dual controls in the copilot seat, Bailey trimmed the rudder, keeping the Otter on course. She was grateful that it was a fairly clear day without much chance of turbulence above the occasional fluffy cumulus cloud. This flight should be a piece of cake.

Still, Bailey was concerned enough that she made a bid to take the controls. "Tell you what, Kate, you're having a rough day here. Why don't you settle back and nap? This is a quick hop, I'll take care of it."

Kate snapped suddenly awake. "You'd like that, wouldn't you?"

"Sure, I would," Bailey said, casually. "I always like flying."

"That's not what we're talking about here. You're telling me I can't do my job. Aren't you?"

"No insult intended."

"The hell there isn't! I know what you're doing, Bailey. You take over the controls, then you report me to Claude for not doing my job."

"Keep your voice down." There was only a curtain separating them from the passengers. Though the people in the cabin couldn't hear their conversation over the engine, they would sure as heck know something was wrong if they were shouting at each other. "I would never report you, Kate. We're both women pilots, and the last thing I want is to give the men the satisfaction of saying that you were heavy into PMS and couldn't fly the plane."

Kate turned to her. Her big green eyes were filled with rage and pain. And something more. The pupils were dilated, unfocused, wavering. "I don't know why I expected you to understand. You're little miss pilot, aren't you? You don't have a life outside the sky."

"Back off."

"All I want from you is an opinion. Should I dump Joe?"

Bailey wanted to shout yes! With Kate out of the picture, she might have a chance. Here was a silver-platter opportunity to shove Kate aside and slide herself into Joe's waiting arms.

But Bailey hadn't ever been able to manage the manipulative games that some women played with such cleverness. Probably because she'd been brought up by Grandpa Mac, she'd never learned feminine wiles. She blurted, "Here's my opinion, Kate. Your husband is a handsome son of a gun. More than that, he's got something special to him. A spirit, a fire in his belly. If you divorced him, I'd go after him like a hound dog on a possum."

"You have the hots for Joe?" Kate's beautiful mouth curved in an ugly sneer. "Oh, Bailey, that's rich. You're not his type at all."

Her words stung like a slap across Bailey's face. Truth hurts, she thought. She wasn't Joe's type. Sometimes, it seemed that she wasn't anybody's type. Bailey unfastened her seat belt. "Take the controls, Kate. I'm going to see the passengers."

Before she could slip through the curtains that separated the cockpit from the cabin, Kate grabbed her arm. Her fingernails pinched hard. "You don't know what it's like to be me, Bailey."

"That's for doggoned sure, lady. And I don't want to know."

As she stepped into the rear cabin, Bailey suppressed a twinge of guilt. Probably, she should have pressured Kate into giving up the controls, should have insisted. Kate really did look as if she was sick or something.

Oh, heck, she'd be fine, just fine. Kate could manage the Otter. She was just having a bad day.

Of course, that wasn't a detail Bailey would share with the passengers. People liked to think that pilots were totally cool and without emotion. Never panicky. Never in mourning. Never depressed.

Though Bailey served packaged nuts and handed out drinks, including a vodka for Charles Valente, with a cheerful, upbeat manner, Joe's blue eyes shot a questioning glance in her direction. Had he sensed something? Did he know that his wife was planning to hit him with a separation? That must have been what Kate meant when she referred to a rough flight.

Quickly, Bailey looked away from him. A marital squabble wasn't any of her affair. All she needed to think about was the safety of the aircraft. Was Kate really depressed? Was she overdramatizing? Was her ability to fly impaired?

They hadn't flown together often enough for Bailey to have a clear idea of Kate's attitudes. Usually, the schedule avoided having both female pilot and copilot. They were the only two women who worked for Rocky Mountain Sky Air, and too many passengers had the same reaction as the nervous congressional aide.

The last thing Bailey wanted was an incident while they were both flying. She'd gone through hell to get this job. Even though she'd been flying since she was a kid, even though she'd passed all the certification procedures with high scores, there just weren't enough pilot jobs to go around. If Bailey got fired at Sky Air, it was unlikely she'd ever fly commercial again. She'd be stuck doing the twice-a-year shows for Mac Augustine's World War II Airshow, dressing up like a kamikaze pilot and zooming around in a detailed replica of a Japanese Zero. She needed more than that. She needed to fly at least twice a week. Twice a day would be better.

She'd just finished serving the handsome actor guy in the back of the plane when she felt a hard bump and had to grab the edge of his seat to keep from sprawling flat on her face.

"What was that?" he demanded. The coy joking was gone from his attitude.

"A little turbulence," she replied.

"The hell it is." He stared through the porthole window. "Something's wrong. The propeller isn't turning."

Joe was standing right beside her. "He's right, Bailey. That's a stall on the right engine."

"We'll handle it," she said. "You gentlemen sit back down."

The Otter wavered dangerously, tilting back and forth like a canoe on storm-tossed high seas. Bailey hurried up the narrow aisle to the cockpit. "Nothing to worry about, folks. Stay in your seats. Keep your seat belts fastened."

In the cockpit, Kate shook her head and blinked furiously at the multitude of dials and switches as if she'd never seen them before.

"What happened?" Bailey demanded.

The beautiful face was wild-eyed, frightened. Intensely, she whispered, "Oh, my god, I don't want to die."

Bailey strapped herself in. The warning lights and instruments told her one story, but years of flying and working on planes gave her the truth. "We're losing manifold pressure. One engine's out. No problem. We can bring it in. Where are we?"

"I'm off course. Wasn't paying attention."

"We've lost altitude," Bailey said. The horizon was much too low.

Kate jerked back on the yoke and brought the nose up. The sudden angle was too steep.

"Not like that," Bailey said. She kept her voice calm, but her heart was beating in double time. From her co-pilot seat, Bailey tried to even them out, but she was fighting Kate's controls. If they kept this up, they'd stall the other engine for sure. "Kate, give me the stick. We can still make it to Aspen."

"I'm the pilot. This is my plane."

Kate shook her head as if trying to clear it. Her feet on the rudder induced a rocking motion, like a baby's cradle. *And when the bough breaks* . . .

Once again, Kate yanked up.

The Otter made a ragged ascent, wobbling like a bird with a broken wing.

"Damn you, Kate. Let me take it!"

Sobbing, Kate obeyed. She folded her arms beneath her breasts, pulled her feet away from the pedals.

Now Bailey was flying the Otter. Within seconds, she pushed the rudder hard to the left and cranked the yoke. The plane stabilized. But the damage had been done. The one operating engine coughed and sputtered. They were still losing power as if the plane were fuel starved.

Bailey spoke into her headset. "Mayday, Mayday. This is November Six Four Two Sierra Alfa. We've lost the starboard engine and might need to make a landing. Anybody down there hear me?"

She scanned the mountainous landscape below them. She had copiloted this route often enough to know that they were way off course. There was nothing resembling an airfield in sight. She never should have left Kate up here alone.

"Mayday, Mayday. I need assistance."

Nothing but static on the headset answered her plea.

The pressure dial indicated they were losing more power. Bailey could only hope that the fuel in the wing tanks was draining, that they wouldn't explode upon landing.

"Kate, I need to bring it down. We're losing the other engine. We've got to land."

"That's my job. I'm the pilot. I can do it." Kate's hands grasped the yoke with a shivering, hysterical strength. "I've got to make it. For my baby."

Her baby? What on God's green earth was she talking about? "Kate, you're not well. Let me land."

"I'm six weeks' pregnant!" She was shouting now, but it didn't matter. From the cabin behind them, Bailey could hear the passengers yelling and crying.

"Calm down, Kate. You settle back and—"

"I don't want a baby. It was a mistake! I've been on antidepressants. Oh, God, I pray my baby isn't deformed."

As the Otter bucked and lurched, Bailey held on tight. She had to take the controls away from Kate, whose face was ashen and eyes were wavering. "Kate, you can't handle this."

"Shut up, Bailey. I'm the pilot here. I can do it."

But she pointed the nose downward.

Bailey could feel the beginning of a spiral roll. A crash descent. She drew back her fist and jabbed at Kate's perfect jaw. One punch and the pilot was out cold.

Bailey had the controls. Using every bit of her skill, she eased them out of the spin. They were flying low, barely four hundred feet above the floor of a valley with rugged peaks rising up on either side, cutting off radio transmission. The ground winds in the mountains swooped in treacherous downdrafts. She tried to take it up, but the Otter was losing power. The left engine cut out, then started again. She had to land. Had to find an open space.

A mountain field would be a disaster, full of ruts and holes that would catch the landing gear and jerk them to a sudden halt before the momentum was gone. The plane would break apart. But there wasn't any choice.

The Otter didn't have enough lift to make it over the next ridge.

Bailey sighted in on a long field of hay and prepared for landing. But something was wrong! Her instrument panel was blinking!

Fighting the wind, flying on sheer instinct, Bailey knew what she had to do—glide the plane in without hitting any rocks. She'd made that kind of landing before, but that was in Florida on water, not on hard, unforgiving earth, where the fuel tanks could scrape on rock and explode in a fireball. Oh, sweet Lord, she didn't want to die.

Determined, Bailey sighted in on a field of tall grass. The tortured whine of the engine went dead. She cut the power. Behind her, in the cabin, the passengers screamed. And, silently, Bailey begged for their forgiveness.

She forgot all the proper procedures she'd been taught in flight school and reverted to the lessons of her youth, when she and Grandpa Mac had made a living in ancient planes held together by baling wire and duct tape. Her instincts took over, determining the distances, feathering her touch.

The ground was coming up fast.

She hauled back on the yoke, keeping the the nose up as she felt the earth beneath the landing gear. There was a huge rock in front of them. No steering. No brakes. Bailey yanked back. The plane bounced. She could feel the gear break away. On their belly, they careered toward a wall of pine trees. The plane was breaking up. There was a jolt that threw her forward in her seat belt. They slammed to a halt.

They weren't dead.

Bailey grabbed Kate's shoulder and shook. "Wake up! Come on, Kate. You've got to get out of here before we explode."

The passengers!

Bailey fought her way free of her seat belt and charged back into the cabin. They'd lost the tail section, but the Otter was otherwise in one piece. She fought with the hatch, flinging it open. "Everyone out. Now!"

Dazed, frightened eyes stared back at her.

Then Joe took over. His voice was urgent. "Now, ladies and gentlemen. Now! Get through that door fast and run like hell."

They didn't need more instruction. The Otter emptied its belly fast. Bailey heard a piercing wail from the woman who had been concerned abut her husband's drinking. "He's had a heart attack," she shrieked. "Help me! Charles, wake up! He's dying."

Behind her, Bailey saw the actor type. He was slumped on the floor, unconscious. In the front of the plane, the congresswoman struggled to assist her mother, who couldn't seem to rise from her seat.

"Help me," Jillian Grambling shouted.

"Joe!" Bailey called to him.

He turned away from the hatch door, where he was urging passengers out of the plane. "What, Bailey?"

She pointed at the actor.

"I've got him," Joe responded, moving swiftly to the rear.

The actor must have been out of his seat when they'd landed. He was bleeding profusely from a gash on his forehead.

Joe hoisted him over his shoulder, fireman style, and carried him off the plane.

Bailey went to the congresswoman. There couldn't be more than a few seconds left. They were lucky that the tanks hadn't exploded upon impact. No time to waste.

The woman at the rear had her husband on his feet. He doubled over in pain, grabbing at his chest.

The congresswoman sobbed, "Please, help me. I think my mother's ankle is broken."

Bailey unfastened the seat belt of the tiny gray-haired woman. "Congresswoman, you get out. I'll take care of your mother."

"I won't leave her."

"You go," the elderly woman said.

There wasn't time for discussion. Bailey managed to lift the woman. "Don't put your weight on that leg."

"Tell my daughter to get out."

"Come on, let's go."

Bailey got her to the hatch. With Joe's assistance, she helped the older woman down the few stairs. There was a smell in the air of heat, of impending explosion.

She saw the actor, groaning on the ground. Too close. He was too close. They still weren't clear of the plane. Bailey had to get back inside. There was still the man with the heart attack. And his wife.

And Kate, unconscious at the controls. Bailey had to go back and rescue the pilot.

The explosion hit.

A red inferno blinded Bailey and seared away the tears. She felt an intense pain. Then she felt nothing at all.

Chapter Two

After two months' recuperation in Florida, her burns and bruises had pretty much healed. Bailey's physical injuries could be cured, leaving only a few scars that would fade with time and be forgotten. But her guilt was an open wound, a pain that would be with her forever.

She was startled awake in the long hour before dawn. Her breath rasped in her throat. The nightmare! Again! Awake or asleep, she would never forget the instant of silence when the engine on the Otter died, and they passed the point of no return.

In her nightmare, she was surrounded by a sky of purest blue that darkened, then flared into hellish orange, pressing down upon her with tremendous force.

Bailey groaned, covered her eyes with her hands, trying to hold back the wrenching agony. Even when she wasn't thinking about the crash, her ears echoed with the screams of the survivors. Always, at the edge of her vision, she saw a burning mountainside with hot flames like fingers that clawed deep slashes into her vulnerable soul.

This constant panic had to end. She needed to get on with her life. But how could she?

Bailey crept from her bed in the secluded, two-bedroom house on the Gulf Coast of Florida's panhandle. Through the closed door of his bedroom, she heard Grandpa Mac snoring like a chain saw, and she smiled. Mac Augustine, the eccentric World War II flying ace, was the one bright spot in this tragedy. He'd been diligent in caring for her, had even put aside his whiskey bottle in order to devote himself one hundred percent to Bailey.

Without him, she wasn't sure that she could have found the strength to go on. Five people on Rocky Mountain Sky Airlines 642 had died. Their epitaphs were engraved in Bailey's heart.

Congresswoman Jillian Grambling had been mourned by her colleagues and supporters in the nation's capital. Ironically, this woman who had supported firearm-control regulations was given a twenty-one-gun salute at her burial service. A special election had been held, and her term in the House of Representatives would be completed by her attorney husband, Ted Grambling.

Jillian's mother, Eleanor Pearl Gordon, was buried beside her husband in Denver.

The older couple, Charles and Dee Valente, were survived by a grown daughter who had not wished to take over the family business and had left the disbursement of her parents' estate to the attorneys. There had been a large insurance settlement.

The fifth person who had died was Kate Rivers.

Jillian. Eleanor. Charles. Dee. Kate.

Five people. Five human lives. All had perished. None would be forgotten.

It wasn't Bailey's fault. That was what Grandpa Mac said. Over and over, he told her that she wasn't to blame.

Grandpa Mac had taken her to grief counselors, old buddies of his from the Veterans' Administration, and they had talked about posttraumatic stress disorder, flashbacks and survivor's guilt.

Nice labels, Bailey thought. But the words didn't make her feel one whit better. Her parents had both been killed in a car accident when she was eight, and—as a child—she'd always treasured the hope that someday they'd come back. She'd wanted to believe that death was a game like hide-and-seek. One day, it would end, and her parents would be whole and well and happy.

As an adult, she knew better. Dead was dead. There were no second chances. She wasn't going to look up and see Kate striding through the door with a confident smile on her lips.

Nor was Bailey relieved when the preliminary FAA investigation indicated mechanical failure as the cause for the crash. The Otter's logs, detailing maintenance and repair, were completely in order. The problem with the fuel flow was just something that happened, an unforeseeable failure of the equipment.

Far from being blamed, Bailey was hailed as a heroine. Testimony from the passengers who survived cited her skillful landing and her action in getting most of them free from the plane before the wing tanks exploded.

Though the praise for her was almost unanimous, Joe Rivers had said nothing. He gave his statement for the FAA. To Bailey, he spoke not a word, and his silence was an accusation.

Since the crash, Bailey had only seen him once face-to-face. It was when she'd been in the hospital, sleeping in tortured fits, floating in and out of consciousness.

The memory was sharp as a knife blade. She had wakened to Joe standing beside her bed, looking down at her. A sling held his left arm tight to his body. There was a small scratch on his cheek. An ocean of misery reflected in the blue of his eyes, but he held back the wash of tears. His gaze hardened. The fingers on his right hand clenched on the rail of her hospital bed, holding so hard that his knuckles went white.

He had spoken in a whisper. "I need to know the truth," he'd said. "How did it happen, Bailey? How did my wife die?"

Bailey would take that truth to the grave. She could never tell Joe that Kate's death was her fault, that she'd knocked Kate unconscious and left her, strapped into her seat, unable to escape.

During the FAA investigations, she had testified that Kate wasn't feeling well. Therefore, Bailey had taken over the controls and performed the crash landing.

And why, the investigators asked, hadn't Kate left the cockpit? Why hadn't she escaped the explosion?

Bailey had said that Kate was unconscious and wouldn't wake up when she shook her.

The FAA investigators probed. How had Kate lost consciousness? Was the windshield broken? They asked about visible injuries, about damage to the cockpit.

Bailey had lied. She said she didn't know why Kate passed out.

The lie would haunt her forever. The lie negated the FAA citations for heroism. The lie made it impossible for her to refute the accusations of those who doubted her.

There were two.

The handsome actor, whose name was Ross O'Shea, was suing the airline and Bailey, as well, for his debilitating injuries that supposedly caused him to lose out on an important role—though his survival in the highly publicized crash made him a favorite on the talk-show circuit.

And the congresswoman's aide, Martin Harvey-Barr, said that Bailey could have done more.

They were right, she thought as she went through the motions of grinding coffee beans and brewing the first pot of the day. She could have done more. Five people had died in a horrible inferno. Bailey should have found a way to save them.

Sunrise peeked through the window above the sink, and Bailey closed her eyes against the rising scarlet of the sky. Why should she be allowed to marvel at another dawn?

In her mind, she saw Kate Rivers, strapped in her seat belt in the cockpit and unconscious. The fire surrounded her, burning in her shining blond hair, charring her peaches-and-cream complexion. There had been nothing left to bury.

"Forgive me," Bailey whispered. "Oh, God, forgive me."

Taking her coffee cup, Bailey went outside to the long, wide runway surrounded by lush Florida foliage and palm trees. At the end of the tarmac were two ramshackle hangars where Grandpa Mac kept his World War II replica airplanes.

Bailey walked slowly, trying not to favor her left leg. Though she couldn't remember the few seconds before the plane went up in flames, she must have been standing when the full force hit her. The witnesses said she'd been flung through the air. Her ankle had been badly sprained. Her forearms had been singed, but her face and body were spared, except for a deep scar that snaked down the right side of her back, from her shoulder to her waist.

At the end of the airstrip, with her back to the planes, Bailey lowered herself on creaking joints and sat cross-legged, contemplating the skies. A wide-winged gull dipped and glided across the gold-and-pink dawn. A second bird joined the first, performing aerial acrobatics that were magnificent in their simplicity.

Bailey yearned toward the heavens, wished to spread her arms and gather a piece of wind that would breathe new life into her body. She longed to soar, to return to the air, the only place she'd ever felt at home.

But now, everything was different.

She was afraid. The thrill, the anticipation, was gone. The skies were her enemy. The crash of Sky Air 642 had exiled her to earth.

Logically, she knew that she had to fly again. Grandpa Mac had been after her every day this week, urging her to try out his latest acquisition—a totally refurbished, single-engine, World War II Spitfire with a Rolls-Royce engine.

Bailey couldn't do it. She'd gone so far as to climb into the one-person cockpit and taxi the Spitfire onto the end of the runway. And there she sat, trembling with terror, drenched in sweat. She couldn't bring herself to take off.

But she had to do it. She was scheduled to return to work at Rocky Mountain Sky Air in five days.

"Damn." She wasn't ready. Not yet. Maybe never. This wasn't like hopping back onto your bicycle after you'd lost your balance and fallen off. Five people had died. Bailey had no right to pilot an airplane again.

She saw a car parked at the end of the runway. The driver's-side door opened, and a man stepped out. He stretched and yawned, then reached back into the car and retrieved his suit jacket, which he shrugged into. He flexed his shoulders, tugged at the seams, then fiddled around with the Windsor knot on his necktie. He combed his fingers through his thick black hair.

As he walked toward her, his silhouette against the sky became more clear. His stride was long. His movements purposeful and direct. Bailey thought she must still be dreaming, at the edge of a nightmare.

The man who approached was Joe Rivers.

She felt that she ought to be standing when she faced him, but her legs felt impossibly weak. How he must despise her! Bailey had been responsible for his beautiful wife's death.

When he was near enough for her to discern his features, she saw the hard glitter of his ice blue eyes. No trace of an acknowledging smile touched his lips. In one hand, he carried a briefcase. The other arm swung stiffly at his side. His fingers curled into a fist.

She could read his intention clearly. He was coming for her like an executioner. He was here to accuse her.

Resistance fired within her like a jet burner. She couldn't sit here on the runway, cowering before him like a pathetic and helpless little girl. Summoning up the shreds of her confidence like a limp and tattered banner, she forced herself to stand.

"Hi, Joe."

"Bailey." He nodded. "I understand that you haven't been flying."

"That is correct."

"Good." He stopped four feet away from her, as if he couldn't abide coming any closer. "Do you intend to pilot a plane again?"

Bailey lifted her chin. "Yes."

"Private plane?"

A decision snapped through her. "I intend to return to my job at Sky Air in five days."

"Don't pack your bags just yet." His challenge was clear and harsh.

"What do you mean, Joe? Have you got a problem with me going back to work?"

"I want the truth," he said. "And I'll keep you grounded until I get it."

"I've been cleared, Joe."

"Not until the investigation is over. As you know, Bailey, I work for the FAA. I've asked to be assigned to the ongoing investigation of the crash of Sky Air 642."

She was shocked by this revelation. Though she knew Joe worked as a sky cop for the FAA, it seemed highly irregular to assign the husband of a victim to look into the cause of a crash. Plus, she'd thought the cause of the crash had been officially determined: mechanical failure.

"I have questions." His words ground out, harsh as a rasp against steel. He cleared his throat. "I'm here to take your statement."

"I ALREADY DID my talking," Bailey said. "Weeks ago."

"I've listened to the tape." Joe had played it over and over, endlessly repeating her words, trying to find the answer. "There were details missing. I need to hear it from you, from your mouth."

"Should I have an attorney present?"

"If you need one, yes."

She glared up at him. Her eyes were black as charcoal, sullen as slowly burning embers.

He remembered that anger. Once before, he'd seen evidence of her hot temper. The first time he'd met Bailey Fielding was at a Sky Air hangar party at the airfield. One of the guys had been teasing her, and she'd flared up at him like a rocket taking off for the moon. Without using one word of profanity, she'd read him up one side and down the other, called him a low-life, skunk-tailed son of a river rat. She had been so consumed by her outrage that she hadn't even noticed that the entire party had come to a halt while everyone stood and listened to her fiery, Southern-accented speech. When she stopped, she looked around, embarrassed, and had flushed a bright crimson.

At the time, Joe remembered, he and Kate had laughed about the incident. Bailey Fielding was a character—a tall, wiry woman with angular arms and incredibly long legs. Her long, straight hair was always skimmed back in a no-nonsense ponytail. Though Kate had been disdainful of Bailey's lack of femininity, Joe thought she looked exactly like a female pilot should look. No matter how clumsy she was in her personal life, there was an unshakable confidence in her manner.

If she'd been flying with anyone but his wife, Joe would have assumed that Bailey had acted properly in the crash. He couldn't have done better himself in landing the stalled Otter. But something had happened in that cockpit. Something that caused Kate to fly way off course. Something that caused the dips and dives that lost precious feet of altitude after the initial stall of the starboard engine.

Joe needed to know how and why. Was the crash Kate's fault? Had she screwed up? Joe was well aware that the investigators had given his wife every benefit of the doubt. But he wanted to know the truth.

"Come with me," she said. "If you're going to ask me questions, we might as well go inside and sit down."

When she turned away from him, her shoulders were stiff with tension. She wore a sleeveless, long-tailed shirt and baggy shorts. Though she walked slowly, there was a halt in her step.

Instinctively, he found himself admiring the long legs and slender, lanky body of Bailey Fielding. He felt a strange stirring, a warmth. Joe pulled his eyes away. He didn't want to start liking her.

At the wood-frame beach house, they were greeted by a tall, silver-haired man with an eagle beak of a nose. He wore the most god-awful Hawaiian patterned shirt that Joe had ever seen.

"This is my grandfather," Bailey said. "Mac Augustine, this is Joe Rivers with the FAA."

The old man shook his hand with an iron grip. His eyes, dark as Bailey's, bored into Joe's. "What the hell are you doing here, son?"

"I'm an FAA investigator."

"An investigator? I thought this case was closed."

"We don't have all the answers. The file stays open until we fill in all the blanks."

"Why are you bothering Bailey?" Mac bristled, ready to defend his granddaughter. "She's a damn sight better pilot than anyone else I know, and I've known them all. Been flying since the forties."

"Yes, sir. I'm familiar with Mac Augustine's Airshow. And your reputation, sir."

That appeased the man enough that he stepped aside and allowed them to enter the kitchen. "Joe Rivers, huh? You a pilot?"

"Yes, sir," Joe said. "I flew for the navy. On a carrier."

"One of those top-gun pretty boys," Mac said with a chuckle. "You got so much computerized junk on those planes that you can't even feel the air. Not like the old days. Flying on a wing and a prayer. That's when being a pilot was something to be proud of."

Bailey placed a mug of coffee in front of him and turned to Joe. "Cream and sugar?"

"Black."

Mac Augustine continued, "My little Bailey here took to the air like a bird. I raised her from the time she was eight, and this girl was flying by the time she was eleven. Solo at thirteen. A mighty fine little wing walker, too." He leaned toward Joe. "I don't suppose an official hotshot like yourself knows what a wing walker is."

Joe knew he was being put in his place by the old man.

"A wing walker," Mac continued, "is somebody who goes out on the wing, usually a fearless lady in a skimpy bathing suit, and she stands on the wing of the plane, hooked on by a couple of wires, while the pilot does rolls and dives and corkscrews. Takes guts."

"And safety regulations," Joe reminded him. "The FAA has rules. Even for stunt pilots."

"Regulations? Rules?" Mac Augustine slugged back his coffee, wiped his mouth with the back of his hand

and beamed at his granddaughter. "Tell this fed what we think of his regs."

"They're necessary," Bailey said.

Joe couldn't be sure, but he thought she kicked Mac under the table before she continued in a serious tone, "There's a time and place for aerial stunts, and it's not while you're working for a commercial airline."

"I suppose so," Mac muttered.

"Or a charter," she said.

Mac rose to his feet and hefted his mug. "I'll leave you two alone to talk about all the rules that take the fun out of life. See you around, Rivers."

Joe rose. "A pleasure to meet you, sir."

"No, it's not. I appreciate your respect, son. But I know I'm a winged dinosaur. One of an almost extinct breed who has a hard time making way for you fast-flying whiz kids." He lumbered toward the door. His parting glance was calm and somehow powerful. "We sure had a fine time, though. We owned the sky, from the ozone to the horizon. A fine time."

Joe couldn't help grinning as he watched the old flying ace in his ridiculous Hawaiian shirt heading out the door. No wonder Bailey was a character. This was the stock from which she had sprung.

Her attitude was all business. "What are your questions, Joe?"

He flipped open his briefcase, consulting notes that he'd gone over so many times that they were committed to memory. "According to the surviving passengers and you, the first jolt came while you were in the cabin and Kate was alone in the cockpit."

"Correct." She frowned at him. "Joe, you were there. Don't you remember?"

"Just answer my questions."

"Okay." Her fingers tightened around the coffee mug. "But it seems to me like you're playing games."

"Why were you out of your copilot's chair?"

"In flight, the Otter only requires one pilot," she said. "The copilot is recommended for takeoff and landing. During the rest of the flight, it was one of my duties to see to the comfort of the passengers."

"No hostess?"

"Not on an Otter. There's only room for twenty passengers, max." Exasperation was evident in her voice. "You know that, Joe. It's not required. Why are you really here?"

"This is my job."

"Is it?"

"I don't have to answer to you, Bailey. It's my job to protect the public safety. If I determine that you're a danger to yourself or to others—"

"A danger?" She set down her mug so hard that the dark liquid sloshed over the rim and spilled on the kitchen table. "Let me tell you about danger, Joe Rivers. Harassing me is going to be real hazardous to your continued well-being."

"In your opinion, Bailey, could the crash have been averted if you had remained in your copilot chair?"

"According to the FAA investigation, the crash was due to mechanical failure. We lost pressure. The right engine stalled, then malfunctioned entirely."

"That's not what I asked," he said. "If you had stayed in the cockpit, could you have averted the crash?"

"I don't know." She smoothed the thick hair at her temple back into the ponytail at the nape of her neck. "I wasn't in the cockpit, but I assume that Kate did everything that could be done."

"The Otter was off course. When did that happen?"

"I don't know. When I returned to the cockpit, I realized we had drifted to the north. It wasn't really a big deal. It could have been easily corrected if the plane had been functioning properly."

He studied her carefully. There was really only one question he was burning to ask, only one pain-filled query. But Joe bided his time, building slowly, asking her to repeat every procedure along the way. Her account of the incident was exactly the same as it had been several weeks ago.

According to Bailey, she'd returned to the cockpit, discovered that one engine was already gone. The plane was beginning to roll. Kate turned the controls over to Bailey.

"Why?" he demanded. In listening to the tapes, he knew that this was the point when Bailey's account faltered. "Kate was proud of her ability as a pilot. Why would she relinquish the controls to you?"

"She wasn't feeling well."

Joe noticed a flicker at the corner of her steady brown eyes. It was an infinitesimal tic. If he hadn't been watching carefully, he wouldn't have noticed the movement. A first signal of anger? He was certain that Bailey had something to hide.

"She wasn't feeing well," he repeated the words as he scribbled them in his notebook. "That's very strange, Bailey. I was with Kate that morning, and she didn't say anything about feeling ill. You wouldn't lie to me, would you?"

"I'd advise you to knock it off, Joe Rivers. Right now."

"What?" He spread his hands, all innocence. "What are you talking about?"

"You know perfectly well what I'm saying here." Her dark eyes flared. "You know what was wrong with her."

"Do I?"

She leaned forward, her elbows rested on the tabletop. "I'm talking about her medication, Joe."

A sickening sense of triumph churned in his gut. This was a new piece of information from Bailey. She hadn't mentioned medication before. Smoothly, he pressed for more detail. "Exactly what medication was that? Do you remember?"

"Some kind of antidepressants."

"And why didn't you mention this in the prior FAA investigation?"

"I didn't see any reason to smear the reputation of a good pilot who had died in the line of duty." She leveled a hard glare at him. "Obviously, you think differently."

"I want the truth. And, as far as I know, Kate wasn't taking any prescription drugs."

Bailey sipped her coffee. She crossed her long legs. Stalling? "Then I must be mistaken. You were her husband, Joe. You should have known her better than anybody."

Should have, he thought. But the sad truth was that he and Kate had grown apart. He'd been on a lot of long assignments out of state. "Just for the sake of argument," he said, "let's assume that Kate was taking medication. What was it for?"

"Just assuming..." She mocked his tone. "I'd say the usual reason for antidepressants is that somebody's depressed."

"Was Kate depressed?"

"She was...moody." Bailey pushed away from the table and went to the sink, where she rinsed out her mug and stuck it in the dishwasher. "I don't know. I'm not a medical person. But it sure seemed to me, on the day of the crash, that Kate was sick. If it wasn't the pills, maybe she was just coming down with something, a flu or something. Her eyes were unfocused. Her hands shook. And she said something about being unhappy."

"Kate?" She'd been vivacious and enthusiastic. Even when they argued, which they'd done with great frequency in the last year of their marriage, she fought with vigor. "She wasn't a sad kind of person."

"Listen, Joe. I don't know why you're asking me these questions if you think you already know the answers."

He leaned back in his chair, knowing that she was right. His interrogation technique was sloppy. He was too much involved. Usually, Joe was renowned for being cool and incisive. But this was about Kate, about her death.

Joe took a deep breath, prepared himself to be more professional. "All right, Bailey, let's go back to the cockpit. When you were both aware of the mechanical problem, you were the one who landed the plane."

"Yes," she said.

"After the plane landed, you returned to the cabin, popped the hatch and ordered the passengers to get out as quickly as possible."

"Yes. That's right."

He stared into the dark depths of her eyes, trying to see the truth. This was the one question that had plagued him since the beginning of the investigation, since the crash itself. "Where was Kate? Why wasn't she helping you?"

"She was unconscious."

"Injured?" he pressed. "Did she hit her head in the landing?"

"I don't remember."

"But you knew she was unconscious, strapped into the pilot's chair by her seat belt and shoulder harness."

"Yes."

"And you didn't go back to get her."

"I didn't know how much time I had." Bailey's voice went flat. "Everything was happening fast. I don't remember what I was thinking."

"How was Kate injured?"

"I don't remember."

Joe knew that she was lying. He could feel it in the marrow of his bones. Bailey wasn't telling him the truth. She'd left something out, and that was the key to why his wife hadn't escaped the explosion, why she'd burned to death.

It might take weeks, might take months or years. But he was determined to break through Bailey's deception. He'd make her eat those lies. Before this investigation was over, he would know the truth.

"Joe," she said quietly.

His frustration, his disgust for her, was thunderous. He hoped like hell that she wasn't going to try to pull some kind of "poor little me" routine. "What is it?" he snapped. "Has your memory finally returned?"

"Joe, I'm so sorry. Kate told me, just before we went down."

"What did she tell you?"

"About the baby. About her pregnancy. Six weeks along."

Though her voice was soft, the words echoed in his head.

"Joe, I'm so very sorry for your tragedy. You must have found out just before she died."

"That's impossible, Bailey." A knife-edged sadness plunged between his shoulder blades and twisted painfully. "Kate couldn't have been six weeks pregnant. I was out of town for two months before the crash."

Chapter Three

"You're wrong," he repeated.

As he spoke, Bailey saw a transformation in Joe Rivers. He was enraged. And he was dangerous.

His civilized veneer was gone, stripped away to reveal a primal fury that burned as steadily as the unblinking stare of a predator about to strike. The edge to his anger was manifested in a lethal calm. He lifted the coffee mug to his lips. His breathing didn't falter. His darkly tanned skin paled only slightly. The light in his blue eyes flashed once, then stilled.

The silence that filled the room felt like the prelude to a hurricane. Bailey's skin prickled. Her rib cage tightened as the storm gathered and sucked the air from her lungs.

His baritone voice dropped a key as he slowly spoke. "You're telling me that my wife was having an affair. That she was carrying another man's child."

Though Bailey was proud of her own self-control, she was no match for him. His edge, razor sharp, frightened her.

A shiver, deeper than fear, racked her body. She felt exposed to him. Her knees were suddenly too weak to stand, and she braced herself on the edge of the kitchen sink. Why had she spoken? Why had she mentioned any part of the conversation she and Kate had had in the cockpit?

Throughout the interrogations with the other FAA officials, Bailey had been able to keep Kate's secrets. But there was a strength in Joe, an overwhelming persuasive power, that compelled her to speak.

"Bailey, tell me the truth."

She needed to escape from him before she said too much. She needed to run. "This conversation is over, Joe."

"No."

"It's not important."

"What did Kate say?" Joe demanded in that hypnotic voice. "What else did she tell you?"

"It's not important. Whatever Kate told me doesn't have anything to do with the crash."

"What happened in that cockpit?"

Bailey pushed away from the sink. The screen door was only a few paces away. If she went outside, she could find Grandpa Mac; Joe's fearful spell over her would be broken. Hesitantly, she moved toward the door.

"Answer me." His voice was like low, distant thunder.

Just a few more steps, she thought. Outside, she could escape his questions and his power. Her hand reached for the doorknob.

There was a crash as Joe's chair hit the kitchen floor. In an instant, he was beside her. His hands grasped her upper arm, and he whipped her around. He held her tight, only inches away from his face. "What did she say?"

Bailey swallowed the cry that rose in her throat. She didn't struggle in Joe's grip, wouldn't give him the satisfaction of behaving like a scared rabbit. She looked him straight in the eye and repeated, "Kate told me, right before we went down, that she was pregnant."

"Six weeks pregnant," he clarified.

"That was what she said."

His grasp loosened. He stepped back, away from her. Slowly, he turned his chair upright and sat at the kitchen table.

Now, she was free to escape. But Bailey didn't want to. His rage ebbed as quickly as it had appeared. Quietly, she sat opposite him and said, "I'm sorry, Joe."

"I don't need your sympathy."

Nor did he need to count the days. After Kate died, he had replayed their last months together, dozens of times. Each time, he had cursed himself for being gone too often and too long. Eight weeks.

They had made love on the night before she died, but it had been eight weeks before that. He'd been on an assignment in Alaska, and on the two weekends he came home, Kate had once been out of town with a charter flight and once they'd fought.

He'd suspected the affair. Though Kate hadn't confessed, she'd been evasive. For the past year, she'd been hinting that there might be another man.

His gaze rested on Bailey, not seeing her as a woman or even as a human being. She was the answer. "Who?"

"I don't know."

He stared through her, seeking to burn away all the petty subterfuge. "Stop protecting her, Bailey. She's dead."

"I'm not protecting her."

"Tell me."

"I can't." She slammed the flat of her hand down on the tabletop. "I don't know."

"Here's something you do know," he said. "As an FAA investigator, I have the authority to pull your pilot's license."

"Are you threatening me?"

"Tell me what you know about Kate's boyfriend, and you'll never have to find out how many ways I can mess up your life."

"Why would you do that? It's not fair."

"Hey, you're a big girl, Bailey. You must know by now that life isn't fair. All I need to pull your license is my own judgment that you're incompetent. Sure, you can petition to get the license back. But it might take months, and you'd always have that stain on your record."

"But that's a lie!"

"You were piloting a plane that crashed," he said. "Five people died."

"I did everything I could. You were there, Joe. You know that I did the right stuff."

"Do I? As I recall, you didn't want me in the cockpit."

"I didn't know how bad it was. Not at first."

"But later, you knew. You could have called me up there."

A horrible doubt slithered through her mind like a venomous reptile. If she'd called Joe into the cockpit, could the crash have been prevented? He might have been able to reason with Kate, might have brought her to her senses and kept her from pulling strange maneuvers. If Kate hadn't been jerking on the controls, they might have prevented the stress on the engine. They might have made it to an airfield.

"Even if I had called you forward," she whispered, "I don't think you could have done anything differently than I did."

Seeking affirmation, she searched his expression, tried to read his mind. But he said nothing.

With heartfelt fervor, she added, "I sure as heck wish you had been the one flying the Otter, Joe. Then you could live with these nightmares."

"Guilt," he said.

"I keep backing up and thinking there was something else I could have done."

"You made mistakes," he said.

"We all do."

His simple statements were torture for her—sharp darts with barbed edges that stuck in her flesh and spread poison through her mind. Yes, she felt guilty. Yes, she'd made mistakes.

"If you could do it over," he said, "what would you change? What would you do differently?"

"When I first noticed that Kate wasn't feeling right, I would have taken over the controls. I should have overridden Kate's authority as pilot."

Too well, she remembered that precise moment. Bailey had been foolish enough to confess that she was interested in Joe. Kate had told her, point-blank, that she "wasn't his type."

Pride and humiliation had driven Bailey from the cockpit. Somewhere in the back of her head, she knew better than to let her emotions get the better of her. But she'd left Kate, depressed and shaky, alone in the cockpit. The next thing she knew, they were on the verge of going down.

Joe's low voice was almost seductive. "Tell me about it, Bailey. Why didn't you take the controls?"

Her jaw thrust at a stubborn angle. She sure as heck wasn't going to tell him that she'd been embarrassed by having a crush on him. "Kate was the pilot. The plane went down because of mechanical failure."

"But there was something you could have done."

"No."

"Tell me the truth. What were you and Kate talking about in the cockpit?"

"Nothing important."

"Tell me about Kate. Who was her lover?"

Or else he'd take away her license. Bailey glared back at him. Her temper ignited. Take away her license? He might as well take away her life. Without flying, there was no reason to go on living. She couldn't be grounded, couldn't bear to walk through life when she could fly.

"Listen here, Joe Rivers, you might have some kind of high muckamuck authority with the FAA, but you're acting like a long-tongued, scaly, disgusting swamp lizard, fighting in the ooze with the snakes for a carrion bite of rotten meat. You come here, to my grandpa Mac's home, and you threaten me? As if you had the right? I'm done talking. If you were smart, you'd pack up your briefcase and hit the road."

"Then, you prefer a formal hearing."

"I prefer a reasonable attitude. You don't give two hoots and a holler about the crash. What about the other people who died? Jillian, Eleanor, Charles and Dee Valente? Do you care about them?"

"Of course."

She surged to her feet. "You don't. Right now, all you're concerned about is your hotshot, fly-boy male pride. You're struck to the very depths of your festering soul by the fact that your wife was messing around.

I'll tell you right now, Joe Rivers, that's not my problem.''

Her temper gave her strength. She didn't limp as she circled the table and pushed open the screen door. Now she was leaving, but she wasn't running away. She was simply choosing another direction, away from Joe Rivers.

Bailey marched through the grasses and the beach palms to the edge of the tarmac runway. The thick heat of a Florida summer was nowhere near as hot as the blazing inferno of her fury.

''Bailey!''

She heard him calling her name, but she just kept walking. There was nothing else she could say to Joe Rivers. Talk about misjudging a man! She'd thought he was somebody she might care about; she'd been attracted to him, believed he was a good guy. Wrong, wrong, wrong, oh, my gracious, she'd been wrong.

When Joe ran up beside her and caught hold of her arm, she yanked away. ''Don't make me hit you, Joe.''

''What?''

She spun around. ''You heard me. If you don't cease to pester me, I'm going to land a roundhouse right smack in the center of your sorry face.''

But it wasn't a sorry-looking face, she realized as her dark eyes clashed again with his. He was probably the most handsome man she'd ever known. His black hair was mussed. His jaw was tight. And his eyes, oh Lord, his eyes were the deepest, purest blue. They penetrated straight to her soul. She longed to touch him, to collapse against his strong shoulder and sob until the pain had passed.

But she couldn't. Not now. Not ever.

''I won't tell you I'm sorry,'' he said.

"Then we've got no reason to stand here jawing. Think about this, Joe. Why would Kate and I share confidences? We didn't have anything in common. You knew that, didn't you?"

He shrugged.

"Come on, Joe. Apart from the fact that we were both female pilots, we couldn't have been more different. She had men coming after her like fleas to a hound. They were drawn to her. She was pretty and flashy and bright."

"So are you," he said.

He couldn't have shocked her more if he'd smacked her up the side of the head with a two-by-four. She actually fell back a pace. "What?"

"You're pretty, too. In a different way than Kate. In a quiet way."

Her eyes narrowed. "You're making fun."

"I'm just telling the truth. It's an observation. Don't get all carried away."

"No, sir. I wouldn't do that." But the day seemed suddenly brighter, as if the sun had come out from behind a cloud. Joe thought she was pretty?

"All I want is the truth," he said. "Now if Kate really was pregnant, she might have been airsick. What do you call it—morning sickness? That might have impaired her judgment. How can I find out if it's true?"

"Check with her doctor," Bailey said. That was so obvious.

"The only doctor I know was the one she was required to see for annual physicals."

"I happen to know the name of her gynecologist because I was looking for somebody when I moved to Denver and Kate recommended her doc. She's at the

Lakewood Women's Clinic, and her name is Rose Quarry."

"Thanks. Can I use your phone? I'll put it on my credit card."

He'd already started back toward the house when she called to him. "Joe?"

He pivoted and faced her. "Yes?"

"There was another doctor, too. I don't know his name. But he was a psychiatrist."

"I see." Joe was beginning to think he didn't know anything about his deceased wife. She was going to a psychiatrist, and she hadn't seen fit to inform him. "Bailey, do you remember anything about this doctor?"

She shook her head. "Kate mentioned his name a couple of times, but I can't recall it. Oh, I almost met him once. Kate pointed out his plane, a Beechcraft Bonanza, that he hangared at Centennial Airfield."

"Would you remember that plane if you saw it again?"

"Probably better than I'd remember the man," she admitted. "The plane had a silver tail. Oh, yeah, and the call letters included Delta Romeo. 'DR.' Which I thought was kind of cute since he was a doctor. Anyhow, I guess that was how Kate bumped into him in the first place. At the airport. He specializes in helping people who are afraid of flying."

"I might need you to identify the guy."

"Sure."

A tiny frown played at the corner of her wide mouth, and Joe found her expression to be strangely endearing. Unlike Kate, Bailey displayed her every emotion. Right now, he could tell that she was puzzled. "What?" he asked.

"Well, if you're thinking I might ID this shrink, that must mean you're thinking I'll be back in Denver. And that," she concluded, "means I'd be working as a pilot for Sky Air again."

He nodded.

"So you're not going to pull my pilot's license?"

When he gazed down into her bright eyes and saw a glimmer of hope, Joe almost wished he could reassure her. He almost shared her hopefulness.

He steeled himself. Bailey Fielding was his adversary. She was holding him back from the truth.

Harshly, he said, "I'm not making any promises."

To her credit, she didn't argue or beg. Bailey turned on her heel and strode toward one of the hangars at the end of the runway.

Joe trudged back to the small beach house. Though he was still tense, Bailey's outburst had brought him back from the outer boundaries of his anger. He was sane enough to realize that investigating the crash probably didn't have much to do with Kate's pregnancy. But it was still something he needed to verify. For himself.

After a call to information, he reached the Lakewood Women's Clinic and was put on hold for Dr. Quarry, listening to recorded music. The song was a classic. "You Are So Beautiful." That certainly had applied to Kate. Blond and utterly lovely. When they had married, he thought she was the most perfect creature he'd ever seen. Now, seven years later, he still paid homage to a beauty that would never fade in his memory. But she hadn't been perfect.

"Hello?" a female voice came over the phone. "This is Dr. Rose Quarry."

"My name is Joe Rivers, and I believe my wife—"

"I'm sorry for your tragedy, Joe."

"My wife," he said, "was pregnant."

"Yes. We'd talked about how long it would be safe for her to pilot an aircraft and about the recovery time after delivery."

His heart pounded in his throat. "How far along was she?"

"Let me pull up her file on the computer. I already had her scheduled for an amnio because of the possible complications from her antidepressants."

Joe swallowed hard. "Right."

"Here we are," said Dr. Quarry. "Kate was about six weeks pregnant. That was what we had figured."

"Thank you, Doctor." The confirmation of the worst news a husband can have about his wife burrowed into his skin. He'd have to live with it. "By the way, could you give me the name of the doctor who prescribed the antidepressant medication?"

"Why?"

"I wanted to talk with him. He's a psychiatrist, isn't he? It's been difficult for me to deal with Kate's death."

"I understand," she said. "But I can't give you that information, Joe. Kate's medical records are privileged. Again, I'm sorry for your loss."

He could have pressed. He could have told her that he was with the FAA and doing an investigation into the crash, but Joe wasn't in the mood to pull all the official strings. "Thank you, Doctor."

He hung up the telephone receiver. The fight drained from him as he accepted the cold, hard facts. His wife had been pregnant with another man's child. He had been completely blind. He had somehow missed the signals that their marriage was over. Their love was gone. Dead.

Mac Augustine strode through the door and poured himself another cup of coffee. Standing over the sink, he struck a sulfurous kitchen match, lit a cigarette and inhaled deeply before blowing the smoke through his nostrils like an aging dragon. "Bailey only lets me smoke five times a day. Makes a man savor his nicotine."

Joe said nothing. His private thoughts blanked the surface of his mind.

"Women, eh?" Mac relished another drag on his smoke. "Can't live with 'em, can't live without 'em."

Joe might have been willing to try living without the female of the species.

"Know what I think?" Mac continued. "Looks to me like Bailey has a little bit of a crush on you."

"Doubtful," Joe said. "She just called me a long-tongued, scaly, disgusting swamp lizard."

Mac laughed. "For Bailey, that's a term of endearment."

"Yeah? I don't think I want to hear what she says when she really hates you."

"I think maybe you like her, too." Mac's drawl curled around his smile. "I bet that's why you came down here, all the way to Florida."

"It's my job," Joe said. "I'm investigating the crash."

Mac blew smoke toward the lazily turning blades of the ceiling fan. "That's what you say. But since my little girl was flying the plane, I know there wasn't a chance of pilot error. And the cause, according to you FAA boys, was mechanical failure. How come you're really here, Joe?"

"There's something about this case that doesn't fit."

"Are you thinking of sabotage?"

Joe looked up sharply. Of course, the potential for sabotage was investigated in every crash. But the FAA had pretty much dismissed that possibility in this situation. There hadn't been a bomb on board. No terrorist groups had claimed responsibility. Losing power was not an unheard-of occurrence. Mechanical problems happened far more often than pilots liked to admit. Usually, you only lost one engine. Usually, the pilot was able to find a field and bring the plane down safely. But in the mountains, there weren't good landing areas.

"Sabotage," Joe said. "No."

Couldn't be. Even if the engines had been tampered with, it would be impossible to prove. The Otter had been demolished when the fuel tanks exploded. On a small plane, there wasn't evidence from a black box, because there was no such instrument on board.

"I wouldn't rule it out," Mac said. "It wouldn't be too hard to do. The fuel line could be weakened so it would break during the expansion and contraction at high altitude."

"There was nothing left of the fuel lines," Joe said.

"Keep sabotage in mind," Mac said. "There was a powerful woman on that plane. That congresswoman. And she had some mighty powerful enemies."

And Jillian had been replaced by her husband, Ted, whose stance on certain key issues was the opposite to the way Jillian would have voted. Still, Joe mentally refuted the suggestion. "Doesn't seem possible. I've investigated hundreds of crashes, and there was only one that I'd say was sabotage. That involved a small explosive device.'

"Only one that you know about," Mac said. "There might have been others. It's hard to prove."

"In this case, impossible. There was nothing to indicate sabotage in the wreckage of flight 642." Joe allowed his mind to wander along this path. "Of course, there are the people involved. I could refocus on questioning the survivors, then expand the field of involvement."

"You could." Mac inhaled deeply. "Somehow, I don't think our new congressman from Colorado, Ted Grambling, would take kindly to that kind of poking and prodding."

"I'll keep it in mind," Joe said.

"You'd have to be careful, son. You might provoke the wrong people and get Bailey in trouble. If somebody screwed up the Otter and they think she knows something about it, they'd come after her."

"Maybe."

"Let me tell you something, Joe. If you do anything, and I do mean anything, to hurt my granddaughter, I swear to the good Lord above that I will crush you." He ground out his cigarette in the sink and washed the residue of ash down the drain. "Do you read me?"

"Loud and clear."

OUTSIDE THE RAMSHACKLE hangar within sniffing distance of the salt-sprayed beach, Bailey strapped herself into the single-person cockpit of the perfectly renovated Spitfire. The seat fit her like a glove. She should have felt completely at home. While she and Grandpa Mac had been barnstorming the country with the airshow, she'd logged more hours in this old plane than most teenagers spend behind the wheel of an automobile.

She knew every dial, every gauge, every switch inside this machine. And yet, the instrument panel seemed as foreign as a flying saucer. What was wrong with her? Why couldn't she think? She wanted to believe there was a simple explanation. Maybe the heat had clogged her brain. She was sweating from every pore.

Tension. Mental paralysis. She knew what was wrong. She knew, but didn't want to face it. Bailey couldn't remember the first thing about flying because she couldn't get past the fear. That was her problem. Fear.

What if she could never fly again? What if the fear was too much for her?

An agonized growl tore from her throat and hung derisively in the air. What, in the name of all the creatures that walked and swam and flew, was wrong with her? She was behaving like a sissy, a baby, a girly-girl. Never before had she lacked for courage when it came to flying. And now? What was the matter with her?

She needed to prove to herself that she could do it. To grab on to a handful of self-respect and hold on tight.

Staring down the runway, she saw Joe come out of the house with Grandpa Mac. They were two tall men standing side by side, and somewhere in the back of her mind, Bailey knew the picture was right. Ever since she was eight, her grandpa had always been the only person she could trust and love unconditionally. And Joe? What was he to her? The husband of her dead friend, a man who had reason to hate Bailey. An FAA investigator who suspected her.

A man who thought she was pretty.

Bailey pushed that thought out of her head. Pretty? It didn't matter.

Joe was her enemy. He could take her license away. He could ground her. And yet, every feminine instinct in her body yearned toward him.

"I'm crazy," she muttered.

Joe wasn't her friend, and he could never be anything more to her. If she were smart, she'd concentrate on learning to distrust him and to run away fast when she saw him coming.

Bailey cranked the ignition on the Spitfire and felt the power of the engine. Before she had time to be scared, she taxied down the tarmac runway. Her fear was momentarily forgotten as she ran through the routine safety checks. All systems were go.

Takeoff.

She held her breath.

She had to do it now. Take off.

She was up in the sky, poking a hole through the clouds. Delighted laughter spilled from her lips. Home, Bailey realized. Everything was going to be all right. She'd come home.

Chapter Four

Back in Colorado, Joe returned to the mountains and viewed the site of the crash landing. He went over every inch of the field, searching for a clue, a piece of engine that had broken free.

In a government storage area, he combed through the wreckage of Rocky Mountain Sky Airlines 642, searching for proof of sabotage that might have been overlooked in the earlier investigation. There wasn't much left. The engines were charred, twisted hunks of metal. The entire remains of the plane fit in a large wooden crate.

Joe studied every nut and bolt. He conferred with mechanics, studied the specs for the Otter, reviewed the maintenance history. The end result? Nothing.

Dead remains, he thought, the Otter was nothing if not symbolic of the dead remains of his hopeless life.

At night, every night, in the town house he'd shared with Kate, he had never felt so alone and confused. And helpless. He couldn't change what had happened. He couldn't revise the past and come out with a happy ending.

The nights were hell. He couldn't stand to sleep in the bed. The soft, pastel, patterned sheets, Kate's bed linens, itched him. Since her death, he had pretty much confined himself to the brown plaid sofa in the den, which was also his home office.

It was weekend. Half-awake, Joe stared at the fading sunlight that sliced through the window blinds. What time was it? He held up his wristwatch. After six o'clock. And what day? He turned his head toward the small black-and-white television on the bookshelves. The program was "Sixty Minutes." It must be Sunday.

His head hurt, and he tried to remember the last time he'd eaten. Maybe yesterday. He needed to get some food, to pull himself together. Tomorrow was another day. A Monday, fresh start on the week.

With some effort, he dragged himself to a sitting position with his shoulders bowed, his elbows resting on his knees. He stank of unchanged clothes and old sweat. It must have been a couple of days since he'd showered.

Staring at the soundless television screen, he thought of the crash. Why hadn't he gone into the cockpit? Why hadn't he carried his wife to safety?

There were reasons. Of course there were reasons. Logic was on his side. He hadn't known that she needed help. He had assumed that, because she was the pilot, Kate knew what to do. But he'd been wrong.

Accept it. She was gone.

He might as well give up. Everybody else had.

Joe hauled his carcass off the sofa. The crash was two months and one week ago. Concerned friends and family members had ceased their efforts to comfort him. After a couple of weeks of phone calls and visits and gifts of casseroles with microwave instructions taped to the lid, they'd grown impatient with his incessant sorrow. He wasn't a fun dinner guest. Too obsessed, too guilty. *Get on with your life.*

But the guilt imprisoned him, ladened his spirit, trapped him in shadows of doubt. He should have saved her.

Joe opened the door and stumbled into the hallway. He hated leaving the den. That had always been his private lair, but out here, everywhere, there were signs of Kate. He'd closed off all the rooms he could, keeping a corridor from the den to the bathroom to the closet in the upstairs bedroom. But the kitchen was on the other side of the front room, and he had to walk past Kate's living room, furnished with a tastefully striped sofa and chairs.

He glanced into the living room. It looked shrouded with the drapes closed. In here was the entertainment center with the wide-screen color television with cable and the CD player. Joe remembered sitting beside Kate on the sofa, watching a video, drinking wine.

When he looked at the sofa and tried to imagine her there, he couldn't. He was beginning to forget what she looked like, and he didn't want to forget. He wanted to be loyal to her memory. But she'd been disloyal, hadn't she?

He'd been a fool to trust her. She'd been carrying on an affair, laughing at his steadfast working self as he dressed like a trained monkey in his necktie and suit and went to the office every day. Damn her! It was Kate who insisted he settle down to a regular job. Kate told him she couldn't stand his dangerous work as a test pilot.

But how could he blame her? She was dead.

He glanced back into the living room. A trick of shadows and light seemed to move the drapes. A breeze? But that was impossible. He kept the town house sealed like a tomb.

Yet, there was a difference. A freshness.

He didn't actually hear a voice calling his name, but he felt beckoned. A silent whisper compelled him to stare through the eternal dusk of the living room Kate had furnished.

There was the form of a woman on the sofa. At the corner of the sofa, she sat with her legs curled beneath her.

Great, Joe thought, now he was seeing ghosts.

But it wasn't Kate. The shape was long legged with her long brown hair pulled back in a ponytail and a hint of laughter in her huge brown eyes. Bailey.

"What are you doing here?"

The rusty sound of his own voice startled him. Obviously, he was losing his mind. There was nobody here. But she looked real. Had she come to help him or to mock him?

Truth, he thought. That was what Bailey—or this dream of Bailey—had come to hear. It was time for Joe to tell the truth.

"Look," he said. "I know it wasn't all Kate's fault. The affair. Her pregnancy. I don't know why I should tell you this. You're not even real. I made you up. I should just shut up and get back to work."

But he had to say the truth.

"I quit loving her. I had loved her once, but it was gone. And I tried to get that feeling back, but . . . things changed. We were both hanging on to a shell of a marriage."

The shape of Bailey was quiet. And that was a damn good thing, Joe thought, because if she started talking to him, he would be obliged to dial the lunatic hot line.

He closed his eyes against the insanity and the pain. "I wasn't a good husband. I didn't bring her flowers and champagne. She had to look elsewhere. It was my fault. I wasn't rich enough, caring enough, sensitive enough."

But he wouldn't make that mistake again. He would not quit this investigation until he knew all the answers to the crash, until he knew why Kate had died. He owed her that much.

When he knew, he could lay Kate to rest and get on with his life.

He opened his eyes. Bailey was gone.

Joe turned on all the lights to search, but he was alone again in a cluttered, messy town house, filled with mementos of a life he could barely remember living.

He had to get this over with. He had to find out what happened. Discover why Kate had died.

THE NEXT MORNING, Joe decided to try a different tactic of investigation. Instead of studying the mechanical equipment, he would seek answers in the people involved. His first phone call was to the Denver offices of the new congressman, Ted Gambling. Though he had filled his wife's seat in the House of Representatives, he had not chosen to fill her shoes. His political sympathies were far different from those of his late wife, Jillian Gambling.

On the telephone, Joe introduced himself, and the two men exchanged condolences on their mutual tragedy. Then Joe said, "I'm sorry to bring up this painful subject, Congressman, but I'm investigating the possible causes of the crash."

"Mechanical failure, wasn't it?"

"I am not ruling out sabotage."

The new congressman swore. His tone was harsh and suddenly hostile. "Can't you leave this alone? I've been through enough. Don't open this investigation again, please."

"I need to get at the truth, sir." Joe took a deep breath. "Your wife had enemies, powerful enemies."

"What are you saying?"

"Can you give me some idea of who I might talk to? Who was desperate to get your wife out of the way?"

"Are you suggesting murder?"

"Your wife was a strong woman who aroused strong feelings from her supporters and her detractors. Do you have any reason to suspect that someone or some group might have wanted to harm her?"

"No," he said tersely.

"Were there death threats?"

"There's always some crackpot threatening something or another."

"So," Joe said, "there were death threats."

"Nothing to take seriously."

"Could you give me specifics?"

"No."

"Were there any unusual events surrounding her departure for Aspen?"

"No."

"Perhaps you could run through the events of the day of the crash."

There was a pause as the new congressman caught his breath. "I don't have to put up with this."

"Sir, I'm with the FAA. I'm an investigator."

"Is that why you're calling me, Joe? Or is it because you can't accept the death or possible incompetence of your own wife."

"Just answer the questions, Congressman."

"I'm not saying one more word to you. And if you contact me again, I'll have your job."

The phone went dead, and Joe hung up. Okay, there were death threats, the usual death threats. And Congressman Grambling was a cranky, self-important man who wasn't afraid to issue threats of his own. This wasn't much to go on, but Joe felt as if he was making progress, breaking some eggs to make an omelet.

It was ten o'clock in Denver when he dialed the phone number for Mac Augustine's home in Florida.

When Mac answered, he sounded as irritable as a hibernating grizzly. "What do you want, Joe?"

"More questions. No answers. Is Bailey there?"

"She's back in Denver. Getting ready to start work for Sky Air again. After you left, that girl got herself back in gear, flying every day. She's ready."

"You sound happy about that, Mac."

"You bet I am. The sky's where Bailey belongs. She's a pilot, Joe. No matter what happens, she can't keep both feet on the ground.'

"You say she's going back to work?"

"Starting today."

Joe experienced a sinking sensation in the pit of his belly, almost like fear. "I guess I knew that. But I'd forgotten."

"Have I got any reason to worry?" Mac asked. "Joe, have you found sabotage?"

"Nope. I've got nothing."

But he was tense when he thought about Bailey going back to work. He couldn't exactly explain why. It was an instinct, a gut feeling. During those years when he'd been flying low and fast as a test pilot, he'd learned to trust those split-second impulses. And he did so right now.

After saying goodbye to Mac, Joe hurried through his shower and shave, then dressed in a navy blue suit with a lightly starched white shirt and a bright paisley necktie. Within minutes, he was headed toward the airfield at the southeastern edge of Denver's suburbs.

As he neared the field, he peered through the windshield, scanning the dreamy blue skies overhead, watching the small planes—some like angry, buzzing hornets and others like big-bellied horseflies—taking off and landing. Was one of them Bailey? Why was he so worried about her?

Must have been that ghost he'd encountered last night. But that hadn't been Bailey. Only a vision.

The real Bailey wouldn't have been able to sit quietly for that long. The real Bailey was a stubborn, tough woman who probably had the key to this puzzle in the back pocket of her snug-fitting jeans. Not that Joe had noticed how nicely her jeans outlined her butt. Not that he cared. Joe rationalized to himself that he didn't want anything to happen to her before he had the answers.

Besides, this trip to Sky Air had another purpose. Joe wanted to question the owner of Rocky Mountain Sky Air, Claude Whistler. Claude was still young, with only a touch of silver in his wavy golden hair, but he'd established a comfortable niche in the competitive business of air travel. Most certainly, he was a clever player who had learned to manipulate the necessary political channels to get licensing. He was a smart businessman who courted the travel agents. Was he also a profiteer? Some people claimed that his operation made far too much money to be believed, but the FAA kept a careful watch and there was no indication of impropriety.

Joe stepped inside the air-conditioned offices of Rocky Mountain Sky Air, where Galloping Greta, the wiry marathon runner who made out the schedules, perched behind a wide counter. Arrayed in front of her, he knew, were computer screens and equipment for communicating with the various aircraft. But Greta wasn't wearing a headset right now.

She was unabashedly eavesdropping on a conversation that spilled through the opened door of Claude's office. Smiling at Joe, she raised her eyebrows, and they both listened to Bailey's drawl.

"...just plain in-and-out unreasonable," she said. "You know I'm fully qualified to handle a Cessna Citation II. The only thing I don't fly is jets."

"She's right," Greta whispered to Joe. "Best pilot we've got working for us."

"But this charter would be solo." Joe recognized the smooth baritone of Claude Whistler, coolly persuasive. "Bailey, you're a copilot, not a pilot."

"Promote me," she demanded.

Joe almost laughed. It would take more than Claude's suave, sophisticated logic to dissuade Bailey.

She continued, "Listen here, Claude. I didn't hustle myself back to work here in Denver so I could sit on my tailbone, twiddling my thumbs."

"But I—"

"Tell you what. You can promote me to pilot and still pay me a copilot salary. Fair enough? I'd say that's a deal you can't refuse."

Joe winked at Greta and stepped forward to tap on the opened door. He walked into the room as if he belonged there.

Bailey turned around, hands on hips and jaw thrust forward. From the stubborn expression in her eyes and the red flush beneath her Florida tan, Joe could see that she was determined to get her way.

But there was something else in her look, as well. In the instant her eyes met his, there was a sizzle. Unless Joe was very much mistaken, the bolt of electricity that shot from her was a purely sexual heat. He heard a tiny gasp in the back of her throat. Not a whimper of weakness or fear, not from Bailey. The sound was more like the demand a woman makes when she wants to be caressed, stroked and satisfied.

Her lips pressed together. She straightened her spine and tossed her head, causing her ponytail to swing and erasing the impression that she might be glad to see him. "I wasn't expecting you, Joe."

Claude unfolded his tall, muscular, perfectly tailored body from behind his desk and stuck out his hand. "How are you doing, Joe?"

"I'm okay. And yourself?"

He glanced at Bailey. "I've been better."

Joe nodded. "I'm familiar with this particular problem."

"Excuse me." Bailey leaned across the desk, almost sticking her head between the two men. "I do not appreciate being referred to as a problem when I am standing right here. As it so happens, I am a solution."

"How so?" Claude asked.

"You need a pilot on that charter. And here I am."

In her jeans with her pale blue Sky Air cotton shirt, she looked long legged and lean, but feminine at the same time. Her shoulders moved while she talked. She gestured expansively. Energy radiated from her in waves.

This woman, Joe thought, was fully recovered. She was no longer the tragic, self-pitying creature he'd visited in Florida. Bailey Fielding was a force to be reckoned with, and he could feel himself rising to the challenge.

"What do you think, Joe?" Claude asked. "Do you think I should let Bailey take a solo charter flight on the Cessna?"

Bailey sniped at her employer. "There's no need for you to be condescending, Claude. No need to ask someone who doesn't even work at Sky Air if I should be given the opportunity to fly a plane that I've been piloting since I was a girl. Either you trust me or you don't. Which is it?"

"I'll take you up on the offer to fly pilot on copilot wages. Your departure is at 5:25. You have three passengers. Take them to Pueblo, stay overnight, bring them back here tomorrow morning."

Her smile was radiant. "Thanks, Claude. You won't regret this. I promise."

She nodded curtly to Joe as she left.

He closed the door behind her. Seeing Bailey again hadn't been what he expected. When he heard her voice, saw her stubborn face, it was as if the darkness had been vanquished as easily as the sunrise banishes night. She was a relief.

Such feelings were dangerous, he thought. He was sure that she knew more than she was saying. Bailey was the worst woman on the face of the earth for him to be attracted to. Bailey might have been responsible for his wife's death, and she was haunting him.

"Joe? How can I help you?"

Joe didn't sit in the chair opposite Claude's desk. He wanted to talk to the man as an equal, and that was difficult from the employee seat. Instead, Joe paced in Claude's large, elegant office, glancing at Claude's bookshelf without bothering to read the titles on the spines. He studied framed certificates of merit and a wall of photographs. Nonchalantly, he said, "I'm still investigating."

"Whatever I can do to help, I'm ready."

"So, you wouldn't prefer to put this crash behind you?"

"I want to know why it happened. We're still flying an Otter, you know. If there's a correctable problem with the plane, we need to know. This accident caused us a great deal of grief."

His words sounded rehearsed, but Joe wasn't surprised. The owner of Sky Air had probably repeated those words a million times since the funerals. Claude knew the right things to say, the right places to go. Surely, he had arranged his mature but all-American features into an appropriate expression of sorrow as he spoke of his grief at the tragedy and offered condolences.

And all the while, Joe thought, Claude Whistler's bright blue eyes were directly focused on the bottom line. How would the crash affect his small airline and charter service? Would he lose business? How could he turn disaster into a coup?

Joe's glance rested on an enlarged snapshot of Claude Whistler shaking hands with former president George Bush. Beside it, hanging on the wall, was a formal portrait of Claude, his wife and three grown daughters—all blond and perfect, haloed in the artfully arranged backlighting from a photographer's studio.

Claude Whistler seemed above reproach, which was exactly why Joe had to wonder about him. Nobody's hands were that clean.

One of Claude's official statements about the crash was elaborate praise for the valiant efforts of Kate Rivers in rescuing her passengers, giving her own life to save them. He'd made sure that Kate had died a heroine's death.

And that was a lie.

Kate had been unconscious. She hadn't landed the plane.

Though Joe had not refuted him at the time, he wondered how many other shiny-clean deceptions were protecting Sky Air.

"Talk to me about Kate," he said. "Before the crash, how was she doing?"

"As a pilot? She was damn good, Joe. You saw her files. In the four years she worked for me, there were only two reported incidents of carelessness, both by a guy who quit shortly after the second incident."

Joe dug into his suit-coat pocket and produced a small spiral notebook. "The guy's name?"

"Get real, Joe. You're not going to follow up on this."

"Sure, I am. Two incidents of carelessness. And the third was a disaster involving fatalities."

"Whoa, there. Let's not lay the blame for the crash at Kate's door. Or engrave it on her tombstone."

There was an accusation in his tone. How dare Joe speak unkindly of his dear, departed wife? It was ungallant. It was cruel. But Joe was beyond caring about appearances.

He stood before a newly positioned photograph on the office wall. Claude Whistler and Kate. They were arm in arm, laughing. God, she'd been so breathtakingly beautiful. Joe turned away from the photograph. He couldn't stand to look at it.

He faced Claude. His notebook was ready. "Why wasn't she flying the plane?"

"You know all this. Don't you, Joe?"

"I want to hear it from you."

"Okay." He leaned back in the chair behind his desk and steepled his fingertips. "According to Bailey, Kate turned over the landing to her. Which was probably extremely wise. Bailey has a background of stunt flying, a feel for unusual conditions. Though she has very little commercial experience, I couldn't have asked for a better pilot to handle a crash landing. All in all, I think Kate made a good decision."

"But that wasn't the kind of decision Kate would make. You know it and so do I. She was uncomfortable riding as a passenger in a car. Kate sure as hell wouldn't trust someone else to do a crash landing."

"Most of the time, I'd agree with you. But Bailey said Kate was kind of sick."

"With what?"

"I had the feeling that it was, you know, female problems."

"Oh, well, then. That explains the whole thing." Joe's voice was harsh with sarcasm. "Female problems. Should I make a note of that on the FAA report. Pilot crashes plane, cramps suspected."

"There's no need to be hostile."

"Or stupid," Joe said. "Are you sure Kate's illness wasn't due to her medication? The antidepressants?"

Joe watched Claude for a reaction, and he didn't have to look too deeply. Claude made no attempt at a poker face. He tilted forward in his chair with a jolt. His eyebrows raised. It was almost too much reaction. "What medication?"

"Prescribed by her shrink."

"I didn't know anything about that, Joe." He stood. "My God, are you saying Kate was drugged?"

"She was taking medication."

"And you knew about it. Well, of course you did. You were her husband." He stood and braced his knuckles on the desk top. A drugged pilot, they both knew, represented a serious situation. If it was true, Claude was open for lawsuits. He could lose his airline and charter service. "How could you let her fly like that, Joe? You're FAA. Dammit, you should have known better."

Joe could have protested, could have articulated the simple truth that he was unaware of his wife's medications, her visits to a psychiatrist, her affair with another man. But he refused to be manipulated into a defensive position by this slick, successful businessman. Especially since he was sure, in his gut, that Claude was lying.

"Hard to believe she didn't tell you," Joe said. "She liked to confide in you. I know that she valued her relationship with you."

"But Kate never mentioned drugs. If I'd known she was under a doctor's medication, I would have given her sick leave."

"How much did she tell you, Claude?"

"About what?"

Joe's temper simmered, but he kept the lid on. "Did she mention the troubles in our marriage?"

"She was my employee, Joe."

Clever sidestepping. Claude was smart enough not to answer directly, but Joe goaded. "Come on, you were one of her best buddies. I'm sure she told you what a bastard I was. What a boring, dull slob."

"Frankly, I think this conversation is unprofessional and unproductive. You've got to let this go."

"I'm not quite ready to do that, Claude. Not yet."
Joe lobbed a parting shot. "I am considering the possibility of sabotage in the crash of Sky Air 642."

Now he had planted the seeds in Claude's mind, and
Joe would wait until the small lies they'd told each other
bore fruit. "One more thing," Joe said. "If you don't
mind."

Coldly, Claude asked, "What else?"

"I'll be passenger number four on Bailey's charter,"
Joe said. "I want to run a quick check of her piloting
skills. She is qualified to fly passengers on the Cessna
Citation, isn't she?"

"Of course. All her licensing is in order, and Greta
has the information on file."

"Good."

"As always, I want to cooperate with the FAA."
Claude sat back down behind his desk and busied himself with paperwork. "I saw how you were looking at
her, Joe. Are you sure that all you want to check is her
skill level?"

Maybe not, but Joe didn't mention that he wanted to
convince Bailey in whatever way necessary that she
should tell him the truth about the crash.

JOE CAUGHT UP WITH HER in the hangar where she was
laughing and yakking with a couple of the mechanics in
grease-stained overalls. Her presence here was a clear
reminder of how very different she and Kate were. His
wife would never have chosen to spend her free time in
the hangar. Kate never got her hands dirty.

"Miss Fielding, please come with me."

"Right now?"

"I don't have time for games. Do I need to remind
you that I am in charge of this FAA investigation?"

"No, sir," she said in that lazy Southern drawl. "You most certainly do not."

She fell into step beside him, matching her stride to his as they marched at the perimeter of the airfield.

For a moment, Joe allowed himself to believe that they were just two people out for a stroll on a summer day. Beyond the end of the runways were lightly rolling hills. Though the ground cover was still green and dotted with splashes of wildflowers, this untended land would soon be parched brown in the arid heat of July. On a ridge, a respectable distance from the noise of air traffic, a row of two-story development housing serrated the edge of the horizon.

Just a man and a woman walking, he thought. Nothing could be more natural. Nothing could be further from the truth.

"Well?" she questioned. "Let the games begin."

Joe phrased his question carefully, trying not to set off the human time bomb beside him. "Give me your opinion. Do you think Kate and Claude Whistler were . . . close?"

"Claude?" She rolled her big brown eyes. "Honestly, Joe! You're barking up the wrong tree if you think there was anything going on between Kate and Claude. He's married and has three grown daughters."

"Kate was married, too," he argued.

"But Claude is *married* married. And Kate was only flirting with him." She stopped herself. "That was her nature, Joe. I don't mean any disrespect."

"Tell me this. Would Claude have known about the medication Kate was taking?"

"I doubt it. Kate wasn't about to jeopardize her job by blabbing to the boss that she was on drugs. He would have grounded her."

"Or he could have chosen to ignore it."

"That would be illegal."

"But we both know it happens all the time."

When she cocked her head and looked at him, Joe decided that her eyes were her best feature. The irises were dark, liquid, expressive. And intelligent, he thought. There was an unquenchable curiosity in her manner.

Though he wished that he could have known her under different circumstances, Joe suspected that such a circumstance never would have arisen. Bailey wasn't the sort of woman he would seek out. Her charm and beauty were more subtle.

"Joe? What have you got against Claude?"

"He's too damn perfect. So clean he squeaks. There's got to be something he's hiding."

"Why can't you just accept things the way they are?"

"Because I want to know the truth."

"Fair enough," she said.

She looked straight ahead, studying the high, feathery cirrus clouds to the north, presaging a warm front and good weather for flying. Bailey was ready to confess the truth.

She had decided, before she left Florida, that she couldn't hide from her conscience. If Joe wanted to hear the whole horrible story of what had really happened in the cockpit, so be it.

Even if the telling meant she'd be grounded, Bailey knew she couldn't bear the guilt of lying. It was better to spill the story out into the open air, and see if the stink drew flies.

"Bailey, I need to ask you something."

"Shoot."

She was ready. All he needed to do was ask.

Chapter Five

Bailey was waiting for the bomb to drop. Joe had the authority to take away her pilot's license. He had the power to explode her career into fragments of shrapnel. But what was he going to do?

She'd thought about Joe after he left Florida, thought about him with more frequency than was necessarily healthy. Grandpa Mac kept teasing her that she was hot for the hotshot test pilot. He made little jokes about it, hinting that she might need to brush up on her cooking skills if she wanted to snag a man. And he'd mentioned that "Fielding-Rivers" would be an interesting last name, akin to field and stream. Finally, she'd buzzed so low in the Spitfire that Grandpa Mac hit the dirt. Intimating that she might have a relationship with Joe wasn't funny. Joe Rivers was a man she could never have.

She walked vigorously beside him, ignoring the stitch in her side and the occasional throb in her still-healing ankle.

She could never have any kind of relationship with Joe. Because, when the truth was told, she would have to confess that she and Kate had argued in the cockpit, that they'd fought over the controls and Bailey had knocked Joe's wife unconscious. The reason Kate hadn't escaped from the explosion after the crash landing was Bailey. It was almost as if she'd killed his wife.

How in the name of all creation was she going to tell him? She couldn't forgive herself. How could Joe ever forgive her? Fighting her anxiety, she asked, "What did you want to talk about?"

He glanced at his wristwatch. "Lunch."

"Lunch?" Talk about throwing her off guard! Lunch most definitely did not sound like a real terrific idea to her. Sharing a bite wasn't going to make it any easier if he yanked her license. "I already ate," she said. "Is that all you needed?"

"Come with me to Centennial Airfield and point out the plane that belongs to Kate's psychiatrist."

Reprieve, she thought. He wasn't interested in her end of the story; he was still obsessed with Kate. "Sure, I'll do that as long as I'm back here by three-thirty." Warily, she asked, "Is that all?"

"For now."

And what about later? Was he biding his time, waiting for exactly the most painful moment to drop the ax? She wanted to get this over with. She wanted to know. When would he turn to her, catch her in the hard light of his blue eyes and demand that she tell the truth?

She followed him to the parking lot, wondering and waiting. But he didn't say anything. He was stringing her along, toying with her like a cat plays with a mouse.

Well, he'd better watch out, she thought as she climbed into the passenger side of his flashy red Mustang, because this little brown-haired mouse had big, sharp teeth.

She fastened her seat belt and watched as Joe buckled up and keyed the ignition. As the Mustang purred, he went through a series of procedures with the efficiency of a pilot preparing for takeoff. Seat belt, fastened. Air-conditioning, on. Car radio, scanned and jazz station selected. Volume, adjusted. His gaze flicked over the white leather dashboard, checking gas, oil and RPM. The final touch came when he donned his sunglasses and squinted into the distance.

The top pilots never lost that cocky attitude, she thought. They conquered speed and altitude. Faster than sound, they were masters of the sky. So arrogant. So doggoned sexy.

Bailey looked away from him. She glided her long, slender fingers across the white leather upholstery. "This car is exactly what I would expect you to drive. Of course, a former test pilot would have to drive a glamorous vehicle."

"What do you drive?"

"A 1971 Volkswagen bug." She grinned. "She's mostly held together by coat hangers and duct tape."

"Typical."

"Was that meant to be an insult, Joe?"

"You stunt fliers are all the same. You'll climb into any machine with an engine."

She shrugged. "Some psychic guy from Boulder told me that you are what you drive. I guess that's true. I don't mind being a plain, old, steady Volks."

"Yeah," he agreed. "It's a car with a lot of spunk."

"And what about you?" She cast him a sideways glance. "Are you a Mustang, Joe? High performance? With lots of flash and dash and horsepower?"

"Not anymore. I hung up my wings."

"Get out of town!" She stared, taken aback. "You mean to tell me that you never fly anymore?"

"On occasion. But most of the time, I'm just a working stiff for the FAA."

"Still glamorous," she said.

"What do you mean?"

"You're a lawman, Joe. And not just a traffic policeman, either. You're a sky cop."

They covered the distance to Centennial quickly and parked. Strolling among the many private planes, charters and helicopters that were tethered and hangared there, she quickly located the psychiatrist's Beechcraft Bonanza with the silver tail and the "DR" call letters. "That's the one," she said.

"You're sure?" he asked as he jotted down the identification numbers.

"I might not recognize the man, but I do know my planes. That is one homely-looking machine."

"You don't like the Beech?"

"I like a little more zip and a little shorter runway."

He grinned. "You're a fast woman, Bailey Fielding."

For a second, she thought he was going to give her a little hug. His arm reached toward her, hovered, then dropped back to his side. *What was going on here?*

"Okay," Joe said. "Let's go to the office. I'll get this shrink's name and address."

Bailey entered with him, but held back while he showed his FAA credentials and asked questions. She was quiet, watching, trying to figure out why Joe was being so friendly. He'd shed the jacket of his navy blue suit. Without it, he looked far more comfortable. Her gaze drifted down his backside, from his broad shoulders to his tailbone. He'd look mighty nice in tight blue jeans.

Joe seemed more unkempt than usual, which, she supposed, wasn't strange when she considered the strain he was working under. He'd lost some weight. The waist of his trousers must have been loose, because he hitched up his belt. His black hair needed a trim.

Her fingers itched to touch that hair, to soothe the tense lines that crisscrossed his forehead and radiated from the corners of his eyes. The poor guy looked tired, battered.

Doggone it all, she was beginning to like Joe Rivers. She was beginning to want to help him, to somehow ease his pain.

When he finished talking to the man behind the desk, he was smiling, and his warmth melted through her like hot butter. She hadn't heard him laugh since before the crash.

"Dr. Lawrence Salton," he informed her as they stepped outside. "His offices are at the Tech Center, which isn't far from here. Do you mind coming with me?"

"I've got the time," she drawled. "But I don't quite understand what's going on here, Joe."

His expression was all innocence. "About what?"

Slowly, she said, "You're an FAA official. If you wanted an ID on a pilot, a shrink who owned a Bonanza, hangared at Centennial, you could find out without a look-see from me."

"True."

"And it does seem mighty odd that—while you're in the middle of an investigation—you're taking me along on a visit to this character. How come?"

"Maybe I like spending time with you, Bailey."

She pulled back and studied him, looking for signals of insincerity. "Come again, hotshot?"

"Why wouldn't I like being with you? You're smart and insightful. Maybe you'll give me a new way of looking at this investigation."

"And maybe you're trying to lull me into a false sense of security before you drop the boom."

"Only if you've got something to hide."

Now, she thought, now was the moment when she should tell him what had happened in the cockpit. She should get it over with.

But Bailey hesitated. She didn't want these pleasant moments with Joe to end.

Looking away from him, she scanned the field and noticed that the Bonanza had been taxied right beside them for fueling. "But I don't think the trip to the Tech Center will be necessary. That's the shrink's plane they're getting ready for a takeoff."

"Salton must be here," Joe said. "Do you recognize him?"

Bailey tried to recall what the man looked like. Vaguely, she had the impression that he was brown haired, brown eyed and average height. With a mustache. She spotted such a man at the far end of the field. He was accompanied by four other people, and he was clearly the leader of this tight little cluster. She pointed. "There. I think that's him."

She and Joe approached the group.

The man she'd assumed was Salton was speaking in a gentle tone. "Visualize," he said. "Touch the wings, imagine the flight of a soaring eagle, strong and brave. A mythical creature, dominating the atmosphere. Just as you will dominate—"

Joe interrupted, "May I have a word with you, Dr. Salton?"

"Not now. I have a group."

"I insist," Joe said as he flipped out his wallet and displayed his credentials. "I'm with the FAA."

"I knew it!" wailed a tiny woman who was wearing huge sunglasses. "Something's wrong with the plane."

Salton patted her arm. "I assure you, Emily, that there is nothing, absolutely nothing, wrong with my plane."

"I'm afraid."

"Maybe you're not quite ready for this flight," he said.

"I've got to do it." She reached up behind her sunglasses to swab at her eyes. "I'm going to New York with my husband. I need to be able to fly. I'm all right."

Salton turned toward Joe. "I can't talk. This is a very important stage for these individuals. They're altitude impaired."

"What's that?" Bailey questioned.

A husky man who looked big enough to play football for the Denver Broncos answered her, "Fear of flying."

"Well, that's nothing to be ashamed of," Bailey said. She was annoyed that the doctor found it necessary to make up some ludicrous name for this very real phobia. Altitude impaired? "I think you're brave to be here. Fear of flying is a terrible thing. I just got over my own fear. And I'm a pilot."

Salton glared at her. "That's very interesting, but—"

"Why?" asked the Bronco-size guy. "What made you scared?"

This probably wasn't a good time to mention crashing, she thought. If these people were going up for the first time in a small plane, they didn't need vivid images of the worst possible thing that could happen to them. "I guess your doctor is right. I had a bad experience, but I don't need to talk about my stuff."

"Go ahead," said Dr. Salton. "We've discussed the dangers of flight."

They all turned expectantly toward Bailey. Apart from talks with Grandpa Mac's grief counselors from the Veterans' Administration, she'd never been analyzed, never been in group therapy, and she felt self-conscious talking about herself. On the other hand, if she could help these people, she would.

"I was in a crash," she said.

The doctor was quick to point out that though her plane had gone down, Bailey was standing here before them. Whole and very much alive. "Continue," he said.

"I can't get the picture out of my head. Or the sound of the engine running rough, then cutting out. Then I hear the screams. I feel the air disappearing beneath me and see the ground coming up fast, too fast. And there's nothing I can do. I'm out of control." Talking about the crash brought back the dizzy sensation of terror. "That's the worst part. Being out of control. I dreamed about it, then I convinced myself that I could never fly again."

"Let me get this straight," said the big guy. "You're a pilot, and you were still scared?"

"Only a fool never knows fear."

"How did you get over it?"

"I wanted to fly. More than anything. More than fear. It's beautiful in the sky. The light is clean and pure, wide open to an endless horizon. I love the power of being able to dip and swerve and climb like a rocket. And I love to glide, floating on a gentle breeze, hanging there like a star." Bailey realized that she'd been gesturing. Her arm had lifted above her head to place an imaginary planet in the faraway skies. "Anyway, I'm willing to face the very demons of hell to get myself airborne."

When she glanced over at Salton, he nodded to her, then said to the group, "Primal experiences. We are living in a wonderful time, being able to soar like the birds. Can you visualize the images?"

The small woman clutched Joe's arm. "There's nothing wrong with the doctor's plane, is there?"

"I'm sure there isn't, ma'am. All planes, even private planes, are required to log maintenance and repair work. These machines are less likely to develop a mechanical problem than your car."

"But you haven't personally inspected it, have you?"

"I'm investigating a totally different incident."

"Incident?"

"An air accident."

"A crash?" Emily squeaked. She faced the group. "Doesn't this seem strange to any of you? We run into two people at the airport, and they've both been involved in crashes."

The others made placating noises, and the doctor rested his hand on her shoulder, but it seemed to Bailey that they'd all had enough of this lady and her brittle, demanding panic.

When she tore off her sunglasses and stared with tense eyes, she looked somewhat familiar. "I don't believe any of this stuff about being safer in a plane than in your car. If we go up in the sky, we're all going to die."

"Shut up," one of the others snapped. "We're visualizing an eagle."

"Visualize this." She stuck out her fist, middle finger raised. "It's a bird!"

"Stop it!" The doctor turned to her. Softly, he said, "Perhaps, Emily, you're not quite ready for this phase of the treatment."

"Fine. I'm leaving." She turned on her heel and marched toward the office.

"And the rest of you?" the doctor questioned. "Are you ready to soar?"

Hesitantly, they nodded.

"Wait here," he instructed as he stepped up beside Joe and walked a few paces. "What the hell is this all about?"

"Kate Rivers," he said. "I'm her husband."

"I see." He observed Joe with far more interest. "Still speaking of her in the present tense, aren't you? She *was* your wife. Isn't it time to let go?"

"She's still my wife," Joe said stiffly.

"You're a widower. Kate's dead. You need to deal with it."

Away from his group, Dr. Lawrence Salton was hard. Bailey didn't like him, didn't like the way his brown mustache covered his upper lip and made him look as if he was sneering.

"I'm investigating the accident," Joe said. "And I—"

"That seems highly irregular," Salton said. "Why would the FAA assign an investigator who was so personally involved?"

"I requested the assignment."

"You really are a glutton for punishment, aren't you? What's your name? It's Joe, isn't it? Listen, Joe, let's make this fast."

"I need some information about the medication you prescribed for Kate."

"That's confidential."

"Not when it involves public safety."

"Call my office and make an appointment," Salton growled. "If we have privacy, we can be more honest. Can't we, Joe? We can talk about what this is really about."

"Which is?"

"It's obvious." He displayed prominent white teeth beneath the mustache. "You're jealous of my relationship with your wife."

Without another word, he returned to his group.

"What a sleaze," Bailey mumbled. "Visualize a jackass."

Joe wasn't laughing. He turned to her. "Let's go."

THOUGH JOE HADN'T intended to spend the day searching for men who might have been Kate's lover, that was the way these hours were beginning to shape up. He wasn't sure that Kate's love life had any connection to the crash, and he was certain that the FAA would not sanction his actions in pursuing that area of investigation.

Still, he rationalized as he eased the Mustang out of the Centennial parking lot and headed southeast, Kate's state of mind had affected her piloting ability, especially since she'd been taking medication. Judgment impaired, he thought. Reflexes slowed. How long had this been going on? Who else, besides Bailey, knew?

The lover. Kate's lover knew everything. If he found that man, that back-stabbing son of a . . .

"Joe?"

"What is it, Bailey?"

"I don't think Kate was involved with the doctor."

"That's swell," he said tersely. If his wife had preferred Dr. Lawrence Salton over him, Joe figured he needed to seriously consider self-exile. "Why don't you think so?"

"She always called him 'Doctor.' Not by his first name. That seems formal, doesn't it? I mean, if they were . . ."

"Lovers." Joe supplied the word that gnawed at his soul. "Yeah, you're probably right. If they were lovers, she'd call him by his first name."

He was relieved to find himself agreeing with Bailey.

In Joe's mind, Claude Whistler was a more obvious choice for the role of Kate's lover, the father of her baby. Claude had money and power, two assets that attracted Kate like a magnet.

He glanced over at Bailey in the passenger seat. "You really don't know who it was?"

"No. And that's the whole truth. Now will you be as honest with me?"

"Sure," he said.

"Why'd you bring me over here to Centennial?"

"I needed for you to identify the plane."

"You could have found out in another way. Like finding one of Kate's prescription bottles and checking the name. Or using your authority to get Salton's name from her gynecologist."

"I could have done that," he said, "but I've been concentrating on the wreckage. This is the first time I've really gone into the field."

"After two months and two weeks?" she questioned. "This is the first time you've gotten around to talking to people?"

"The other investigators did that part. They took statements immediately following the accident. I've only been actively involved for a little over a week."

"Why did the FAA reopen active investigating?"

"You know the government," he said. "Why do they do anything?"

It was an easy answer, and Joe hoped that, for a while longer, everyone would believe it. He needed time. He needed to figure this out.

"Are you really considering sabotage?" she asked. "Like Grandpa Mac said?"

"Maybe."

"So you're going to be talking with the survivors."

"Yes, and with the families of those who died." Like the new congressman, Ted Gambling.

A visible shudder convulsed her shoulders. "I feel so bad for those people."

"The survivors. Like me?"

"I feel the worst for you, Joe." He heard a catch in her voice. "For your loss. I wish I could take your misery and carry it up into the sky, beyond the ozone, so you wouldn't have to be hurting anymore."

As he pulled up at a stoplight, she touched his arm and he reluctantly turned his head toward her. After Kate's death, he avoided pity. He'd brushed away the shallow condolences of friends and family. They couldn't know how he felt. They couldn't understand.

"I'm sorry, Joe. Really sorry."

"I'm okay." He hardened himself against remorse and pain. "I can take care of myself."

But when he looked into Bailey's eyes, he saw a glimmer of real emotion, of tears wept from the heart but not shed. She wasn't just saying the words; she believed them. In her, his grief found a mate.

Or was he just seeing what he wanted to see?

"Bailey, do you really care so much?"

"Of course I do. I wouldn't be much of a human being if I didn't have concern for other people. If I see somebody starving, I'm going to feed them. If I see somebody in pain, I want to make it better."

"Like Salton's group?"

"I wanted to help." She frowned. "I'm not sure that I did."

"I'm not sure that he did, either."

Joe cleared his throat and returned his gaze to the road. He was beginning to get a clear picture about Bailey. She was, quite simply, a good person. In her plainspoken, commonsensical way, she was kind. She was helpful, trying to do the right thing.

"So, tell me, Bailey, have you been in touch with any of the survivors?"

"I sent cards and condolences, then I backed off. Oh, but there's one of the survivors who's been in touch with me. Ross O'Shea."

"The actor?"

"The guy you carried off the plane. If you talk to him during the course of your investigation, be sure you give him my worst. All he got from the crash was a sprained arm and a small scar near his hairline, but he's claiming all kinds of damages. Did you know he's been on talk shows?"

"I saw one of the shows," he said. "Something about 'Living with the Nightmare: Survivors of Disasters.' At the time, I didn't think it was funny."

"But now?"

"There were four people who had been in various freak accidents, sitting in a row with neck braces and splints and casts. One guy survived having a piano dropped on him."

"Really?"

"It's not funny," he said. "But I kept thinking of cartoons. Like Wile E. Coyote and the Roadrunner. Another one had fallen down a well. Then there was Ross. His account of the plane crash featured him as superhero, pulling people from the wreckage."

Bailey snorted. "That no-account actor has been trying to make his career on almost being killed in a plane crash."

"Has he been bothering you?"

"Until I got back to Denver, it was only his lawyers. Since I've arrived here three days ago, he's left half a dozen messages on my answering machine."

"That's harassment. You don't have to put up with it."

"He'll go away," she said. "Besides, his phone calls give my answering machine something to do."

At the intersection, he turned north.

"Wrong way," she said. "Where are we headed?"

"I need to stop by my place and pick up my toothbrush. Don't worry, we have plenty of time before you have to file your flight plan."

"Are you taking a trip?"

"I'm your fourth passenger on the flight this afternoon to Pueblo."

"What for?"

"Routine," he said. "Checking you out on skills. This is the first time you've solo piloted a Cessna."

"Excuse me, Joe Rivers, but I thought I just heard you say that you were doing a fly-along to see if I'm a capable pilot. That can't be right."

"It's no big deal, Bailey. I'm just—"

"Bull! I don't need checking out."

He hadn't expected an explosion. Maybe he'd even deluded himself into believing that he and Bailey were on the same side. But the dark glare in her eyes told him that, on some level, she still considered him the enemy.

He flared back at her. "That's my decision. The last time you had a commercial flight, there were five deaths."

"That's not the reason," she said. "You know I'm capable. You know it! Why are you really flying along?"

He wasn't entirely sure. But he knew he needed to stick close to Bailey. He wanted to stick close. "Call it instinct."

Chapter Six

Bailey sputtered. Sitting beside him in the slick Mustang, she had never been so confused in all her life. In the first place, she felt sorry for Joe. Her heart went out to him. But she could not ignore his overweening authority. Riding along with her? Checking out her skills? How could he insult her like that! She didn't need a doggoned FAA baby-sitter.

And she really hated that he was taking her to his town house, as if they were friends who found nothing unusual in visiting each other's home. He was taking her emotions on a barnstorming stunt ride where they went up and down and loop-the-loop, eliciting gasps from onlookers. She wanted to scream for him to stop. At the same time, she wanted the ride to go on forever.

When they pulled up in front of Joe's redbrick, Colonial-style town house, Bailey remembered the last time, the only time, she'd been here with Kate.

"Bailey, do you want to come in?"

"No," she snapped.

"Fine. I'll be right back."

She changed her mind. "Yes," she said. "I ought to see the bathroom."

The real reason was that she was curious. In her recollection, the town house was—like Kate herself—lovely and perfect. It was the kind of home a cheerleader might aspire to own someday when she was ready to hang up her pom-poms. Bailey remembered matched furniture, drapes and wall decoration, clean and pretty with everything in a proper place. The first time she'd been here, the well-tended town house caused Bailey to jealously imagine a marriage that was exactly the same way.

Now Bailey was more inclined to believe that these bright surroundings were a facade that masked Kate's unhappiness, her need for antidepressants, her affair with another man. But what did this town house mean to Joe?

She wanted to see what it looked like, maybe to get a focus on this man who was driving her to the edge of distraction.

Though Bailey didn't expect the place to look the same as when Kate was alive, she was unprepared for the debacle that greeted her when Joe opened the door. It was dark, dusty and didn't smell too terrific, either. A pile of yellowed newspapers spilled across the foyer. The Scandinavian table near the door was piled high with a dead bird-of-paradise plant and a heap of unopened mail.

A quick glance into the kitchen showed countertops stacked with dirty dishes, pizza boxes and remnants of snacks. The trash can overflowed.

She wrinkled her nose as she surveyed the scene of bachelor dishabille. "Either your home has been ransacked or you haven't cleaned in here for months."

"I wish it had been burglars," he said.

When he walked inside, he shielded his eyes, avoiding even a quick peek into the front room. Staring at a well-worn path on the carpet, he trekked down the short hallway and up the stairs.

"The guest bathroom is next to the kitchen," he said. "I'll be right back."

Bailey thought his tone was unusually subdued.

Resting her hand on the newel post, she stood at the bottom of the stairs, staring after him. It must be painful for him to live here. All these things—the tables and chairs and lamps and knickknacks—must have brought back memories of Kate.

Bailey frowned at the dismal clutter and shook her head. This wasn't right! Of course, she respected Joe's feelings and his mourning. But he couldn't live like this. Nobody should.

An exasperated sigh puffed through her lips. She wanted to hate Joe, to dismiss him from her mind and heart. But she couldn't help wanting to comfort him.

Marching into the kitchen, she dug under the sink for extralarge garbage bags, then made a first vigorous assault by emptying the kitchen trash can. Tying off the top of the bag, she deposited the refuse on the front porch.

Joe clattered down the stairway with a small carryon, which he dropped on the unswept kitchen linoleum. "What do you think you're doing?"

She scooped the newspapers, half of them not even out of their rubber bands, into another sack. "You listen here, Joe Rivers. Maybe you don't want to change a single stitch in this place because that's the way Kate left it and you've got some kind of insane idea that this is a memorial, but you can't live like this."

"I can't?"

"It's downright unsanitary. I mean, look at this kitchen! You could catch some dread disease by eating in here."

"Bailey, don't bother with this stuff."

She might be overstepping her boundaries by attacking the litter in his life, but she couldn't just leave it. If she turned her back and walked away, she would be plagued by the thought of Joe, rotting in this house, wallowing in sadness until the trash was knee deep, then up to his waist, then over his head.

She had enough guilt without adding his pain and suffering to the list. "We've got an hour before we have to leave for the airport, and that's enough to make a difference."

"I didn't bring you here to clean."

"Well, I surely can't guess what your motives were." She handed him the bag of newspapers. "This is for recycling."

"Do I have a choice?"

"Absolutely not. Recycling is good for the environment." She hustled back into the kitchen. "While I'm doing this, you go into the front room and open up those drapes."

"The front room?"

"That's right," she drawled. "I believe you'll find it right next to the foyer."

"Yeah, sure," he said. "Open the drapes."

He peered into the darkened living room. Though it had always been Kate's room, last night he'd imagined Bailey sitting on the sofa with her legs tucked demurely beneath her and her mouth closed. That incarnation was definitely a fantasy. The healthy reality of her presence was anything but docile.

She called out to him, "Might open a window or two, as well. It smells like something died in here."

Something had died in here. His marriage.

Bailey stalked out of the kitchen and stood beside him. "Come on, Joe. It's just stuff. Chairs and tables and a really nice entertainment unit."

"Kate picked it out, all of it."

"Your wife had excellent taste. After all, she picked you out, too." She patted his shoulder. "But this isn't ancient Egypt. You don't have to bury her possessions with her in a pyramid tomb. Now, you go open those drapes."

She returned to the kitchen, muttering about dead houseplants and air freshener.

He went to the window and yanked on the cord.

The afternoon light splashed harshly on the beige-and-white-striped sofa and chairs. The colors had complemented Kate. When she'd bought the furniture set, she remarked on how well it went with her hair. For a moment, he tried to imagine her sashaying through the entry, humming while she dusted her shelves and her mosaic-topped coffee table. His mind struggled to conjure an image of her, but he failed.

She wasn't coming back. She didn't live here anymore.

"Oh, my sweet hallelujah!" Bailey exclaimed from the kitchen. "Joe, get your lazy rump in here."

He hadn't even been able to tiptoe into this memory-filled room in weeks, but now he strode across the plush carpet. Somehow, he felt lighter, as if his center of gravity had changed.

He poked his head into the kitchen, where Bailey stood with the refrigerator door wide open. She pointed with disgust at the contents. "What is this junk?"

"Casseroles," he said defensively. "After Kate died, people kept bringing me food. And it wasn't really anything I wanted or liked."

"I see. Most of these well-meaning gifts were brought here a couple of months ago?"

He nodded.

She pulled one out. "I would guess that this is scalloped potatoes à la mold. And here's a tray of fungus burritos. Oh, and look at this lump! Either it's bread made from blue corn—"

"Or a culture for penicillin," he said. "Let's get rid of it. All of it."

"Actually, I think you should bequeath the whole refrigerator to medical science and start over with a new one." Platter after platter, she emptied the contents of the refrigerator into a garbage bag. "Honestly, Joe, Grandpa Mac is a widower, too, and he never got himself into such a sorry state. Now, you take these toxic casseroles and dispose of them right away."

Dutifully, he carted the trash bags to the Dumpster behind the town houses and tossed them inside. It felt good to dig out from the mess his life had become.

Joe inhaled deeply, caught a whiff of the garbage and took a step back. Okay, maybe it wasn't a perfectly fragrant world. But, for a moment, he'd had a glimpse of clarity.

And he had Bailey to thank for it.

By the time he returned to the town house, she'd almost finished loading the dishwasher. The countertops were cleared.

"Looks good in here."

"We've barely made a dent," she said. "You know, I've been thinking about your investigation."

"Have you?"

"Best place in the world for contemplation is standing over the kitchen sink."

"I'll make a note of that. For the FAA."

"Anyhow, Joe, it seems to me like you're spending a lot of time figuring out the identity of Kate's lover."

"I haven't meant to. Things just keep circling back in that direction."

"I suggest you find that piece to the puzzle. Get it out of your system," she said. "It's the only way you'll move on."

"Like cleaning out the town house," he said.

She glanced up. "I suppose you've already gone through her things. You know, to search for a clue to her lover's identity."

He hadn't. He couldn't stand the thought of pawing through her drawers, touching her clothes, looking at the things she'd selected with such care. "I don't know where to start."

"What about her jewelry box? I know Kate had some nice pieces. Diamond earrings?"

"I bought those for her on our first anniversary. On the fifth, I got her a tennis bracelet to match."

"Check it out," Bailey said. "I'll finish up in here."

"Hold on," he said. "Let's keep in mind that I'm the one who's running this investigation."

"From the looks of this place, you can't even run a vacuum cleaner, but I will try to remember my place, sir."

Joe went to the office and unlocked his desk. In the rear of the bottom drawer was a locked box. As he touched the cold metal handle, a shock went up his arm. He recalled the argument they'd had when he had insisted on putting Kate's good jewelry in here with their important papers. For safety.

Safety? What a joke! He'd been so careful to guard her diamonds, but he had failed to keep her precious self safe from harm. Dammit! Would he never be free from grief? From guilt?

He unlocked the box. Inside were three smaller velvet-covered boxes. One contained the diamond stud earrings with two different gold cuffs. He held them in his palm, watching the flash of reflected light from the sharp-cut facets. Then he removed the sparkling bracelet.

"Joe? Where are you?"

"In the den," he called out.

"My gracious Lord! This room is a total pit."

Joe held up the earrings and bracelet. "Kate loved these. She really liked beautiful, expensive things."

"Who wouldn't?" But Bailey hardly glanced at the jewels. "We're going to need a backhoe to clear this mess."

Absently, he picked up the third box. What was in here? He couldn't remember. He'd only bought her the two pieces.

Displayed against a background of black velvet were her wedding and engagement rings. She hadn't been wearing them in the crash. Apparently, she hadn't been wearing them too frequently in the past six weeks while she dated another man.

He closed the box with a snap. "There's nothing resembling a clue in this collection."

"Try the bedroom," Bailey advised. "I always keep my special things in the top drawer of my bureau."

"The underwear drawer," he said dully. "You and every other woman in the world. That's the first place burglars check."

"Then I guess it's worth taking a gander. We're at least as smart as your average burglar, aren't we?"

Joe really didn't want to start digging around in the bedroom. All Kate's clothes still hung in the closet. The air still held the cloying fragrance of her favorite perfume.

"Come on, Joe. We haven't got much time."

Apparently, he realized, Bailey wasn't going to allow him to avoid this confrontation.

She went first. Again, she adjusted the curtains and opened a window, bathing the room in light and the sun-warmed air of a July afternoon. Her gaze scanned quickly. "No books," she said. "Guess it would have been too much to hope for a diary."

"She wasn't much on writing letters, either."

Before he could think, Joe went to Kate's dresser and opened the top drawer. Though he would have rather stuck his hand into a box full of rattlesnakes, he felt among her silky underthings until he touched the wood base of the drawer. His fingertips encountered a flat box, and he pulled it out.

About the size of a cigar box, it was patterned with pink roses and lace. "I don't think I've seen this before."

"So? What's inside?"

There were three one-dollar tokens from a Central City casino. A plastic amber vial containing Kate's prescription for antidepressant drugs. And a pendant. A little golden airplane, similar to a Cessna Citation, with a diamond where the single propeller should have been.

Distastefully, Joe lifted it from the box by its chain. "She must have picked this up for herself. It looks like a souvenir-shop toy. But it must be expensive, or Kate wouldn't have kept it."

"Do you think that's a real diamond?"

"Must be." He idly turned the pendant in his hand. "I don't get it. This pendant isn't Kate's taste."

"Might have been a gift," she said. "I think it's kind of cute."

"Do you?" He turned toward her and held out the pendant. "It's yours, Bailey."

"I can't accept it. A real diamond would be valuable."

"I don't want it."

He held the necklace at eye level. The chain seemed to burn his fingers. The little golden airplane seemed poised to fly into his eyes like a stinging hornet. A gift from Kate's lover? The thought enraged him. That bastard!

And what about his unfaithful wife? She'd betrayed him in the worst way a woman can cheat on a man.

"Joe? Are you all right?"

"I want you to have this necklace, Bailey. I want you to wear it often, and every time I see it, I'll remember."

"I really don't think that's a good—"

"It's an important lesson. Every time I see this little airplane, I'll know what happens when a man is dumb enough, blind enough, to trust a woman."

"Not every woman, Joe. That was just Kate."

He reached behind her. "Let me put it on you."

"No!" She shoved against his chest, and he looked into her face. "Don't ask me to be a substitute for Kate. I'm not her. I never will be."

The pendant fell from his grasp. "I didn't mean to—"

"I know."

"I wish things could be different."

She tilted away from him, gazed up at him with a strangely puzzled expression. They were scant inches apart, and Joe breathed in the scent of Bailey. Fresh and clean. He hadn't noticed before that her lashes were thick and long. Her cheekbones, high and fine. Her skin was a marvel. The closer he got, the better she looked.

Her lips parted. He couldn't resist.

Her eyelids didn't close until the last second, and he saw himself reflected in her eyes, wondering and fearful. When their lips met, a flash of arousal fired his senses, blanked his mind. Her long, slender body glided close. Closer, he wanted her closer. He tightened his embrace. Her breasts crushed against him. Her legs pressed against his loins, and the friction excited him even more.

Joe was gasping when their kiss ended.

"No," she said. "Joe, we can't."

He held her shoulders and kissed her again. His tongue probed, and she responded.

When they separated, her gaze was dark, mysterious and liquid. Bailey was a creature of the air, but she reminded him of a mermaid, a siren, an enchantress. She was remarkable. Why hadn't he seen it before? "You're beautiful, Bailey."

She looked away from him. Slowly, she took a backward step. "This can't be happening."

"But it is."

"Damn," she said.

It was the first time he'd ever heard her use real profanity. "What's wrong?"

"We need to leave. I have to file my flight plan."

"Cancel it," he said hoarsely. "Stay with me."

"After all that fuss I made with Claude? I think not."

She stepped away from him. The motion of her long

body was sinuous, graceful. "Now, you skedaddle down the stairs, and I'll finish up searching in here for clues. Go on."

Joe nodded. There were a lot of thoughts going through his head, but they were too nebulous to put into words. He went to the door of his bedroom.

She made a shooing motion with her hand. "Get out of here, Joe. I'll be done in a minute."

As soon as he left the room, she sank down on the bed. Kate's bed. She placed her hand over her rib cage and felt her heart fluttering like a captive bird. He'd kissed her.

But had he really been kissing Bailey? Or was it Kate? Was he trying to revive the memory of Kate?

No matter how much Joe tried to remove Kate from his life, she would always be lurking at the edges of his consciousness. She had been his wife for seven years, and nothing could erase that fact. Even though she'd been disloyal, even though they'd fought and squabbled and their sex life had dwindled, he couldn't forget her. Somewhere in his mind, he still loved her a lot.

There would never be a chance for Bailey. She could never compete with a perfect memory that would only grow more wonderful with every passing year. Beautiful Kate shimmered in his recollections.

And Bailey, in all her imperfect reality, was left to compete with a ghost of the ideal woman. She didn't stand a chance!

After a quick glance in the closet, where Kate's beautiful clothes offered a smug affront to Bailey's minimal wardrobe, she picked up the pendant necklace from the carpet and dropped it in her shirt pocket.

At the bottom of the stairs, Joe stood waiting, but she barely looked at him. "Let's get out of here."

"Bailey, about what happened upstairs—"

"Forget it, Joe." She wrapped her hand around the front-door knob. "Now, here's what I think you should do. Forget this trip to Pueblo with me, stay here and get this place into livable condition."

"It'll wait." He leaned against the door, holding it shut.

"I beg your pardon, Joe, but that's what this mess has been doing. Waiting."

"It's not important," he said.

She was important. Joe could feel his priorities straightening out. Right now, Bailey was number one.

Her eyebrows raised above her teasing brown eyes. The irises were lighter, less troubled. When she pushed her hair off her forehead and smoothed the sides back into her tight ponytail, she looked so cute. With her hands on her hips, energy sparked from her like tiny lightning bolts.

"I apologize if I made you uncomfortable," he said.

"Accepted," she snapped. "Now, let's go."

"But I'm not sorry I kissed you, Bailey."

"Whatever." She grabbed the door handle again.

"Dammit, woman, I'm trying to talk to you. Hold still!"

"There's nothing to say."

"The hell there isn't."

"Listen up, Joe. You can't even vacuum your carpet because you feel like Kate's here in this room, haunting the sofa and the coffee table. And I'm just as bad. When I'm with you, I feel like she's in my head, watching and laughing at me and telling me that I'm not your type."

"What?"

"Besides, you're into the middle of an investigation. As you've pointed out lots of times, I was piloting the plane that crashed. There can't be anything between you and me until this case is all wrapped up. It wouldn't be right."

But the way he felt couldn't be wrong. For the first time since the crash, he had red blood flowing through his veins instead of ice water.

"Bailey, I'm not investigating you. Nobody blames you for the crash." What was the matter with her? Why was she equivocating? "If there's one consistent opinion from everyone involved, with the exception of that worthless Ross O'Shea, it's that you performed well."

"Oh, really? And if I performed well, why did you want to come with me on the charter flight to Pueblo? I seem to recall some comment about checking me out."

"It's routine." God, she was the most stubborn, most infuriating woman in the world. "Why can't you let go of it?"

"How can I? You might take away my pilot's license."

"Trust me, Bailey, I wouldn't let my feelings for you influence my judgment."

"Your judgment?"

Her dark eyes flashed with obsidian brilliance. With her fists on hips and legs widespread, Joe didn't think he'd ever seen a sexier woman in his life.

"What's your point, Bailey?"

"You have all the power, Joe. You could take away my ability to fly. And I can't live with that."

He could have protested. He could have promised that he wouldn't take her license, no matter what. But that wasn't the way it worked. "What are you saying? That you want to be the boss?"

"That's right. Won't work the other way."

"Forget it." He bent down and picked up his carry-on bag. He opened the front door. "I guess you were right. There won't be anything between us. You're not my type."

"Is that so?" His words were a slap in the face, and she hardened herself.

"Yes, it is so."

"And what type is your type? Fast and flashy, like your car?" Like Kate, she thought. Joe would be embarrassed to be seen with someone who was less than gorgeous, someone like herself. "Well, you're not my type, either. Someday, Joe Rivers, I'm going to find myself a man who's kind and gentle and caring."

"A wimp," he said.

"Not at all," she continued. "This man is going to be strong enough to stand up for himself and what he believes in without hurting anybody else. Without hurting me. He'll be a man I can trust. Somebody smart and good."

"The perfect man," Joe said.

"And that's not you."

She stalked down the sidewalk from the town house and flung herself into the passenger side of his car. Thus ended the shortest, most intense relationship of her life. For the space of one hour, she'd been happy with Joe. They had both actually been smiling and laughing.

Bailey rolled her eyes. She'd been cleaning, for goodness' sake. Doing a woman's work. That was probably the only way he could relate to a female. Hotshot Joe Rivers, former test pilot and current sky cop, could only engage in male-female relations when the female was fulfilling one of those so-called traditional roles, like cooking or cleaning or ironing his starched white shirts.

"And I'll tell you one more thing," she said. "You need to have your suits tailored."

"Why?"

"Because you never look like the shoulders fit. When you've got on a suit jacket, you're always shrugging and twitching. Like a kid wearing long pants for the first time."

"And you're an expert on fashion?"

"I just might be. You've never seen me dressed up."

At the airfield, she slammed the passenger door of his high-performance Mustang, but she made sure, when she sauntered away from his car, that she walked cool and slow. When a lady left a man, she needed to look good, to give him something to think about. Bailey had had enough practice in walking away. The problem was that she hadn't mastered the special, serious, committed part of a relationship.

Bailey hadn't been brought up to cater to a man. Grandpa Mac had taught her all the skills she needed for survival, which happened to include cooking and cleaning, but he'd also shown her how to change the oil in her car and repair her aircraft. He'd even taught her how to defend herself, how to fell an opponent with one well-placed, hard jab.

What he hadn't been able to explain was how to seduce a man, how to hold a lover close and dear. One time, he'd told her that sex would come naturally when she found the right man. But the only thing she'd figured out about relationships thus far in her life was how to say goodbye and get on with her life.

As she went through the preflight check with the mechanics at Sky Air, Bailey was sure that none of them could tell that she was hurt and confused. None of them would guess, for instance, that when she licked her lips, she was still tasting the pleasure of Joe's kisses. The amazing, awesome pleasure.

But as soon as she walked into the Sky Air offices, Greta knew something was different. Her lips pursed. "You've been with Joe all this time?"

"Helping with his investigation."

"That's a strange procedure for the FAA," she said. "You be careful with him, Bailey. Watch yourself, or he's going to get you in trouble."

"I know," Bailey said.

Greta pointed to three people who were sitting in the lounge area. "Here's your charter. The Benedict family."

Bailey greeted her passengers with a firm handshake and a confident smile. Two men and a woman, all in their sixties.

"We're going down to Pueblo for a birthday party," the woman said. "My grandbaby is four."

The heavy-jowled older gentleman scowled. "A damn waste of time. Right in the middle of the week. Messes up my schedule. We'll need to return early tomorrow. Seven in the morning?"

"I'll be ready," Bailey said.

After she loaded their luggage and the masses of presents for their granddaughter, she informed them, "We'll be having another passenger. A gentleman from the FAA."

"Good," said the older Benedict. "Then we'll be safe, won't we?"

"Absolutely," Joe said as he joined them.

He was just as arrogant as he could be. Bailey wanted to slap that superior expression off his face as he introduced himself and nodded to her as if nothing had happened between them.

The younger man, a cousin, asked him, "And why is it that you're riding along?"

"Routine inspection," he said.

After her passengers were comfortably boarded, Bailey strapped herself into the left cockpit seat. Joe was right beside her, riding shotgun. That was his job, to observe, and it was her job to ignore him. But she was achingly aware of his presence, his nearness, even his scent. Her body yearned for his touch. He made her feel tense and tender at the same time.

Bailey made sure that she went through every pre-flight procedure with painstaking precision. She didn't want to give Joe a single reason for complaint.

As she taxied away from the hangar, she went through the usual equipment checks. Revving the engine. Checking the steering and the flaps and tail rudder. Pointing her toe, she tapped the brakes on the right side of the landing gear. Then the left.

The left side was loose. She pressed harder. The left brake did not respond at all. Under her breath, she muttered, "Oh, my sweet Mississippi, I cannot believe this."

Joe leaned close. "A problem?"

One dead brake in the gear really wasn't a big deal. But she couldn't ignore the mechanical failure with Joe aboard. No matter what else she thought about him, he was an FAA investigator, and he would surely pull her license if she ignored a basic safety precaution like this one."

With a sigh, she said, "I've got no left brake."

"Take her in," Joe ordered.

"I was just about to, sir."

She held down the right brake, and the aircraft pivoted on one wheel, circling 180 degrees to head back to the Sky Air hangar.

To her passengers, she announced, "I'm sorry, folks. I'm having a problem with the braking system. We'll have to find you another charter."

"Great," said the old Benedict. "I might get out of this birthday party yet."

Bailey radioed back to the office. "Greta, my left brake is screwed up. You're going to have to come up with another plane for this charter."

"Can do."

"I'll take the flight," Bailey said. "Whichever plane you come up with."

"Sorry, Bailey. I'm checking my lists, and I don't think we've got anything available except an Otter, and that's too big to fly with only three passengers. Besides, we need it tomorrow morning."

"We'd be back by ten. I promise. Please, Greta."

"I'm afraid not. I'm going to have to contact another charter service. Tell your passengers."

"There's nothing? What about that little Piper Cub that Claude uses?"

"Too small."

Bailey's frustration peaked. "I cannot believe this. How could something as simple as a brake check slip by the mechanics?"

"It happens." Greta signed off with a warning. "Be nice to the passengers, Bailey."

"Why wouldn't I be sweet as pecan pie?"

"Because you're angry about the plane. I can hear it in your voice."

"What you're hearing is a little bit of static and a lot of gloom."

But she managed to be pleasant as she escorted her passengers to the neighboring hangar and turned them over to a one-man charter service who was delighted to have the business.

After she waved her friendly goodbye to the Benedicts, she erased the false optimism from her face and stormed back to the Sky Air hangar. Her luck had been running bad all day. First, the scene with Joe. Now this.

Since it was well after five o'clock in the afternoon, she wouldn't even have the satisfaction of chewing out the mechanics and ground crew. All Sky Air employees, except for Greta, had been gone for a couple of hours.

Even though Bailey wasn't authorized to work on the planes, she intended to go over the Cessna and figure out the problem so the plane would be ready in case there was a flight tomorrow. Come hell or high wind, she wasn't going to spend another day on the ground.

Joe had beaten her to the job. His suit coat was off, and his white shirt was rolled up past the elbows. It was clear he had checked out the plane himself the minute her back was turned.

"With all due respect," she drawled, "what in blue blazes are you doing here? It's not the FAA's job to mess with the planes."

"We should repair the brake ourselves," he said.

"Whoa, hold it. Is this some kind of test? I know my regs, and I'm not officially licensed to—"

"It was cut."

"What are you talking about?"

"The brake line was sliced through. Deliberately."

"Sabotage," she said.

Chapter Seven

She'd said the word. Sabotage! But Bailey still couldn't believe it. "Joe, are you sure?"

"Somebody tampered with the brakes. The line wasn't frayed, wasn't worn, it was cut." He made a slashing motion with his hand. "A deliberate act."

But it didn't make sense. They were in Denver, not some international hotbed of terrorists. This was a lousy little Cessna Citation, owned by a Colorado-based airline. Why would someone sabotage this plane? "I guess we'd better report it."

"No."

She stared at him. "What do you mean?"

"I don't want this incident reported."

"You know the rules, Joe. You're an FAA official." Was he trying to trick her? Was this some kind of harebrained, half-witted ploy to test her competence? "Any air accident, even a dumbo attempt at sabotage like this one—which I was sure to catch before I left the ground—needs to be reported and investigated."

"I'm an investigator," he said. "Consider it reported, and don't say anything to anyone else."

"I can't ignore procedure." Accident forms were required by the FAA and the insurance company, filled out and filed in triplicate. "I'll lose my pilot's license."

He paced toward the plane, then back toward her again. The sound of his footfalls echoed on the concrete floor in the empty hangar. Beyond the opened doors, the very first hints of dusk had begun to settle as the sun dipped behind the jagged horizon of the Rocky Mountains.

Though Joe looked at her, his gaze turned inward, as if he were searching for exactly the right phrase. "I guess I haven't given you any reason to trust me, Bailey."

"No, sir. You have not." That was an understatement of the highest order.

"I won't ask you to forgive me," he said. "Just trust me. I don't have any right to ask for this. But trust me enough to give me this chance."

"What chance?"

"If we report this sabotage, I won't be able to investigate the crash."

"I don't understand. Why would your supervisor pull you off the crash investigation because you found something that looks like sabotage? Besides, these two incidents might even be related—"

He held up his hand, staunching the flow of her objections. "My supervisor doesn't know I'm here."

Bailey's energy faltered. She had a sour taste in the back of her mouth. "What are you telling me, Joe?"

"I haven't been assigned to this case. Not now. Not ever."

She swallowed hard. "Explain."

"I wanted to investigate, right from the start. But my request was turned down. My boss said I was too involved, that I couldn't be objective, that he didn't want me to have to relive Kate's death day after day.''

"Seems reasonable."

"But that's not how I feel about it. I want the crash out of my system.'' He straightened his broad shoulders. His bearing was erect, almost military. "I want her out of my life for good."

The blue-eyed gaze he leveled at Bailey was calm but determined. His were the eyes of a man who had faced death. The eyes of a test pilot. The eyes of a hero. He lacked the dangerous edge that she'd seen in Florida, but this coolness was even more scary because he seemed unshakable, willing to go to any lengths to achieve his goals.

He continued, "Kate and I didn't have the world's greatest marriage. If she'd lived, we probably would have separated or even divorced. But she was killed. Suddenly. Tragically. Her death has tied me to her more permanently than our life together.''

As he calmly, quietly poured out his soul, Bailey caught a glimpse of the real Joe Rivers. The flash and fireworks were absent. His trademark arrogance was gone. She felt, for the first time, that he was being completely honest with her.

"During this past couple of months," he said, "I thought I was crazy, insane. My supervisor called it an obsession.''

"With Kate's death."

"Right. My boss told me to take some time off. I've accumulated about two months' vacation."

"And you're on vacation right now."

"It started with my trip to Florida to see you." He stood before her and took both her hands in his. "Don't make me stop. Not now. Let me find out why the Otter crashed."

He was almost pleading with her. Joe Rivers was not the sort of man who would ever beg, but he was coming close.

"You lied to me, Joe. Out-and-out lied."

He squeezed her fingertips, and she felt an annoying thrill that climbed her arms and set her whole body to tingling.

"Please, Bailey."

His voice struck a low, compelling note that resonated within her. She didn't want to be attracted to this man, but his blue-eyed gaze shattered her defenses.

Still, she said, "No."

"This is more than a cut brake line," he said. "This is the first real clue to the crash."

"A clue? How do you figure?"

"Whoever cut that line didn't mean to cause a crash. As you said, you'd notice the problem in preflight. And since I was riding along with you, you couldn't ignore the defective brake even if you were inclined to do so."

"Me?" She pulled her hands out of his grasp. "I would never take such a risk."

"Come on, Bailey, you're a stunt pilot who's accustomed to making do with whatever flying machine you've got on hand. If I hadn't been on board, you might have decided to take off anyway and deal with the defective brake on landing."

"It crossed my mind," she admitted. "I could have managed a landing on one brake, but it would have been swerving and would have scared the Benedict family half to death."

"So," he said, "why would someone bother to set up such an obvious sabotage? I'll tell you why. It was meant as a warning. Somebody doesn't want you flying."

"Are you telling me that somebody hates me enough to mess with every plane I intend to fly?"

"It's possible."

She couldn't believe it. "I might not be the most popular gal in Denver, but I don't have enemies like that."

"Think about it," he said. "You had a rough time after the crash. You were scared. Afraid to fly. Maybe the person who caused the first crash is trying to scare you off, keep you out of the air."

"Well, that person surely does not know me very well. I don't scare easy." The very thought spiked her temper. "I do not back down."

"Good," he said.

"But this still doesn't make sense. Why would somebody want me out of the sky?"

"Maybe you witnessed something. A clue that would explain the crash."

She shook her head. "I can't think of anything."

"Maybe you saw a person who happened to be in the wrong place at the wrong time. Or overheard an implicating remark."

"Or maybe," she said, "this isn't about me at all."

"What else could it be?"

"You," she said. "Maybe the theat was meant for you."

"Dammit, you're right." His eyes flared with excitement. "This attempt at sabotage is supposed to warn me off. Somebody wants to end my investigation. That's good thinking, Bailey. That's damn brilliant."

Maybe not brilliant, but . . .

"Who have you been poking at with your investigating?"

"That shrink. The congressman. And Claude."

"Claude?" Bailey objected. "He'd never mess with one of his own planes."

"Give me the chance to find out," he said. "Don't report the cut brake line. Will you do it? Will you trust me?"

She allowed his question to hang unanswered for a moment while she considered. If they got caught, he'd probably get a slap on the wrist. She, however, would lose her pilot's license. She'd be grounded flatter than road kill on the side of a highway.

But if they figured out this case, they could both lay their ghosts to rest. Was it worth the risk?

Bailey heard the click-click of heels as someone approached the hangar from the south side where the doors were wide open.

Greta came around the corner. "Let's take a look at those brakes," she said. "I need to make up my schedule for tomorrow, and I want to see if this plane will be ready to roll."

It was time for a decision.

Bailey licked her lips. She didn't like lying, especially not to Greta, who had never done her any harm. "I already checked. You know what?"

"What?" Greta said.

"The line was kind of frayed and loose, and I figured I could fix it, but I screwed up and accidentally cut the brake line instead."

"I don't believe you, Bailey."

Her nerve plummeted into her shoes. "You don't?"

"How could you do such a silly thing?" She turned to Joe. "And I suppose you just stood there and watched her."

"I did. It happened just the way she said."

"Accidentally cut the line?" Her glance passed swiftly between them. "Well, I suppose that's why we have mechanics. And, since it was worn, we probably needed to replace it anyway. I'll tell Duffy to come in early and replace it. We'll see what he has to say about this frayed brake line."

A deep voice rumbled from behind her shoulder. "Excuse me, ma'am. I don't think there's any need for that."

Greta pivoted and faced Mac Augustine. Immediately, her face lost the slightly worried, pinched look. Her smile was warm and inviting. "Well, hello there."

"Hello yourself, sweet thing."

He gave her a long hug. To Bailey's amazement, Grandpa Mac dropped a light but lingering kiss on Greta's forehead.

"Grandpa Mac?"

He winked at her, but his attention focused on Greta. "You're looking mighty fit, pretty lady."

"I'll take that as a compliment, Mac. Any time you want to come running with me, you're welcome."

"I don't think I could keep up. But I'd like to try."

He sauntered over to Bailey, draped his arm around her shoulder. "You run along, honey, and take this sorry excuse for a test pilot along with you. I'm going to stay here and fix the brakes on this Cessna."

"Now, Mac," Greta said, "I shouldn't let you do that."

"I'm a certified mechanic." He grinned at her. "Besides, I was hoping you'd offer to stay and help me with my tools."

"As a matter of fact, I think I will." She turned to Bailey and Joe. "Both of you, get out of here. We'll have the Cessna up and running by tomorrow. And, Bailey, after tonight cancelled, I put you down for a morning flight. Be here by nine o'clock."

Mac walked them to the front of the hangar.

"Grandpa Mac, what are you doing here?"

"When I got that call from Joe this morning, I thought I'd come up here and keep an eye on things. Good thing I did."

She looked up at him. "Why do you say that?"

"The next time you two have a private conversation, don't do it standing in front of an open door." He patted her shoulder. "You run along. Be careful, honey."

"Thank you, sir," Joe said.

"Yeah," he growled. "And Joe, keep in mind that if anything happens to Bailey, I'll kill you with my bare hands."

"I'd expect that."

Mac chuckled and strolled back to where Greta was waiting for him. The doors to the hangar were closing before Bailey and Joe left the field.

Bailey couldn't believe it. "Grandpa Mac and Greta? He's old enough to be her father!"

"Some women prefer experience," Joe said.

"The man is in his sixties."

"He's older than that, Bailey. The man was a pilot in World War II."

"But he was just a kid."

"Sure," Joe said. "They were all young men. Brave men."

"No, I mean he was eight years old at the Battle of Britain in 1940. Mac was born in the United States, but his family moved to England. His father helped develop the Spitfire LF Mk IX, one of the greatest fighter planes ever built."

"I thought Mac flew in the war."

"He did. After his father was shot down, Mac started flying. He was twelve."

"Amazing," Joe said. "Your grandpa Mac sure does have the right stuff. No wonder he's going after Greta. You know, Bailey, I have it on good authority that pilots are more active, longer and better than—"

"I don't want to hear this," she said, stepping up her pace to get to the parking lot. "It's like thinking about your parents having sex. I mean, you know they do, but I'd rather consider the copulation rituals of whooping cranes."

"Mac's like a father to you, isn't he?"

"He raised me since I was eight. My parents died in a car accident." She stopped beside her Volkswagen. "Well, Joe, what are we going to do next?"

"As Mac pointed out, we can't be carrying on these private conversations in public places. But we need to come up with a game plan."

"Agreed," she said. Bailey was distinctly uncomfortable with lying to Greta and flaunting FAA regulation about reporting the cut brake line. The longer she was linked with Joe and his renegade investigation, the worse trouble she'd be in. "I want this done fast."

He offered. "My place?"

"Thanks, no." She shuddered. "I couldn't stand to be in there without donning an apron and racing around like Hannah the happy homemaker."

"Then it's got to be your place."

Bailey wasn't sure that was a good alternative. They were not, after all, discussing an after-dinner drink or a date. She and Joe were putting their heads together to figure out who, if anyone, was a saboteur.

Her career was at stake. The last thing on her mind should have been sex, but it was hard to keep her thoughts away from that subject when she noticed the masculine breadth of his chest and shoulders, his flat torso, his narrow hips. Everything about him appealed to her. It always had. How could she possibly work beside him without wanting him?

"Bailey? Your place?"

"All right, Joe, you can come to my apartment. But we've got to make an agreement, right now. We're working together to investigate possible sabotage at Sky Air. That's all. Nothing personal."

"I promise." His slow, sexy grin did not reassure her.

She scribbled down her address on a scrap of paper and handed it to him. "In case you get lost."

"You don't think my Mustang can keep up with your Volks?"

"Grandpa Mac always used to say, 'It's not the plane, it's the pilot.'"

"Don't worry, Bailey. I'll keep up with you."

He filed the scrap of paper with her address in his pocket and hurried to his car. Though she had a head start coming out of the parking lot, he was on her taillights in a moment.

Joe suffered about two seconds' worth of guilt when he realized that he had, once again, lied to her. He'd promised that there would be nothing personal between them, but his intentions were very much the opposite. He wanted to be as close to her as a man could be to a woman.

Pursuing her Volkswagen, he changed lanes and followed her on a right turn. He didn't lose sight of her vehicle until he was hemmed in by two trucks and a minivan. On the first side street, he pulled over and checked the address. Great, he'd never even heard of this street. Joe had never been much of a navigator.

BAILEY CHUCKLED as she pulled into the parking lot outside her apartment building. She'd lost him. Joe's high-performance car and his bragging sure didn't count for much when dealing with the perils of suburban traffic.

It was just as well that she'd have a few minutes to herself before he got there. Though she kept her apartment clean as a sheet of mountain snow, it still hadn't lost the musty scent from being closed up for two months. This way, she had a chance to open the windows and let some summer breezes whip through.

And she could make some coffee. Some of that fancy French-vanilla stuff that she had in the freezer.

What about food? There was that Chinese carryout restaurant that delivered. Or a pizza?

Stop! This wasn't a date.

Bailey had the feeling that she would be reminding herself of that fact often. Though she'd made a firm statement about not getting involved, she hadn't been thinking about the crash or the sabotage or the strange relationship between Mac and Greta. Bailey's imagination had been fully occupied with visions of Joe Rivers.

She'd listened with great attentiveness to every word he'd said about his phony investigation and the possibility that somebody might be after them. But the words that kept repeating in her head were from earlier, when he'd said she was pretty, and just now, when he said she was brilliant. The sensation she recalled with bone-shaking vividness was his kiss.

That moment in his arms had felt close to perfect. His mouth had claimed hers with a passionate demand. When he'd yanked her close, the tension thrilled her right down to her toes. And the second kiss...

The experience would feed her dreams for a long time to come. But that was all. She could allow herself to fantasize, but she didn't dare to allow him that close again. Because, someday, she would have to confess about what had happened in the cockpit. And he would despise her.

After locking her Volks, she followed the sidewalk. Though it was only a little after eight o'clock, there was no one around.

Bailey checked her mailbox at the front of the wrought-iron stair, then sorted through the ''occupant'' mail and the bills as she started to climb to the third floor.

Her apartment complex was four buildings in adobe-colored stucco with red tile roofs. Each building was three stories and faced a central courtyard with a garden and a stone pagoda fountain that was totally out of character with the Spanish-style architecture.

Bailey lived in 306. It was on the third floor, on the end with a view of the mountains. She liked the apartments that had just enough lighting and security to feel safe but not enough to be paranoid. There were lights outside each apartment door.

As she rounded the top of the stair and glanced down toward her apartment, she noticed that her doorway was unlit. The corner was in shadow, and Bailey hesitated.

It might have been a coincidence that her plane had been sabotaged and her bulb had burned out, creating dark places where a person could hide, but Grandpa Mac hadn't raised a fool for a granddaughter. She pivoted and started back down the stairs. Joe would be here soon and he could accompany her.

"Wait!" came a male voice from the darkness beside her door.

Bailey grabbed the railing and flew down the staircase. Her feet, in sneakers, gripped the corrugated metal. She was past the second floor when he called to her again.

"I just want to talk."

She looked up and saw him, silhouetted against the bright lights at the top of the stairs.

"Who are you?"

"Ross O'Shea, the guy you tried to kill in a crash landing."

Bailey snapped, "We've got nothing to talk about."

As he started his descent, she raced to the ground floor. With her feet on pavement, she felt safer.

"Please wait," he repeated. "Miss Fielding, I'm not going to hurt you."

He sounded sane, she thought, but he had been waiting in dark shadows near her apartment, which did not bode well for a friendly conversation.

"It's about this lawsuit," he said. "I want to drop it, but I need information."

"What kind of information?"

He was on the second-floor landing, coming closer but not pursuing her. She could see his features in the light above the stairway, and he didn't look like a psycho.

"Stay there," she said.

"That's fine with me." He stopped dead in his tracks. "I didn't mean to scare you, really."

"What do you want to say to me?"

"I think we can settle this out of court."

What a creep! Though she'd been in Florida and not Denver, Greta told her that he'd been on three local talk shows and the national show that Joe had seen. It seemed that Ross O'Shea's new career was talking about his harrowing escape from a fiery death.

In his version of the story, he had been out of his seat, battling to help everyone else when the engine exploded. He was, of course, the hero. "What's the matter, Ross? Couldn't get on 'Oprah'?"

"Hey, I had to do something, and my agent set up those talk shows when I still had the bandage across my forehead." His rich laugh echoed on the stairs. "What else was I going to do? Because of my injuries, I lost a featured movie role in the next Arnold film."

She was accustomed to hearing the Aspen-bound celebrity wannabes talking themselves up, promoting their nonexistent opportunities. "So, how come you're hanging around in the dark outside my doorway?"

"Could I come down there and talk to you, please?"

"I suppose," she said. Apart from being fatally obnoxious, he seemed harmless. "We'll stand out in the parking lot. I'm expecting company."

Bailey hurried ahead and waited for him in a puddle of light from the security lamps. A spotlight, she thought. That ought to make the actor comfortable. As he came nearer, about four feet from her, she snapped. "That's close enough. Speak your piece."

"My attorneys tell me you have no money worth considering."

"Your attorneys are correct."

"Pursuing this court thing doesn't seem profitable."

He offered a disarming smile. She even thought that the scar across his forehead added an attractive bit of interest to his otherwise precisely symmetrical features.

"So," he said, "instead of the court thing, here's what I want to do."

With a sudden charge, he covered the distance between them. He caught her wrists in his hands and held tight as a pair of handcuffs. "Fooled you, didn't I? I'm a hell of a lot better actor than anybody ever gives me credit for."

"Guess you are," she said. "Now let me go."

"Not a chance."

Before she could physically react, he twisted her left arm high behind her back. His other hand, carefully encased in a thick leather ski glove, covered her mouth. Her arm throbbed. She went up on her toes to alleviate the stress on her shoulder and elbow joints. If she moved too fast, if she struggled to escape, the bones would snap.

Bailey was caught, trapped, helpless. Where was Joe? He should have been here. If ever she had needed the presence of a strong, high-performance male, it was now.

Ross hiked her arm up higher, but she didn't give him the satisfaction of knowing how much it hurt. Ross O'Shea was a cruel bully. If she showed weakness, he'd push harder.

"Here's what I want you to know, Bailey." He was whispering into her ear. His breath was hot. "My scars are going to fade. Some people have even said that they add character. And my sprains are almost one hundred percent resolved."

He lifted her arm higher. Lord, it hurt.

Bailey gathered her strength. She was going to have to defend herself. And when she did, her efforts needed to be quick and effective.

"I want you to hear me, Bailey, to hear every word."

She maintained her immobility.

"There's a pain you caused, Bailey. You did it when that plane exploded. Do you want to know what it was? Do you?"

She wanted to be away from him. His gloved hand over her mouth was smothering her. Ready? She needed to be ready in every fiber of her body. One try. One attack. Swift. Direct. If she failed, he would surely break her arm.

"When that plane exploded, Bailey, you killed the woman I loved. Do you hear me, you—"

She stomped hard on his toes.

His grasp loosened.

She pitched forward and dragged him off balance.

He was forced to release his grip or fall with her.

When Bailey hit the asphalt parking lot, she rolled. In an instant, she was back on her feet, running for all she was worth back to the courtyard.

"Go," he yelled after her. "But know this. I'll be back. When you're least expecting it, I'll be back."

Clattering up the stairs, she didn't stop sprinting until she'd unlocked her apartment door and slammed the door shut behind her. With frantic haste, she locked the door and leaned against it.

Her arm was throbbing. Her ragged breaths sounded like the sobs she'd held back when he was threatening her. Bailey sank to the floor, shuddering.

What had he meant? *The woman he loved.*

Was it Kate? Was Ross O'Shea her lover, the father of her unborn baby?

Chapter Eight

Though Bailey told herself that she wasn't scared, her legs were so limp that she didn't trust herself to stand upright. Her stomach tensed. She gulped down breath after breath, forcing her lungs to heave.

She squeezed her eyelids closed, trying to erase the image of Ross leaping toward her, the predatory gleam in his eye as he easily conquered the scant distance she'd put between them. How could she have been so gullible? My gracious, she knew better. Ross O'Shea had never given her a reason to trust him, and she'd been lulled by his reasonable tone, tricked by his actor's guile. If she hadn't escaped from him, what would Ross have done to her?

Bailey shuddered. His plans for revenge didn't bear thinking about. She was frightened enough as it was.

Forcing herself to stand, she went to the kitchen, poured a glass of orange juice from the fridge and drank slowly. As always, in a crisis, she was able to pick herself up, dust herself off and move on. Her breathing calmed. Her heartbeat returned to a steady, normal thump. She was going to be all right. Now that she knew he was after her, she'd be ready.

When her doorbell chimed, she jumped.

"Who is it?"

"Me. Joe."

She opened the door. "What took you so long?"

"I got kind of turned around." He sauntered inside, oblivious to her goose bumps, not noticing her fear. "I don't know my way around this part of town. Finally, I had to dig my map out of the glove box and trace my route."

"You could have asked for directions." While he'd been playing with his maps and driving down blind streets, she'd been attacked and terrorized. "Why didn't you?"

"I had a map," he said, as if that explained everything.

"Excuse me," she said. "I forgot that men are genetically incapable of asking for directions."

"What's wrong, Bailey?"

"Did you notice my light was burned out?"

"Yes. If you have a bulb, I'll fix it for—"

"I'm not talking about home maintenance." She hadn't meant to shout, but her voice was louder than usual. "When I got here, Ross O'Shea was waiting in the dark. He jumped me, said he was letting me off the hook on the lawsuits and he meant to take his revenge."

"How?"

"I got away from him before I found out."

"My God, Bailey." Joe came toward her. Tenderly, he held her upper arms and peered into her eyes with a fierce, burning gaze. He was a thousand times stronger than Ross. Yet his grasp was gentle, and she was not afraid. "Did he hurt you?"

"I'm all right."

"Oh, honey." He pulled her close. "I'm sorry I wasn't here. God, I'm sorry."

Though he was stroking her back and murmuring comforting words, Bailey held back. Her arms crossed over her breasts. She kept her head turned away from him. If she succumbed to his kindness, her self-control would melt, leaving her utterly without defenses.

"I'm okay," she said.

"Sit down and tell me what happened."

She sat on the end of her navy blue sofa and curled her feet underneath her. Bailey did not intend to relive her foolishness in being tricked into listening to Ross. "He grabbed me and I got away."

"What else?"

Quietly, she said, "He told me that he'd be back."

"I won't leave you alone," Joe said. He felt responsible, as if his absence had somehow caused the assault. Her tension and the flickering of fear in her big brown eyes reproached him. Though she'd said not one word of accusation, he cursed himself for not being more protective. "I'm sticking with you. Night and day."

"That won't be necessary."

"Maybe not for you, but for me." He tried to smile reassuringly. "If anything happens to you, Mac is going to kill me."

"Nothing will happen. I know he's after me. Now I'll be more careful."

Her lips were tight, and he didn't bother to argue. Even if Bailey didn't want his protection, he was going to take care of her. As he watched her, sitting quietly on the sofa, he realized that she had, unconsciously, taken the pose he'd imagined in his vision at the town house. His connection with her seemed almost mystical, mythic. This slender, defiant woman with her plain-spoken manner and her subtle, enticing femininity represented peace for him. He would do anything, absolutely anything, for her.

"There was something else," she said. "Ross said the reason he was going to hurt me was because he'd been hurt. Worse than the bruises and bumps he'd gotten in the crash. He said that the woman he loved had died in the crash."

"Kate?"

"Four women died," Bailey said. "Kate. The congresswoman and her mother. And Dee Valente."

Joe felt a burning need for action. Unable to sit still, he bolted from his chair and trod a path back and forth across her beige carpet. He was tired of passively asking questions and following procedures. He wanted to track down Ross O'Shea and beat the answer out of him. For Bailey's sake, he tried to be objective. "Okay. Ross was in love with a woman who died in the crash."

"Correct. But, Joe, I don't think it's important. If there was sabotage that caused the crash, it wasn't Ross who did it. He's not suicidal."

"But there might be a husband who would sabotage a plane if his wife and her lover were aboard."

"That makes sense." Her eyes narrowed. "So Kate wasn't his lover. Nor was Dee Valente—her husband, Charles, was on board. Oh, Joe, you can't be talking about Jillian Grambling?"

"Who else? Her mother?"

"Don't be so quick to eliminate her. Lots of older women are involved with younger men." Bailey shrugged. "The congresswoman's mother—Eleanor was her name, Eleanor Pearl Gordon. She was recently widowed. Might have been looking for a companion."

"But she also struck me as a woman of taste, a woman with elegant style." As part of the files on the crash, he'd studied the profiles on the victims. Eleanor Pearl Gordon had lived an exemplary life of community service. "Did you know that Eleanor founded and financed two homeless shelters here in town?"

"I know," Bailey said. "Soon as I got back to Denver from Florida, I bundled up all my old Levi's and stuff I don't use and took them to the shelters."

"Can we eliminate her as the lover of Ross O'Shea?"

"Yes," Bailey said, but she was shaking her head. "But Jillian Grambling? I can't believe it."

"Do you prefer Dee Valente?"

"No way. Her husband, Charles, died in the crash with her. And she struck me as a devoted wife who was real concerned about his health."

Again, Joe thought of the information gathered in the files. "But the Valentes had been through some rough times with his business. That puts a strain on a marriage. If Charles thought his wife was messing around, he might have arranged sabotage as a murder and suicide."

"No," Bailey said. "He was looking forward to a drink on the plane. Vodka. He surely didn't behave like a man who was about to die."

"That leaves Congresswoman Jillian Gambling."

"Or Kate. It's possible that Ross didn't have a thing to do with sabotage, that the plane went down because of mechanical failure. His affair might have been just that. An affair."

With Kate.

As Joe considered, he was surprised to find that he wasn't terrifically upset about the idea that his wife had been messing around with the actor. If she'd been attracted to pretty-boy Ross, it reflected her own lousy judgment. It didn't really seem to have much to do with him. Still, he said, "I don't think it was Kate."

Bailey lifted an eyebrow. "Sour grapes?"

"Not at all," he said. Gradually, Joe was straightening out the emotions in his entangled marriage. "I'm remembering Kate the way she really was. She might have even been depressed, but Kate was practical when it came to dollars and cents. No way would she have an affair with a poor, struggling actor."

But Bailey was still skeptical. "Not even if he was really dashing and good-looking?"

"No," he said firmly.

And calmly. His lack of passion in talking about Kate's affair surprised him. It was as if his love for her had been a deep well, and the well had finally run dry. Finally, he thought.

He stopped his pacing, rested his hands on the back of the chair where he'd been sitting and looked at Bailey. The sight of her warmed him. Gazing at her, he felt renewed.

"Something wrong?" she asked.

"Just thinking." About her. Momentarily, he contemplated. Why hadn't he been smart enough to marry a good woman like Bailey instead of Kate?

Joe dragged his mind back to the question at hand. "Here's why I don't think Kate was having an affair with Ross. She'd conceived a child. Ross couldn't support her. However, according to her gynecologist, Kate was planning to carry this child to full term."

"So that leaves Jillian," Bailey said. "I surely would not be shocked to find that a creep like Ross was attracted to her. She was a powerful woman, wealthy and good-looking to boot. But why on earth would she bother with scum like Ross O'Shea?''

Joe thought of his brief conversation with Jillian's husband, Ted Grambling. He had not been impressed. The word *weasel* came to mind. ''Perhaps a meeting with our local congressman might be in order.''

''Oh, my gracious, Joe. What are you thinking?''

''Truth,'' he said. ''I'm looking for the truth.''

''And what are you going to do? March into the congressman's office and demand to know if his wife was having an affair? Accuse him of sabotage?''

''Give me some credit, Bailey. I can be subtle.''

''You be careful. I don't think it's smart for you to run around flashing your FAA credentials when you're not even assigned to this case. And if you get in trouble, I'm in deeper than you.''

''I won't offend the congressman,'' he promised. ''Ross O'Shea is another matter.''

''What are you talking about?''

He slowly straightened his shoulders. His instincts ruled. He knew what needed to be done. Right now. Tonight. ''I think I'm going to pay a visit to O'Shea.''

''Joe, don't.''

''Oh, yes. I think this is necessary.''

''But you don't even know where he lives.''

''Sure, I do. I've got the files for this case in my car.''

A thin smile stretched his lips. This action felt good. A direct confrontation would go a long way toward appeasing the impotence that had plagued him since he first requested to be assigned this case. He wanted to come face-to-face, fist to fist, with somebody. ''I want him to know that you're not vulnerable. If he hurts you, he's going to think that explosion was a walk in the park.''

He strode to the door, feeling good, feeling strong. Feeling like a man.

But Bailey was right behind him.

"I'll be back," he said.

"Forget it, Joe. I'm coming with you."

"You don't need to. I'll handle this."

"Just in case you've forgotten," she said, "it's my career on the line, too. I'd rather you didn't do this but I can see your testosterone is in an uproar and you won't be happy until you've beaten something. I'm just coming along to make sure you don't screw up too bad."

"Thanks for the vote of confidence."

ROSS O'SHEA LIVED a little too far north of Sixth Avenue to be considered part of the fashionable Cherry Creek area. Likewise, his row of apartments was too shoddy to be respectable.

Joe felt the adrenaline pumping as he strode up to the door and pressed the bell. He wished that Bailey hadn't been two paces behind him, but he could understand her need to make sure he didn't kill anyone.

He pressed the doorbell again.

"He's not there," Bailey said. "And I can't say that I'm disappointed. Why don't we just get ourselves a burger and forget about this until tomorrow?"

But there was a young woman approaching the door of the apartment next door. "Excuse me," Joe said. "Do you know Ross O'Shea?"

"Sure. He's my neighbor."

"I really need to get ahold of him. Is there someplace special where he usually hangs out?"

"The bar," she said. "The Coffee Bar down on Third."

"Thanks."

Times had certainly changed, Joe thought as they returned to his car. Just five years ago, a singles bar served whiskey and beer instead of *latte* and cappuccino. He'd been out of the dating scene for the seven years he'd been married, and he wasn't anxious to return to it. "Bailey, do you go to places like that? Coffee bars?"

"Sure, I drink coffee."

"I mean, do you go there to meet people? To meet men?"

She hooted with laughter. Sarcastically, she said, "Sure, Joe. All us single chicks get ourselves wired on espresso and then do mating dances."

"Then how do you meet men?"

"I don't go out of my way," she said. "Maybe I should. Maybe that's why I'm still unmarried and unattached at the ripe age of twenty-seven."

Outside the Coffee Bar were tables and chairs that were mostly occupied by couples enjoying the soft summer night. Most of the patrons, however, preferred to sit inside, where a long-haired woman played her twelve-string guitar and sang in a delicate soprano. Joe found the atmosphere to be pleasing, friendly, touched with the redolence of fresh-baked muffins and brewed coffee. Six different flavors, he noticed on the chalkboard menu. The variety of preparation ranged from white chocolate *latte* to anise espresso.

Bailey stood close to his side. Of course, she didn't have much choice, since the interior of the Coffee Bar was packed with tables, but Joe felt as if they were on a date. Though it wasn't true, he was strangely comforted by her nearness—as if they were supposed to be together.

He'd never felt so comfortable when he escorted Kate. Her bright blond loveliness had attracted admiring stares from the men and disgruntled notice from the women. Joe had been an appendage, the anonymous man who had the privilege of accompanying the best-looking female in the room.

Bailey was different. Better, he thought.

He scanned the crowd until he spotted the back of Ross O'Shea's head. He sat at a table with two attractive females, and he appeared to be engaged in animated conversation.

A rush of anger heated Joe's blood. He had saved the life of this worthless actor when the plane crashed.

Joe tapped him on the shoulder.

Interrupted midsentence, Ross turned his head. When he looked up and recognized Joe and Bailey, the charm that he was aiming at his companions vanished. "What do you want?"

"Let's step outside. We need to talk."

"Talk to me here."

Joe glanced around the Coffee Bar. It wouldn't have been his first choice for a brawl, but he wasn't about to be intimidated by a herd of coffee drinkers.

He didn't bother to keep his voice low. "I saved you, Ross. You were unconscious when the plane went down, and I carried you out of there."

"Thanks. Do you want me to send you roses?"

"I saved you, and my wife died. Burned to death in the explosion."

"Your wife?"

Ross seemed truly puzzled. Was it possible that he was so self-centered that he didn't know anything about the other people who had been killed in the crash?

"Kate Rivers," Joe said. "The pilot. She was my wife."

There was a total lack of reaction from Ross, then a casual shrug. "Sorry, man."

"That's all you have to say?"

"What do you want to hear?" he whined. "It wasn't my fault."

Either he giving an Academy Award-winning performance or he really didn't know that Kate was Joe's wife. So Ross wasn't having an affair with her.

Probably, Joe thought, his lover was the congresswoman. Jillian Grambling. But Joe wanted to hear him say it.

Bailey touched his arm. "Come on, Joe. Let's get out of here."

He patted her hand. "Not yet."

"Leave me alone," Ross said. "Don't you get it? It wasn't my fault. Hey, maybe it was your wife's fault. She was supposed to be flying the damn plane."

Rage flashed inside Joe's head. An intense, white-hot fury swelled and grew until every muscle in his body was tensed for action. Still, he remained in control, total control.

"And look who you're with," Ross said derisively. "Bailey Fielding. She's the one who screwed up. She crashed the plane."

"You've got that wrong. The only reason you and I are still alive is Bailey. You should be kissing her feet."

"Get away from me. Both of you."

Joe wasn't a bully. He would never throw the first punch. But he needed to make Ross understand that if he came near Bailey again, there would be devastating consequences. "Earlier tonight, you threatened this woman. That's never going to happen again."

"You have a crystal ball?" He chuckled. "You can read the future?"

"Read this," Joe said. "If you bother her, if you come near her again, I will make it my business to break every bone in your body."

"You don't scare me."

But he looked like a frightened little kid. His fingers tapped nervously on the tabletop. His mouth was quivering, and his eyes darted.

"If I don't scare you," Joe said, "you're a fool."

Taking Bailey's arm protectively, Joe turned and they moved toward the exit.

"Thank you," she whispered. "I'm glad you didn't hit him."

"The night's not over," Joe said.

He knew that the actor was watching them leave. His vindictive eyes were riveted to the back of Joe's head. Joe had thrown down the challenge. He didn't think Ross would resist.

They were on the street, ten paces away from the outside tables, when he heard Ross's voice.

"Hey, Joe! You can't talk to me like that."

Turning slowly, Joe faced him. "How about if I talk to you like this? You were having an affair with Jillian Grambling."

"She was going to dump her husband and marry me."

"You?"

"She would have married me. I was going to be rich and respected. Big house in Denver. Fancy town house in Arlington for when Congress was in session. Everything was going to be perfect." He seemed to stare through Joe, seeing only Bailey. "You'll pay for that, lady. I'll see to it."

He started toward her, but Joe stepped in the way.

Ross lashed out with a wild jab, but Joe feinted just in time. Ross's fist missed his nose by half an inch.

Joe grinned with hard satisfaction. Now he could fight back.

"No!" Bailey shouted. "Joe, don't."

She couldn't stop him. She knew that it was hopeless to even try. Joe was riding the edge of his anger, the dangerous edge.

Other customers of the Coffee Bar who were sitting outside came toward them. To Bailey, it seemed that they were moving in slow motion, as if in a dream.

Joe's right hand flicked in Ross's face. It was almost a slap. Then Joe drove his left hard into the midsection of his opponent, and Ross doubled over. He fell to his knees.

Onlookers stepped around him, helping him to his feet, trying to talk to him.

"All right," she said quickly. "It's over, Joe. Let's go."

He flexed his fingers, not even breathing hard. Reluctantly, he allowed himself to be pulled away. "Okay, Bailey. I guess you're right."

But they had barely turned their backs when she heard someone shout "Look out! He's got a knife."

Joe whipped around, instantly alert. "Get back," he ordered her. "Stay out of the way."

Ross balanced his weight like a street fighter, making quick thrusts with the blade.

"Come on," Joe said. "Come at me."

Mesmerized with fear, Bailey couldn't look away from the two men who circled each other with deadly intent. If anything happened to Joe, she didn't think she could stand it.

He moved in close, almost teasing with his nearness, and Ross made a vicious lunge.

Joe, still unmarked, caught Ross's knife hand near the wrist and slammed down hard, causing Ross to slash his own thigh. The actor screamed with pain and dropped the knife.

This time, Joe didn't walk away. He delivered a thunderous uppercut to Ross's jaw, and the actor crumpled to the sidewalk outside the Coffee Bar.

The wail of a police siren cut through the night.

Chapter Nine

The next morning, Bailey turned off the alarm clock before the buzzer went off. She stared up at the ceiling in her apartment and groaned. Awakening after a night of tossing and turning was painful. Her left arm ached from when Ross had assaulted her, and there was a faintly blue bruise on her wrist where he'd grabbed hard. In addition, her anxiety seemed to have settled in the pit of her belly. Her gut twisted like a washcloth being wrung out to dry. She groaned again. How had she gotten herself into such a tangled mess?

After the incident at the Coffee Bar, Joe had managed the police questions so skillfully that they'd arrested Ross O'Shea and took him, in custody, to be treated for his knife wound at Denver General Hospital. Though Ross had regained consciousness in time to squeal hysterically that Joe had threatened him, that he had pulled the knife in self-defense, that Joe had stabbed him, the police had had little sympathy. An attitude, Bailey suspected, that came partly from witness statements and partly from the FAA credentials that Joe had not hesitated to show, even though he wasn't investigating.

In any case, Ross was out of the way. For the moment. No doubt he'd be out on bail almost immediately, but Joe said his lawyers would certainly warn him about the legal ramifications he would encounter if he tried to harass her. Unless he was insane, he wouldn't come after Bailey again.

Yet she felt far from safe. She was decidedly nervous, and Bailey had never been a jumpy sort of woman. Her anxiety didn't come from a fear of Ross O'Shea. Nor was it particularly connected to the severed brake line on the Cessna. The name of this gut-churning tension was Joe Rivers.

She was connected to him. The crash had entwined their lives like the roots of a Florida mangrove tree. Yet, because of the crash, they could never grow closer, never form a lasting bond. After the investigation, she and Joe would go their separate ways, and she could only hope that he didn't end up hating her.

After her shower, she forced down a piece of dry toast and orange juice. When she was halfway out the door to the airport, her telephone rang and she grabbed it.

"Hi, Bailey." It was Joe. His voice sounded like morning, husky and as intimate as warmed bed sheets.

"Hi, yourself."

"We're going out tonight."

She wished that were true, that he could call her and make a quick plan, assuming that she'd be there for him. "Joe, I really don't think—"

"To a fund-raising dinner for Congressman Ted Grambling. Not formal, but dressy. I'll pick you up at six."

"Wait a minute," she said. Obviously, this "date" wasn't just a simple evening out. He wasn't proposing dinner and a movie. "What are you plotting?"

"Infiltration," he said. "In the case files on the investigation, I have all the formal statements from the survivors and their families. Now I need to get inside. Poke around. Listen to gossip. I need to turn over some rocks and see what crawls out from underneath."

"Nothing pretty," she assured him. "Are you sure this is a good idea? If Grambling wanted to cause trouble for you, he could."

"Don't worry, I'm not going to make a scene."

"That's what you said last night," she accused. "And that ended up with a knife fight and an arrest."

"See you tonight. Six o'clock."

At the airport, Bailey took the repaired Cessna on a quick and mercifully uneventful charter to Greeley, then returned empty. By three o'clock, she was done for the day.

When she went to the parking lot to pick up her Volks and head for home, she found Grandpa Mac leaning against the front fender, enjoying a cigarette with far too much relish.

"Heard about last night," he said.

"Really? I thought you'd be so busy tomcatting around that nothing much else would attract your attention."

He grinned. "That Greta is one hell of a woman. We go way back, maybe fifteen years."

Though she didn't really want to hear about or think about her grandfather's womanizing exploits, Bailey didn't register disapproval or approval. His life was his own. It had been her good fortune to have him raise her since she was eight, and she loved him unconditionally—in spite of his fondness for whiskey and the occasional cigarette.

"How'd you get up here?" she asked.

"I brought the Spitfire. Made it from Florida to Denver in four quick hops."

She'd suspected as much, and his revelation did not please her. The fully renovated World War II Spitfire with camouflage paint and blue bull's-eyes on each wing wasn't really designed for cross-country travel. "I'm glad you got here in one piece."

"I'm fine," he said. "It's you I'm worried about. I heard about the knife fight. Joe's not getting you into trouble, is he?"

"Trouble was already there," she said. "Joe's part of it, but he's not the cause. Who told you about the fight?"

"Joe. He was going to be busy today, and he suggested that I might want to keep an eye on you, in case this Ross O'Shea character didn't get the message."

"Protecting me?" She bristled. "You two have decided to set up a twenty-four-hour-a-day protection service?"

"Unruffle those feathers, Bailey. I've been watching over you since you were a little girl."

"But I'm a grown woman now. I don't need bodyguards."

He stubbed out his cigarette. "Okay, honey. Let's get serious. I overheard that conversation between you and Joe last night. I know this investigation isn't sanctioned by the FAA, and I know you failed to report a possible sabotage on the Cessna. If you two don't get this investigation settled in a mighty quick manner, you're both going to be in hot water up to your necks. You'll probably lose your pilot's license."

She nodded. "There's a lot riding on the investigation."

"Figure it out. Or drop it. That's my advice." He patted her shoulder. "In the meantime, I'm going to be around whether you want me looking over your shoulder or not. Right now, I'm taking a run down to Colorado Springs to show one of my old buddies the Spitfire, but I'll be in touch. If you need me, you check with Greta."

"Fine," she said, having no intention of calling upon Mac to bail her out.

"I mean it, Bailey. Don't make me get stern with you."

"I'll be okay."

"By the way," he drawled, "if you want to do some interesting flying, this buddy of mine has a souped-up Piper Tomahawk, side-by-side seats, that he uses for stunt flying."

"Interesting," she said. "Claude has a plane like that, too. Do you think your buddy knows him?"

"That's hard for me to say. When you've been flying as long as I have, you know everybody." He stroked the top of her head and gave her ponytail a little tug. "I love you, Bailey. Remember everything I ever taught you. And be careful."

"Do I have a choice?"

"No, ma'am, you do not."

He smiled at her. It was one of those crinkly-eyed, gentle, grandfatherly smiles that bespoke an ocean of caring and a tidal wave of love. Then he gave her a wink, turned and walked back toward the airfield.

She called after him, "Thanks, Mac."

"I haven't done nothing yet."

"Thanks for everything."

She could do a lot worse than having Mac Augustine protecting her rear.

TRYING NOT TO THINK of this evening's infiltration as a date, Bailey scanned her closet, searching for the right stuff for a woman pilot who wanted to look dressy but not formal. Attractive, but not sexy. Most definitely not sexy. Now was not the time to start sending sensuous messages to Joe.

Her best choice was a sleeveless, V-neck, black mini-dress in rayon. Luckily, her legs were darkly tanned from the time she'd spent in Florida, so she wouldn't have to bother with panty hose.

She blew-dry her hair, made a part down the middle and allowed it to fall straight, halfway down her back. Checking out her reflection in the mirror, she hoped that wearing her hair down wouldn't create the wrong impression. It was a simple style—plain and simple.

She frowned. Would Joe think she was trying to look slinky?

When she started fishing through her makeup drawer, she had the same problem, the same question. How could she make herself look appropriate for a fancy dress affair without causing Joe to think she'd done herself up to entice him?

She dug around in the closet until she found a pair of black high-heel sandals that she had worn only once before because they made her tall as an amazon.

Completely ready, she stepped in front of the mirror again. She looked so well put together that she could hardly believe herself. "Damn," Bailey said.

Though it gave her a sense of satisfaction to look good, she needed to keep her distance from Joe. How could she convey that need?

A sudden inspiration struck her. The necklace!

Bailey retrieved the tiny gold airplane with the dia-mond propeller from her mostly empty jewelry box.

Hadn't Joe said that the necklace made him think of women who were cheaters and manipulators? If she wore this necklace as an amulet, it should repel any thoughts he might have of getting close to her.

She fastened the chain around her neck. Perfect! The little airplane glowed against the tan of her breastbone above her cleavage. Now she could be gussied up and not feel guilty about it.

When she heard the bell, she yanked the door open and grabbed her purse. "Okay, let's move 'em out and head 'em up."

She charged out, locked her deadbolt and turned to him.

"Wait a minute," Joe said. "Let me take a look at you."

She lifted her chin, showing off the necklace, and waited while he studied her from head to toe.

Joe wasn't gaping because, after all, he was a grown man, but his blue eyes sparkled with appreciation. Then he noticed the little gold-and-diamond pendant, and his expression darkened.

Good, she thought, he'd gotten her message. Hands off.

Still, he said, "You're a knockout, Bailey."

"Yeah? Does that mean that I look like I could go fifteen rounds without breaking a sweat?"

"That means that you look unbelievable."

"Like something out of science fiction?"

"Something out of a dream," he said.

"Or a nightmare?"

Bailey pivoted and strode along the concrete walkway to the stairs with Joe at her side. Even though she wore her high-heeled sandals, he was taller than she was. As she moved, her long legs felt graceful instead of gawky.

When he opened her car door and helped her inside, she didn't argue about how she could open a doggoned door for herself. And when he slid behind the wheel of his Mustang and glanced at her appreciatively once more, Bailey knew what it was to be a lady who was pampered and cared for. The amazing thing was that it seemed so natural. This was the secret she'd tried so hard to learn and could never seem to grasp. All it took was the right moment. And the right man.

If only this could go on forever. If only they had a future.

Joe aimed the car toward downtown Denver. "So, Bailey. How was your day?"

"I flew to Greeley."

"Tell me about it."

"My return to commercial flying," she said. "It wasn't spectacular. I mean, the heavens didn't open and hosts of angels did not sing a hearty hallelujah chorus."

"Tell me about the sky."

"Oh, the sky. Clear as a breeze. Blue from horizon to horizon." Like his eyes, she thought. "Some puffy clouds. On the way back, I was flying empty, so I dove through one, just so I could come out the other side. I wanted to buzz low to the ground and chase a herd of cows, but there's this big fat Sky Air logo on the tail, and I surely didn't want Claude getting irate phone calls from farmers. That's the problem with flying commercial. You can't let go and play."

"Can't go really fast, either."

She studied the firm set of his jaw. "Do you miss it, Joe? Being a test pilot? Flying fast?"

"No more than once or twice a day."

"So you liked being a rocket man?"

"I never made it that far," he said. "But I always wanted to be an astronaut, to fly the shuttle."

"Why didn't you go for it?"

He shrugged. "I got married."

No further explaining was needed. Not for Bailey. She understood. If she were married to a test pilot, she would have uncomfortable feelings. Uncomfortable? Heck, she'd be downright terrified. It was the job of a test pilot to push the envelope, to break records of altitude and speed and endurance, to take outrageous chances. Every morning when you kissed your husband goodbye, there was a fair-to-middling chance he wouldn't come home that night. "It's like being married to a cop. Or a soldier."

"Or someone like you," he added.

"Me?"

"There's a lot of risk in stunt flying."

"Well, now, if that isn't an example of the pelican saying the bass has a big mouth! How can you possibly compare a couple of harmless loop-the-loops with flying so high that you see the blue sky turn to stars?"

"It's dangerous," he said.

"So's driving a car, but you don't see me sitting here shivering and gasping."

"Life is dangerous," he said. "But if you don't take any risks, you're not really living."

"Amen to that." It occurred to her that it might be fun to go up with Joe. "You know, Grandpa Mac has a friend who's offered the use of his stunt plane. A specially rigged Piper Tomahawk. Maybe this weekend we could take a ride, and I could show you how safe these stunts really are."

"I'd like that," Joe said. "It's a date."

A date? That wasn't what she'd intended. She wasn't going to see Joe on a social basis. No dates! But asking seemed so natural, like being ladylike when she was dressed so pretty. Both were a mistake, Bailey thought. She wasn't really a lovely, well-dressed, desirable female. And she shouldn't be thinking about a date with Joe Rivers.

"Wish I could reciprocate," he said.

"What?"

"I wish I could show you my kind of flying. But I don't think the military is going to let me goof around in a Stealth bomber."

"Probably not." She needed to get back on track, return to the only appropriate subject that existed between them. The investigation. "What did you find out today?"

He acknowledged her change of subject with a nod of his head. "I did a little discreet checking around about Jillian Grambling and her husband, Ted."

"You were discreet?" she asked, disbelievingly.

"I have a few friends in high places. That's how I heard about this fund-raising dinner. Anyway, it seems that Jillian Grambling, although she had an outstanding reputation as a legislator, was prone to messing around. Ross wasn't her first or her most important lover."

"Was she really going to divorce her husband for him?"

"Not a chance. Ted Grambling wasn't blameless. He had a few sweet young things tucked away on the side. According to my source, Jillian and Ted had decided to stay hitched for the sake of both their careers, but it was a marriage in name only."

"Well, then, I guess we can scratch insane jealousy as a motive for sabotage. Seems like she and Ted had made their peace regarding their love life."

"Or the lack thereof."

"It's a shame," she said. "I know their kids are gone and grown, but it's still sad that they stayed together when there really wasn't a marriage left."

"Sad," Joe agreed, though he was familiar with the scenario. "But it happens."

Glittering passions, he thought, have a way of tarnishing over the years. He and Kate had lapsed into a fairly loveless marriage. He was gone all the time. And she had found another man to fill the void. How did it happen? There hadn't been a moment, a single moment, when they woke up and realized that their love was ruined.

"Joe?"

"What, Bailey?"

"If Ted wasn't jealous of her affair, he didn't have a motive for sabotage."

"That's where you're wrong," he said. "Ted's motive for wanting his wife dead was the oldest in the book—money. Not only did he inherit all their joint assets, but he receives double indemnity on an insurance policy that could make a dent in the national debt."

"Plus the political ties make him a quick shoo-in and he becomes a congressman."

"A big plus," Joe said, "for a guy who never progressed beyond second-string lawyer."

"Assuming you're right," she said, "there's still a question in my mind. How did he do it? If the plane went down because of sabotage, it was a neat job. I wasn't in the cockpit when the first jolt hit, but it felt like a natural pressure loss. And you FAA guys went over every piece of wreckage with a fine-tooth comb and couldn't find evidence of sabotage."

"It had to be someone who knows planes. Someone who had access to the Sky Air fleet."

"But who?"

They were still pondering that question when they arrived and Joe turned the Mustang over to a red-coated valet for parking. He showed their invitation, and they stepped inside the Seventeenth Street restaurant that was hung with slightly garish bunting and a banner that announced Ted Grambling, Your Representative.

The first person they bumped into was Claude Whistler, the owner of Sky Air. Joe couldn't have asked for a more obvious answer to Bailey's question. Someone who knew airplanes? That surely was Claude. And he had unlimited access to the Sky Air planes.

He was looking dapper in a summer-weight charcoal gray suit. The silver in his hair shimmered like threads woven into cloth of gold. After a quick nod to Joe, his gaze rested upon Bailey.

"Is that really you?" he asked.

"Why wouldn't it be?" she challenged.

"You look very beautiful, Bailey."

Though he stepped back to fully admire her, his attention was not offensive. His grin was friendly, almost fatherly, as he nodded and said, "Very lovely. I especially like your necklace."

"Thank you," she said.

Joe took her arm. This dressed-up version of Bailey was a remarkable, breathtaking woman, but he almost preferred the way she looked in her Levi's with the denim stretched tight across her firm buttocks and her long legs.

Of course, he was pleased that she cleaned up so nicely, but there was another way he wanted to see Bailey. All day, his imagination had been actively filled with a vision of this woman, stretched out on a clean white sheet, completely naked, her limbs heavy with the languor of their lovemaking. He'd thought of those long, tanned legs being wrapped around him. Her arms would be thrown back in surrender. Her eyes would be dazed with fulfilled passion.

Dangerous thoughts. And inappropriate.

Joe hadn't missed the significance of the airplane necklace. Kate's necklace. It was a golden reminder of unfaithfulness and failed relationships.

Joe turned his attention to Claude Whistler. "So, what are you doing here? I didn't know you were a Grambling supporter."

"I always supported Jillian. I guess Ted's the next step."

"How do they compare?"

Claude drew himself up. "Though I've always liked his wife, my politics are more in line with Ted. I think he'll be a good change."

"A brave new world?" Bailey said.

"Not really," Claude said with disarming honesty. "Ted is more conservative. Nowadays, so am I. When I was first starting out, punching a hole in the established hierarchy of the airline routes, I liked Jillian's focus on the small businessman and his needs. Now I prefer being a well-protected success story."

"Times change," Joe said, and he wondered how aggressive Claude would be in moving the political climate toward his goals. Was it possible that he sabotaged his own plane in order to have a more sympathetic ear in Ted Grambling?

They small talked for a few more minutes, then Joe spotted another individual whom he hadn't expected to see here. The psychiatrist, Dr. Lawrence Salton. Skillfully, he directed Bailey toward their next encounter.

As they neared the doctor, she whispered, "What's he doing here?"

"According to my friend who gave me the tickets, this dinner is the first fund-raising event to be scheduled since Jillian's death. It's a changing of the guard."

"How so?"

"Apparently, when Ted took over his wife's seat in the special election, he made his presence felt. He fired most of her key advisers and replaced them with his own crew. Obviously, there was some resentment. This event is significant, solidifying the basic support group and introducing the new power structure. In the next election, Ted is running on his own."

"So most of these people prefer Ted over his wife," she mused. "How much, I wonder. How much did they want Jillian out of the way?"

"Don't get me wrong, Bailey. I don't think we're looking at a whole roomful of potential murderers. But there might be one among them...."

"Dr. Salton," Bailey said, sticking out her hand. "It's nice to see you, sir."

His mustache twitched in recognition as he shook her hand. "You're the woman at the airport who interrupted my group. Bailey?"

"Yes."

Salton reserved his intense scrutiny for Joe. "And you're the husband, Kate's husband. Did you make an appointment at my office?"

"Tomorrow morning at ten."

Joe didn't believe that Salton was so completely unaware of his schedule. Surely, he knew that Joe was his
ten-o'clock appointment. In asking, he was playing a
game, a mind game. This might be difficult territory—
matching wits with a psychiatrist—but Joe was game to
try. "You're a Grambling supporter?"

"Ted Grambling. I didn't have much use for his
wife."

"Why not?"

"My reasons for not supporting her were my own."

Joe took a guess. "Jillian Grambling was a patient of
yours."

"That's a very good shot in the dark, Joe. However,
as you know, my relationship with my clients is privileged information." He waved to someone across the
room, then turned back to them. "Excuse me."

Bailey tugged on Joe's sleeve, pulling him to one side.
"He did it. I'm sure he did. Salton knows enough about
planes to do sabotage. And he was dosing Kate with
some kind of sedative drug—"

"Antidepressant," Joe said. "That's different."

"He had two patients on the plane. Maybe more. We
should check the whole passenger roster, compare it
with his client list."

"What would that prove?"

"Maybe there was something weird going on with his
practice, and his clients were beginning to figure it out.
Maybe he had a good reason for wanting the plane to go
down."

"Unfortunately," Joe said, "that's highly unlikely.
I've checked into Salton. He's the shrink superstar of
the moment. His clients—many of whom are the same
upper-crust women who would be at this fund-raiser—
speak highly of him."

Bailey shuddered. "Hard to believe. He's so cold. I wouldn't trust him with my grocery list, much less my deepest, most personal problems."

"His approach is a variation on 'tough love.' He's confrontational."

"I'll say he is." Bailey wasn't ready to give up her suspicions when it came to Dr. Lawrence Salton. No matter what he called his therapy, he struck her as a cruel person, one who would not hesitate to shove aside anyone who stood in his way. Plus, he knew about airplanes. He could have arranged sabotage.

And there were the drugs, she thought. As she milled in the attractive crowd, she found herself standing closer and closer to Joe. He seemed solid and real in this crowd of beautiful people who ran on power and dark motivations.

Bailey spied another familiar face. The small woman was standing near Ted Grambling himself. Her face was animated, and her manner was nearly manic. She was the woman in Salton's fear-of-flying group who had refused to go up in the plane. Emily?

Her glance met Bailey's. Suddenly, there was a change in Emily's manner. She'd been joking and laughing with Ted Grambling. As she glared at Bailey, her eyes narrowed. Her lips thinned.

She pushed through the crowd, coming at Bailey, charging at her. Nearly a full head shorter, she stopped in front of Bailey.

Emily's voice was high, nearly hysterical. "How dare you follow me?"

"I'm not," Bailey said. "I'm sorry, ma'am, but you must have me mistaken with someone else."

"Oh, no, I haven't. You showed up at the airport, too. I didn't recognize you then. But afterward, Dr. Salton told me who you were."

"My name's Bailey Fielding." She was thoroughly perplexed. Though there was something familiar about this woman, Bailey couldn't place her.

"Don't play innocent with me. Don't you dare!"

Joe interrupted, "I'm sorry, ma'am, but—"

"How can you be with her? I know you, too. How can you, Joe Rivers? Don't you know? This is Bailey Fielding, and she killed your wife."

"Hold it, lady. You're way out of line."

She reached up and swung at Bailey, who easily dodged the small hand and sharp little fingernails.

People were looking. Conversations stilled.

"Don't you know who I am?" Emily demanded. "Don't you?"

"I'm sorry," Bailey said. "But I really don't recognize you. Can we start over and—"

"Of all the nerve! You're the cruelest, most vicious, most insensitive—"

"Stop!" Joe caught the small woman's arm in a firm grip. "Stop right now, ma'am. We're going to go outside, take a couple of deep breaths and settle whatever you think is your problem. Okay? Now, let's go."

"*You* go," she said. "You leave. Both of you. Nobody wants you here. You're an affront to Ted Grambling. And to me. And to every right-thinking person in this room. You're no better than a murderer."

"Listen, lady. You'd better calm down."

"I'm Emily Valente Raymond. My mother and father were Dee and Charles Valente." She raised her hand and pointed at Bailey. "You killed them."

Chapter Ten

When this tiny woman in her pretty little purple-and-white dress attacked, Bailey couldn't just let it pass. Her fists clenched at her sides. Her chin thrust forward at a hard, stubborn angle.

She wanted to punch Emily on her pert little nose, but she was glad when Dr. Lawrence Salton separated from the crowd. He strode aggressively forward and caught hold of both of Emily's hands. Staring into her eyes, he spoke in a low, hypnotic voice, "Emily, dear, this isn't appropriate behavior."

"Appropriate be damned," she snarled at him. "This woman killed—"

"Stop!" he commanded. "Emily, think. Forget about her. How do you feel? You?"

"I can't stand to be in the same room with her." Emily tugged weakly, trying to pull away from him, but she seemed to be calming down. The fire in her complexion faded to two feverish red dots on her cheeks. "I loathe her."

Salton glanced at Bailey. "Perhaps you should leave."

Not a chance. To leave would be to admit guilt. "Dr. Salton, sir, I don't lay claim to a blameless life. But I've never been one to turn tail and run. Mrs. Raymond has accused me unjustly, and I mean to set the record straight.''

"The issue here," Salton clarified, "is not who's right and who's wrong. There's nothing to be gained for either of you by acting out.''

"Mrs. Raymond," Bailey said. "Please believe me, ma'am. I would give my own life if it would bring your parents back. But I can't. There's nothing I can do. There's nothing I could have done. It was an accident.''

"Precisely," Salton said. "An accident. Did you hear that, Emily?" His manner was firm. He kept hold of her hands, restraining her. It seemed probable to Bailey that he'd had this conversation with Emily before. "Emily, listen to me.''

"You're lying," she said. "Why do you keep lying to me?''

"Truth is painful. We've talked about this, Emily. Remember? We've talked about denial.''

Under her breath, she whispered, "You all keep telling me I'm wrong. An accident? Sure, sure. You're all wrong.''

"Why do you say that?" Joe asked.

"I miss them so much." Her eyes were a little wild. "There were so many things I never got to say.''

Ted Grambling took it upon himself to join them. Though Bailey had never been formally introduced to him, she recognized the condescending, cardboard smile as he strode into their midst like a monitor on a playground. "Well, now," he said in a hearty tone. "What's the problem here, Emily?''

"Her.''

Grambling turned his head toward Bailey. His eyebrows lifted. "Have we met?"

Before she could respond, Emily pulled free from Salton's grasp. "I'll tell you who she is, Ted. Look at the little airplane necklace around her neck. That ought to be a clue to her profession."

"A pilot?" he guessed.

"Duh," said Salton. "Tell you what, Ted. You go stand up on your podium, and I'll handle this."

"Now, Doc, you know that's not the way I am. I take a hands-on approach." Ted, the perfect politician, scowled with the proper degree of concern. "But you could help me out, Doc. Can you tell me what's going on?"

Salton explained, "This young woman was piloting the plane that crashed. She's Bailey Fielding."

Though Ted Grambling was not a tall man, he gave the impression of stature as his spine stiffened. His discomfort was palpable. Apparently, Bailey thought, he'd expected the problem to be something minor. Not the crash.

By now, everyone else in the room was watching, and Ted was aware of that, too. He cleared his throat, seemed to select his words with care. "Emily, we've both suffered a terrible tragedy. You lost your dear parents. I lost my beloved wife. But we must go forward. Our loved ones would have wanted it that way."

"No," she said sharply. "I won't sit down to dinner with this woman. Not her or her buddy from the FAA."

"The FAA?" Again, Ted glanced at Salton, seeming to seek his counsel and advice.

The psychiatrist licked his lower lip below his mustache. His gaze was avid, intent on each of the players in the confrontation. "Ted, this is Joe Rivers of the—"

"Joe Rivers?" Ted Grambling's expression soured as he made the connection. "You're not on the guest list. I'm afraid I'll have to ask you to leave."

"We're going," Joe said.

He took Bailey's arm.

She balked. This wasn't fair. These people had no right to accuse her and pitch her out as if she were some kind of criminal. None of them knew what happened. They had condemned her without benefit of trial or testimony.

Joe leaned close to her ear and whispered, "Pilot's license. Grambling can arrange to pull your license in a minute."

What price dignity? She wanted to stand her ground, but Joe was right. She turned on her heel and linked her arm with his. "Okay. Let's go."

The other people in the restaurant stepped aside to let them pass. None of them knew what was happening or what was true, but they turned away, shunning Bailey and Joe. The atmosphere of celebration stilled as they threaded their way through a gauntlet of cold reproach.

"Murderer!" Emily shouted.

Bailey shivered. The hairs on the back of her neck stood up. Emily's unjust accusation branded her like a hot poker. She could feel the disgust and hatred that radiated in waves from this well-dressed crowd.

The only thing that kept her from blindly lashing out and making a fool of herself was Joe's unflappable calm. His stride didn't falter. His steely, blue-eyed gaze held firm, deflecting the stares from the curious and the cruel. By his very presence, he protected her.

Finally, they made their way to the street. The cool night air stung on her cheeks. "Please, Joe. Let's not stop for the car right now. Let's keep walking."

He didn't argue. Instead, he faced east, and they paced a full block and a half before they both took a deep breath.

"Awful," Bailey said. She kept on walking, wanting to put miles between herself and the restaurant. "That was the most awful nightmare that's ever happened in my whole life."

"It could have been worse," he said. "For a minute there, I thought you were going to punch out Emily."

"Wouldn't have been much of a bout," she said. "I've got eight inches on her in height."

She laced her arm with his, waiting for the adrenaline rush to abate, waiting for her temper to fade. They approached a Mexican restaurant where some sort of party was underway on the patio. A mariachi band in sombreros and fancy, silver-embroidered black costumes played and sang while the patrons danced in the warm July night.

The party mood contrasted with Bailey's inner tension. As her anger began to fade, she felt hollow inside.

Joe nodded toward the miniature fiesta. "Should we join them?"

"I can't think of a single reason why I would want to kick up my heels and dance."

"Come on, Bailey. Lighten up." He shouted over the music. "I'm sure your grandpa Mac has some Forrest Gump kind of saying for this situation."

"He does," she shouted back. "'Don't let the bad guys drag you down.'"

"Good advice."

They crossed another street and walked until they were beyond the twanging of guitars and laughter of dancers.

Bailey leaned heavily on his arm. "But I'm not sure who the bad guys are. I really can't blame Emily."

"Sure, you can. She had no right to come at you like that."

"But her accusations weren't anything I haven't said to myself. My fault. The crash was my fault. If I'd been a better pilot, those people wouldn't have died. In some dark corner of my heart, I feel like she was right. Like I deserve her hatred."

"That's not true."

"I know." But it wasn't as if Bailey considered herself to be a paragon of honesty, either. She'd been holding back the truth, since the moment of the crash.

"That idiot Grambling actually said one good thing. We need to go forward. Never waste time thinking that you were to blame, Bailey."

"I can't help it. I play it over and over in my head, and I imagine all the things I should have done." All those *should haves* haunted her. Hindsight. Second-guessing. But Joe was right. Straight forward was the only direction she could go, and it was time to start being honest with him, no matter what the consequences, no matter what the cost. She had to tell him everything.

She took a deep breath. "I never should have left Kate alone in the cockpit."

"You were the copilot," he reminded. "You didn't have a choice."

"There's always a choice. Kate was upset, and I knew it." Bailey braced herself. As soon as she told him, this closeness would be gone. Joe would hate her. "We were fighting, Joe. In the cockpit, Kate and I were fighting about you."

In a rush, she continued, "I made the mistake of admitting that I thought you seemed like a pretty wonderful mate and she was lucky to have you. Then Kate told me that I was much deluded if I thought a man like you would ever take notice of a woman like me. She said that I wasn't your type."

"She was wrong." He stopped in the glow of a street lamp and faced her. "She was so very wrong."

"It doesn't matter," Bailey said. "What's important is that I couldn't stand what she was saying so I hustled out of the cockpit to mess around with the drinks and honey-roasted peanuts. I should have stayed right there and piloted the Otter."

"Kate wouldn't have let you," he said. "She was the pilot. There was no point in questioning her authority."

"But I didn't even try."

"It wouldn't have made any difference," Joe said.

Though she was grateful to him for saying so, she didn't believe it. She had studied the charts a thousand times and worked out the vectors of their course. She could spell out the route from Denver to Aspen as well as she could form the letters for her own name. "If I had been flying, we would have been on course. It's possible we could have made it to the Loveland airstrip. And I could have brought the plane down safely."

"Even if you had been on course, Loveland was forty miles away. You didn't have enough power to climb. No, Bailey, not on one engine. You couldn't have made it that far. Even if you had been sitting in the pilot's seat, there was nothing you could have done."

When he spoke, she knew that he was telling the truth as he saw it. She was certain that Joe had gone over the topographical maps as often as she had. He'd figured the odds, the weight of plane, the thrust of one turbo-prop.

The FAA would have investigated all those possibilities before deciding that the crash had not been caused, in any way, by pilot error. She couldn't have prevented the forced landing.

She swallowed hard and looked down at the sidewalk beneath her feet. "I've got to go forward. Right?"

"That's right, Bailey."

But would she be walking alone? Or side by side with him?

Finally, she'd begun to tell the truth. So far, it had not been devastating. Now, she would take the next step. Tell him about knocking out Kate. She would explain that she'd left his wife unconscious, helplessly strapped in the pilot's seat.

"Bailey?"

He lifted her chin so she had to meet his gaze. As she gazed at him, marveling at his cheekbones and his firm jaw and the warmth of his blue eyes, she regretted the words she had to say, the truth she had to tell.

"Bailey, do you understand that if there was such a thing as 'my type,' it would be you?"

She couldn't believe what he was saying. His type was a woman like Kate, a flashy blonde who would look right at home in his cherry red Mustang. Not herself. Not Bailey. "You can't mean that, Joe. You're a high-performance man. I'm a Volkswagen."

He grinned. "I like a spunky car."

Her eyebrows pulled into a frown. She had to tell him. No matter how good it felt to bask in his approval, she needed to level with him, even if it meant that she would sever the fragile bond that was growing between them. Already, she'd allowed things to go too far. "Joe, about the crash—"

"We found out a lot tonight, Bailey."

Her intention derailed. "We did?"

"These people are all connected. That's got to mean something."

"Of course it does," she said impatiently. "It means that they're all people who are wealthy enough to be taking charter hops to Aspen. That's kind of an obvious conclusion, Joe."

"But I'm glad we came here."

"Whatever for?"

"For one thing," he said, "I got to see you all dressed up. And you are a beautiful sight."

Deep inside, she winced. His compliment was sheer torture. Ever since she'd met him, she'd dreamed about a relationship with Joe Rivers. Now he seemed to be offering fulfillment. And she could not accept it.

"For another thing, Bailey, I got to see your hair down around your shoulders. Ever since I first met you, I've wanted to pull out that ponytail." With the back of his hand, he caressed her long, straight hair. "It's like silk."

How could she feel so good and so bad at the same time?

He reached around her throat and held the airplane pendant. "Why did you wear this?"

"The truth," she said, "is that I didn't want us to start having a relationship. I knew if you saw the necklace, you'd keep your distance."

"You're not ready yet?"

"No."

"Maybe I can change your mind."

As he leaned closer to her, Bailey knew that he intended to kiss her. She had plenty of time to object, to step away from him. But she allowed herself to be mesmerized by the blue of his eyes.

This might be her only chance, her only moment of happiness with him.

His baritone caressed her. "Can we take off the necklace?"

"Not yet."

"I can be patient."

Bailey sighed. "Joe, would you do me a favor?"

"Anything."

"The next time you have an itch to see me in a fancy dress with my hair down, let's not go to a political dinner where everybody hates us."

"Does that mean you don't want to go back and hang out?"

"I'd rather gut a sow."

He grinned. "I'll take you home. If you want, you can wait here while I go back and get the car."

"I'll come with you. I'd rather not be alone."

"Fair enough." He took her hand, and they retraced their route along Seventeenth Avenue, past the wild mariachi party toward the lights of the restaurant where the fund-raiser for Ted Grambling was being held.

Bailey sighed. "At least that's one little mystery solved."

"What is?"

"Emily looked familiar. I thought so when I saw her at the airport, and I thought so tonight. As soon as she said her name, I recognized her as the daughter of Charles and Dee. I wasn't able to attend their funeral, but I saw photographs of her in the newspaper."

"As I recall," Joe said, "she was pretty cold at the funeral."

"Did you go?"

"I attended all the services. Sat in the back row and kept quiet."

"Then why didn't you recognize Emily?"

"She wore a black veil." He remembered the church pews, shrouded in mourning black. "The Valente funeral was well-attended. There were a lot of men in black business suits. A Catholic service. A rainy day."

"Charles was a successful businessman, wasn't he?"

"He'd had ups and downs. This was a down. He was close to bankruptcy. Now his business is dead. He bequeathed everything to Emily, his only daughter. Within a month, she'd closed down operations and paid out his debts."

"That's sad. He had nothing to leave behind."

"Oh, he left a bundle. According to the notes in the investigator's files, Emily cashed in a huge double-indemnity life-insurance policy on both parents. If I remember correctly, the total was close to a million dollars. Pretty good motive."

"For sabotage?" Bailey recoiled. "I can't believe that, Joe. You saw how upset she was. The woman might be a cuckoo bird, but she didn't kill her parents for the insurance money."

"Probably not. Her husband is a wealthy man."

But there was something strange going on in the mind of Emily Valente Raymond. She seemed convinced that the crash had not been an accident.

Outside the restaurant, Joe handed the claim check to the valet while he and Bailey maintained a low profile, trying not to be noticed.

Fading into the curbside wasn't a problem because there was another disturbance at the event. As Joe and Bailey stood quietly and watched, a handsome man in an expensive tailored suit was unceremoniously hustled through the restaurant door by two husky volunteers. When they released him, he straightened his lapels, smoothed his necktie and stared at Bailey. It was Ross O'Shea.

He cocked his finger like a gun and pointed at her.

Protectively, Joe stepped in front of her. "Move along, O'Shea."

The actor laughed. "Be seeing you, Bailey."

Calmly, he sauntered down Seventeenth Street. There was hardly a trace of a limp from the knife wound Joe had inflicted upon him the night before.

Joe turned to Bailey, ready to comfort her if she needed it.

She didn't. Her fists were braced on her hips, and she glared after the retreating figure. "That Ross O'Shea has some nerve. Imagine him coming here!"

Claude Whistler stepped out of the restaurant. He, too, watched O'Shea's departure, then joined them. "Hell of a night, eh?"

"What happened with O'Shea?" Joe asked.

Claude shrugged. "I don't know. He was talking with Ted Grambling, and it seemed to be amiable enough. Then Ted waved over a couple of volunteers and had O'Shea escorted from the room."

"You didn't hear any of their conversation?"

"Only a parting shot from O'Shea. He said something about this was only a taste of what he could do."

"But you don't know what he was talking about."

"Haven't got a clue." Claude turned to Bailey. "I'm sorry about that scene with Emily. She's a little high-strung."

"It's okay, Claude. I'm fine."

They watched in silence as the Mustang was delivered by the red-coated valet.

Claude held open the door for her. Reassuring and fatherly, he tucked her inside. "I want you to take tomorrow off, Bailey. Recover from this incident."

"I don't need time off," she protested.

"That's my decision," he said firmly. "You need to calm down. Put things in perspective."

"I'll be on call," she said. "I'll carry my beeper tomorrow in case something comes up. A charter you didn't expect."

"That's fine, Bailey. And I'll have Greta put you on the schedule for Friday. Okay?"

"Okay." As if she had a choice . . .

Joe eased the Mustang away from the curb and took the first main intersection headed south. It had been, as Claude said, a hell of a night.

Joe didn't know what he had expected when he snagged these tickets to the political event, but it wasn't the parade of suspects that he got.

Ted Grambling was, as Joe had already determined, a pretentious, obnoxious politician. He wanted to leave the crash behind him and move toward a glittering future without his wife, Jillian, in the way.

Then there was Salton, the psychiatrist. Joe couldn't think of a motive for him, but the shrink was familiar with planes and might have been able to pull off a sabotage.

Emily was a wild card. Not a murderer. But connected with the crash and with Grambling.

Ross O'Shea? Joe could only assume that the actor hadn't come to the political dinner for any high-minded reason. Blackmail seemed likely. He might have something on Grambling.

And then there was Claude. It didn't make sense for him to sabotage his own plane. But Claude was a manipulator with his fingers in a lot of pies.

To Bailey, Joe speculated, "Do you think Claude was lying?"

"About what?"

"About O'Shea. If Claude didn't know why O'Shea was there, why did he come out and make sure O'Shea was gone?"

"I don't know." She leaned her head back on the seat. "Claude has never been one to confide. Not in me, anyway. Gosh darn, I wish he'd let me fly tomorrow."

Joe wasn't entirely displeased with her orders to take the day off. Twice she'd been involved in potential sabotage attempts at Sky Air.

He glanced over at her profile. The curve of her nose and her out-thrust chin appealed to him. His gaze followed the smooth line of her throat, the arch of her shoulders. Her long, graceful arms. Her silken hair.

She was more mysterious than anything else on this case. Why did she keep saying no? Why was she pushing him away?

When they kissed, the message was clear and strong and hotter than the afterburn on a jet turbine. She was attracted to him. In her response, he could feel her desire. She wanted him almost as much as he longed to gently remove that black minidress from her body, to cup her firm breasts in his hands and watch the darkening of her eyes as Bailey's natural passion caught fire.

She gazed toward him. Her eyelids seemed heavy, sultry. "What do you think O'Shea was after?"

"The same thing they all want. Money and power."

"But how could he—?"

"Blackmail," Joe said. "O'Shea was intimate with Jillian. He might have something incriminating on her husband."

At her apartment complex, he helped her from the car and saw her safely to her doorstep.

She fit the key in the lock. Shyly, she peeked up at him. "Can't say 'thank you for a lovely evening,' can I?"

"I wish you could."

"Good night, Joe. See you tomorrow morning."

The door closed. Not even a kiss.

BAILEY WAKENED SUDDENLY. The phone. Her bedside phone was ringing.

She fumbled toward the receiver. A call in the middle of the night couldn't be good news.

"Hello?" She shook herself, fighting the dizziness of a sound sleep. "Hello?"

"I know what you're after."

She could barely hear the voice over the noise of a loud mariachi band.

"Speak up," she said into the receiver. "I can't hear you."

"I'll pay whatever you want."

It was a man's voice. She could tell that much. And the speaker sounded distraught, almost as if he was crying.

She pressed the receiver hard against her ear, straining to listen. "Please talk louder. I can barely hear you."

"Blackmail."

The single word was hard and clear. The two syllables shot through her like a million volts of electricity. She was awake now. Awake and trembling.

The voice on the phone said, "I'll pay. Don't make me kill again."

The mariachis burst into a high-pitched crescendo that matched the screaming in her soul. She was talking to the killer, the person who had sabotaged the Otter. "Who is this?" she shouted. "Who are you?"

The mariachi music ended.

Applause and raucous cheers.

The phone went dead.

Chapter Eleven

For once, Bailey's temper failed to rescue her from the darkness of fear. Terror struck a chord within her and reverberated in her heart. Her fingers clenched around the dead telephone receiver.

She had been talking to a murderer. He had killed once. He didn't want to kill again. And he was willing to pay whatever she wanted. In blackmail? Why had he called her? What had she said? What had she done?

She replaced the telephone on the hook and sat very still on the bed, listening to the night noise in her apartment complex. The creaks and rustles in the building magnified in her imagination. Through her opened bedroom window, she heard the slam of a car door, a voice, laughter, the chirp of crickets, the whisper of wind in the night.

All around her, there was life. And yet she was alone, vulnerable, isolated. What if he came here?

She'd been stupid! When she talked to him, why hadn't she picked up on what he was saying? Why hadn't she played along with him? She should have made an appointment to meet him, should have been smart enough to keep him talking.

Instead, she admitted her ignorance. *Who are you?*

As soon as the killer heard that, he knew she wasn't a potential blackmailer.

The clock beside her bed showed that it was only eleven o'clock. The long hours of the night stretched before her, and Bailey knew she wouldn't sleep.

A shudder trembled through her, and she reached for the bedside lamp, hoping the light would dispel the shadow that loomed over her, a killer's shadow. He knew her. The killer knew her phone number.

Would he come for her?

She pulled the comforter up to her chin. It was a warm night, but she was freezing cold, chilled to the bone.

When Bailey was a little girl, Grandpa Mac always used to tell her that if she closed her eyes, the scary night monsters would go away. But she wasn't a child anymore.

The threat was alive, human and real. He wouldn't go away when she closed her eyes and wished real hard.

She should call Joe. She needed him. More than telling him about the phone call, she needed to hear reassurance in his voice. She needed his arms, holding her, keeping her safe from the unnamed terrors in the night.

Bailey turned on every light in her apartment as she went into the front room and searched her address book until she found his telephone number.

He answered on the second ring. In the background, she could hear the soft jazz he favored, and she imagined him listening to music on the big, fancy entertainment unit in the front room of his town house.

"Joe, I had a phone call."

"What's wrong, Bailey? You sound like hell."

"I was sleeping." She gritted her chattering teeth. Oh, my gracious, she hated being afraid. "Somebody called.

A man. It sounded like he was calling from that Mexican restaurant where they had the band.''

"Slow down," Joe said. "Take a deep breath, then tell me what he said."

"He told me . . ." Panic tightened her throat.

"Breathe."

She gulped down a throatful of air, then exhaled. Another breath. She wished Joe were there with her, that she weren't alone. Another breath. "The man told me that he'd pay the blackmail. Whatever I wanted."

"What?"

"This voice . . ." She felt so helpless. "I didn't recognize him. I couldn't hear very well over the noise of the band. This voice said that he'd pay me whatever I wanted. He said that he didn't want to kill again."

"He thought you were trying to blackmail him?"

"And then . . . I was so dumb! I asked him who he was. And he hung up."

"I'll be right over," Joe said.

Closing her eyes, she thanked the merciful heavens that he was coming to be with her. Though it went against every feminist ideal, she wanted him to vanquish this threat, to rescue her. . . .

"Get dressed, Bailey," he said.

"Why?"

"We need to follow up on this," he said. "We're going back downtown."

Before she could tell him that she was scared to death and she didn't want to investigate, he'd hung up the phone.

"Joe? Of all the—"

Wasn't this a sorry turn of events? Right now, maybe for the first time in her life, she felt like crying on a strong man's shoulder, clinging to him, being weak and helpless while he was brave. But Joe thought she was tough enough to jump out of bed and go charging into the night, chasing a murderer.

Halfheartedly, she fumbled around in her bedroom, looking for clothes. By the time she'd pulled on a pair of Levi's, some sneakers and tucked a white T-shirt into her waistband, her spirits had revived. At least, she wasn't jumping at her own shadow. And she could take four or five consecutive breaths without hyperventilating.

She splashed some water on her face. The makeup from earlier tonight washed down the drain, but she left her hair down instead of pulling it back in a ponytail.

It was one small vanity, she thought. Joe liked her hair down.

When the doorbell rang, she called out. "Who is it?"

"It's me. Joe."

She answered quickly with her purse in hand. "Let's go."

As he drove back toward Seventeenth Street, Joe peppered her with questions: Whom did she talk to at the fund-raiser? Was anyone acting suspicious? What did she say? Repeat the conversation word for word.

"Nothing, nothing, nothing," she said. "I can't think of a single thing that would make anybody think I was trying to blackmail them."

"There must have been something. Just a word."

With this clue between his teeth like a bit, he was off and running. Once again, Bailey realized, he was a sky cop, an investigator whose top priority was solving the case. Her fear and panic were far less important.

As they entered the flow of downtown traffic, he said, "This is great! Now we know for a fact that we're talking about sabotage. Based on this, I might be able to get my boss to officially reopen the case."

"It wasn't great," she said in a small voice. "I was scared."

"Sure, you were." He patted her knee. "If you hadn't been a little nervous, you would have played this guy."

"I don't think you understand, Joe. This person, this murderer, knows who I am. He might think that I recognized his voice. He might come after me."

He parked in front of the restaurant where waiters were removing the garish red-and-white-and-blue bunting. The street was quiet. The valet-parking sign was gone.

"Too late," Joe said. "Damn."

He seemed to be far more annoyed about the fact that they'd missed the bad guys than about her fears and peril. Bailey was beginning to think that he wasn't sensitive or kind or anything else she might be looking for in a man. "Too bad."

"I do understand, Bailey. I know you're in danger, and I won't leave you by yourself until this is over." Reaching toward her, he tucked the long, straight fall of hair behind her ear. "I care about what happens to you. And you're right. This is dangerous. I never should have gotten you involved."

She still wasn't convinced that he cared at all.

"Don't worry," he said. "I won't let anything happen to you. If I did, your grandfather would kill me."

He eased away from the curb and proceeded to the Mexican restaurant that was a block and a half away. He cruised into the parking lot beside the patio and cut the lights. The band had stopped playing, but there were still people outside, eating and drinking.

"Come on," Joe said. "Let's go inside and ask around. Maybe somebody noticed a well-dressed person from the party down the street using the phone."

"No, thank you." She was aware that she was pouting. "I'm tired. I'll stay here."

"Fine." He nodded. "Lock the car doors. If anyone bothers you, lean on the horn."

As soon as he was gone, she rolled down the windows and made a point of unlocking the doors. Childishly, she refused to do as he ordered. Who did he think he was, anyway? And if he thought he was going to use this as an excuse to spend the night at her apartment, he had another think coming.

As she watched the couples on the patio, talking and drinking, she wished that she and Joe could have been like them. Carefree and easy. Out for a date. Having fun. That was never going to happen. Ever.

At the edge of the three-foot-tall adobe wall that surrounded the patio area, she focused on a table that was mostly in shadow. One man sat alone, sipping his dark bottle of Dos Equis beer. She recognized Ross O'Shea.

Bailey sank low behind the Mustang's dashboard, hoping he wouldn't see her. She couldn't imagine that Ross was the person who called. Surely a snake like him wouldn't be concerned about blackmail.

When Joe returned to the car, she hushed him and pointed. "It's O'Shea."

"Good work, Bailey. Looks like he's waiting for somebody."

She whispered, "Did you find anything inside?"

"There's a public telephone near the bathrooms, right by the exit to the patio. Anybody talking on it would be drowned out by the band."

"Did anyone remember a caller?"

"No. This place has been hopping all night. It's the owner's birthday, and she's throwing herself a party."

"What should we do?"

"Might as well wait," he said. "Let's see if anybody shows up to talk with O'Shea."

They sat quietly in the parking lot. Surveillance, she thought. *Good work, Bailey.* She tried not to let the small compliment go to her head.

O'Shea had removed his suit jacket and rolled up the sleeves on his white dress shirt. He ordered another beer and checked his wristwatch.

Bailey did the same. "It's almost midnight," she said.

"Seems like a good time for a meeting," Joe said.

At five minutes after midnight, another man joined O'Shea at the table. He, too, was wearing shirtsleeves, rolled to the elbow. When he lifted his head to order from the waitress, the light caught his profile. Ted Grambling.

But this was a different man than the hearty politician. His features were hard and chiseled, and his unsmiling lips were cruel. He was barely recognizable.

Joe turned off the overhead light in the car so it wouldn't come on when he slipped out. "Stay here, Bailey."

"Like heck I will."

She followed him, carefully closing the door with an inaudible click. As she crept toward the patio, her heart hammered loud as a timpani. With Joe beside her, she knelt behind the adobe wall and listened.

Grambling's tone was businesslike. "Why should I care about my wife's reputation? She's dead."

"It looks bad for you if she was playing around."

"Why the hell would anybody believe you?"

"I have letters from her. Juicy stuff."

"Let me see them."

"Do you think I'm stupid? I don't have them with me."

Bailey pressed her body against the cold adobe wall, straining to be invisible and to catch every word.

"Forget it," Grambling said. "I paid blackmail once, covering up another stupid move that Jillian made, and I'm still trying to rectify that error in judgment."

"It's your choice." O'Shea sounded shaky. "I can sell this stuff to your opponents."

"Don't trade threats with me, O'Shea. You can't win."

There was the sound of a chair being pushed back. Grambling was leaving.

Joe signaled to Bailey, and they moved away from the wall and back to the car. When she'd slipped inside, Bailey placed her hand over her heart, feeling the flutter. "Is this the kind of stuff you do? Surveillance?"

"Never before," Joe said. "I'm a former pilot and a paper pusher. I investigate busted machines. I give citations for misuse of fuel and flying at the wrong altitude. Never once in the five years I've worked for the FAA have I been on a stakeout. I don't even own a gun."

"That's not making me feel safer, Joe."

"Me, neither." He was in way over his head. The closest he'd gotten to life-threatening investigation was a smuggling operation when he had, as required, called in the FBI.

"Now what?" she asked.

"We go back to your place and try to get some sleep."

"We?"

"That's right, Bailey." He nodded at the profile of O'Shea, who downed the last of his beer. "That's a desperate man. And he knows where you live."

Joe started the car and aimed toward Bailey's place.

"It couldn't have been O'Shea who called me," she said. "The person who called said they would pay."

"Then it couldn't have been Grambling, either," Joe said. "He just told O'Shea that he wouldn't be blackmailed."

"Not to protect his wife's reputation. But there might have been something else, something more dangerous."

"Sabotage," Joe said. "Five passengers dead."

IN THE MORNING, Bailey was awake before he was. Joe writhed uncomfortably on her navy blue sofa, trying to cover his head with the pillow, but he could still hear her creeping around the apartment on tiptoe, trying not to disturb him.

Not to disturb him? It was impossible after last night, when he had listened to the sounds of her getting ready for bed and all of his senses were painfully aroused. It was ridiculous to think that a woman brushing her teeth was sexy, but last night Joe had listened with meticulous care to every tiny noise she made. Water rushing in the bathroom sink. In her bedroom, drawers opening and closing. Finally, the bedsprings creaking.

It was all he could do to keep himself prone on the sofa when he wanted to dive into her bedroom and pounce on her delectable body.

Now, with a sliver of morning light parting the drapes on her front window, he listened to the process in reverse. Bedroom noises. Then the rattle of the shower, the whir of her hair dryer.

He held his wristwatch in front of his eyes. Eight o'clock. They were supposed to be at Dr. Salton's office at ten. Plenty of time for a nap. But there wasn't a prayer of going back to sleep.

Untangling himself from the mauve thermal blanket, he sat on her sofa and stretched. He'd stripped to his boxer shorts to sleep, and he considered staying undressed to greet her. Joe rubbed his hand across the stubble on his jaw. Oh, yeah, he was seductive as all hell in the morning. He pulled on his Levi's and buttoned the crotch.

When the phone in her bedroom rang, he heard a muttered curse from the bathroom.

"Bailey, do you want me to answer?"

"Yes, please."

He strode into her feminine bedchamber. Her comforter was still in disarray. Her sheets were peach.

He picked up the telephone. "Hello?"

"I'm sorry," said a female voice. "I must have the wrong number."

"This is Bailey Fielding's home," he said.

"Who's this? Joe?"

"Good guess," he responded. "Who's this?"

"It's Greta. Is Bailey there?"

The young lady in question darted into the bedroom, and Joe held his breath when he saw her. All she wore was an extralarge bath towel in navy blue. Though the towel didn't reveal much more of her body than her black minidress, it was a hundred times more intimate.

"Thanks, Joe." She grabbed the phone. "I'm out of the bathroom if you'd like to use it."

"I'll stay here. I'd better keep an eye on you." He stretched out on her sheets and folded his hands behind his head. "Greta's on the phone."

Into the phone, Bailey said, "Greta, hi. Have you got a flight for me today?"

"Sorry. Claude says you're off."

"What's up?" Bailey eyed Joe's long body. He was wearing jeans, but his chest was bare. Purposely, she averted her eyes. She couldn't concentrate on anything with Joe lying there, looking all warm and sexy.

". . . kind of strange around here."

Bailey turned her attention back to the telephone. "I'm sorry, Greta, I didn't hear what you were saying."

"Claude's all fired up. He's got to make some kind of big payment on a loan, and he's talking about cutting back on two planes and two pilots."

"Oh, no! I was the second-to-last one hired. He's not going to fire me, is he?"

"I don't know what he's going to do. Anyway, that's not why I called. I'm running in a marathon in Aspen on the weekend, and Mac is going to fly me up there after lunch. He'd really like it if you and Joe would come up and join us."

"I doubt we can," Bailey said. She'd stepped away from the bed, but Joe was staring at her. His eyes were so warm that she had to look away from him. He was too distracting.

"Please consider it," Greta said. "Mac has gone to a lot of trouble. He's borrowed a Piper Tomahawk from a friend in Colorado Springs, and it's fueled and ready, right here at Sky Air. And he's got a little map showing the air coordinates for the location of the cabin where we'll be staying."

"Can't I call from the Aspen airfield?" Bailey asked.

"I guess not. From what I understand, there's no phone. The cabin is kind of remote, but it does have its own landing strip, so I'm hoping it's not too primitive. Anyway, I'll leave the keys for the Tomahawk and the map with Claude. Okay?''

"Thanks," Bailey said. Pensively, she stared through the bedroom window to the blue sky. Once again, she was in danger of being unemployed. "Greta?"

"What is it, Bailey?"

"About this loan that Claude has to pay. Can you tell me about it?"

"It's huge. A start-up loan from about ten years ago. From what I understand, it was a silent-partner arrangement."

"Do you know who the partner was?"

"Sure do. It was our new congressman, Ted Grambling."

Scowling, Bailey hung up the phone. She didn't like the way this sounded. Even if Claude had to fire her, she didn't want to see him in trouble.

"Bailey," Joe said, "I've got the bed all warmed up. Why don't you join me?"

"Great idea." She stepped inside the walk-in closet and changed into her oldest, rattiest flannel bathrobe. Then she plunked down at the foot of the bed. "I've got something to tell you. It's about Claude."

AS THEY RODE in the elevator to Dr. Lawrence Salton's fifth-floor office, Bailey was still defending her employer. "You're sniffing up the wrong tree if you suspect him of sabotaging the plane. He lost a lot. In his reputation. And cash, too. I know the insurance payout on the Otter didn't cover the cost of the plane."

"You're the one who mentioned it," Joe said.

"Claude is paying off a loan. That doesn't mean he was working a blackmail scheme on Grambling."

"I still have to wonder." Mentally, Joe referred to the investigation files that he'd committed to memory. All the data on Claude Whistler was in perfect order. He had debts, but he paid on time. "Here's what doesn't make sense. It ought to be the other way around. Seems to me that Claude might have had to bribe Grambling in the early days. It took some major wheeling and dealing to get Sky Air off the ground. So to speak."

"Well, if Grambling was a silent partner, he'd make sure that his wife helped Claude with political favors."

"You said it," Joe declared.

The elevator halted, and Bailey stepped out. For today's sleuthing, she wore her long hair down. She'd outfitted herself in sandals and a loosely fitted, black-and-white-patterned shorts dress that showed off her long, tanned legs.

Though Joe knew enough about women's fashion to understand that the desired effect was casual, he thought she looked wonderfully feminine. Her long, graceful body couldn't be anything but elegant. Escorting her through the door to Salton's office, he placed his hand at her waist, feeling the rayon material slide across her skin.

The reception area was bright with colorful photographs of airplanes. Hanging in one corner was a mobile of Snoopy, wearing goggles and flying his doghouse. The woman who sat at the front desk was a perky redhead with a splash of freckles across her nose. She beamed at him. "May I help you?"

"I'm Joe Rivers. I have an appointment."

"The doctor is waiting. Go on in."

The spacious inner office reflected the same pleasant cheeriness as the reception area, but with none of the airplanes. Two beige sofas and several comfortable-looking chairs were arranged in conversational areas. There wasn't a desk in sight.

The doctor sat cross-legged in the middle of one sofa, concentrating intently on a hand-held video game.

Joe did not find Salton's attitude to be confidence inspiring. If he'd been planning to consult a psychiatrist, he would have wanted someone with a more serious manner.

"Hah!" Salton said, looking up. "I died again. I'm never going to get to the princess at the end of the game."

"My friend's child has one of those," Bailey said. She drew the logical conclusion. "Does that game belong to your kids?"

"I don't have any children." A wide grin spread beneath his bushy brown mustache. "But I guess you could say that this game is for my own inner child. Please sit down."

Joe settled into a seat at the end of the sofa, and Bailey sat beside him.

"Well?" Salton said.

Joe started, "As you know, I'm with the FAA. I'm investigating the crash, and—"

"Wrong," Salton said abruptly.

"Excuse me?" Joe found this guy so offensive, he could hardly sit still and talk to him.

"Well, you might be with the FAA. And you might be investigating the crash. But that's not why you're here." He stretched his legs and rested his Airwalk sneakers on the wood coffee table in front of the sofa. "You're here because you need to know what happened to Kate."

"Thanks for your opinion," he said. "May I continue?"

Salton turned his smug gaze on Bailey. "And you're going along with him because you want to relieve yourself of guilt. It's a heavy burden."

"Yes," she said. "It is."

"Confrontations like last night don't help." He frowned. "I'm sorry about that. Emily is fixated on a belief that her parents were murdered. She can't accept the randomness of fate."

"Why would she be so certain that the crash wasn't an accident?" Joe asked.

Salton paused, then said, "I don't know how much I can tell you without violating her privacy."

"You are aware," Joe said, "that privileged information doesn't apply when the information has relevance to a crime."

"Let me think about it."

But it was clear that Salton intended to make this an exercise in frustration. The psychiatrist was not obligated by law to open his files on his clients without a court order, and he obviously did not intend to be helpful.

Joe leaned back in the chair. "If you're not going to tell me anything, why did you suggest that I make an appointment?"

"I'm fascinated by the dynamics of this crash. The interrelationships. Talk about yourself, too. How do you feel about Kate's death?"

"I didn't come here for therapy."

"All right, then, I'll tell you." He tilted his head back and stared at the ceiling. "You and Kate were married for seven years. The last several months, maybe even a year, were difficult. You argued. She complained. You withdrew, withheld affection."

"You're way off base. I wanted the relationship to work. I was trying."

"You withheld affection," Salton continued. "You accepted lengthy out-of-town assignments. That doesn't sound like someone who was working on the relationship."

Every muscle in Joe's body tensed. "I don't have to listen to this."

"Actually, you do. If you really want to know what was going on with Kate. Don't you want to know why I prescribed medication for her?"

"Why?"

"She was depressed. My God, she had a lot to be depressed about. Her marriage was going to hell in a handbasket. And there was her age. Thirty-three. A difficult time for a beautiful woman who wanted to stay young and beautiful. She was a strong personality. Very interesting."

He lowered his gaze from the ceiling and confronted Bailey. "You understand what I'm saying, don't you?"

"Some."

"Kate was obsessed with winning. If I were to explain it in laymen's terms, I'd say she was a user. She enjoyed using people, manipulating them."

"I understand that," Bailey said.

"A user?" Joe questioned. "Would Kate be capable of blackmail?"

"Bravo," the doctor said. "You catch on fast. Yes, indeed, Kate would be capable of blackmail. If it suited her purposes, she wouldn't see anything wrong in it."

"Blackmail is a crime," Joe said. "If you withhold this information from the authorities, you're an accessory."

"She'd spoken about blackmail, but I don't know if she was actually doing it."

"Who would she have been blackmailing?"

"I don't know that, either."

"Dammit," Joe said. "This isn't getting us anywhere, Dr. Salton. I need information pertinent to the crash. Would the medication you prescribed have interfered with her ability to fly an airplane?"

"Warning," he said with a laugh. "Don't operate heavy equipment or machinery."

"I don't see the humor," Joe said.

"Oh, come on. Medication affects everyone differently. The use is discretionary. When she first started taking these pills, mild antidepressants, I advised her to spend a week on the ground to see how they affected her. That's what she did. And she reported no side effects."

"But it's possible," Joe said, "that she might have been slow in her reflexes. Impaired, in fact."

"Possible," he conceded. "But she'd been on antidepressants for over six months without incident. It seems unlikely that she would have suddenly had an unusual reaction."

"Could she have accidentally overdosed?"

"An overdose would not have been accidental. Are you listening to me, Joe? This could be the very crux of the matter."

"What could?"

"If Kate overdosed, it was on purpose."

"Suicide?"

"Every pilot thinks about it, Joe. If you love the sky, your last memory is air. Close your eyes. Sudden descent. Then, explosion. No chance of survival."

Joe tried to imagine what kind of rage and hatred must have been going on inside Kate for her doctor to even suggest such a thing. The horror overwhelmed him. Behind his eyelids, he saw the searing burst of orange flame. He felt the impact, hurling him off his feet. He heard his own hoarse cry.

"Not with passengers on board." The quiet tone of his voice contrasted the roaring in his head. "That's not suicide. That's murder."

"You were a test pilot, Joe. Have you witnessed other crashes?"

"I know what you're getting at, Doctor. You're saying that pilots are risk takers, and people who choose a potentially dangerous occupation have some kind of death wish."

Salton nodded, encouraging him to talk.

"I investigate crashes for a living," Joe said. "Maybe sometimes a pilot has acted rashly because they thought it would be a thrill to shake hands with the grim reaper. But that doesn't apply to me or to Kate."

"Suicide," the doctor said, "is a possibility that must be considered."

Bailey piped up, "I have one word for your theory, Doctor, and that word is 'Baloney!'"

"Really? And how did you come to this intelligent conclusion? You were riding beside her. If I recall correctly, you were the one who said she seemed ill."

"That's right," Bailey said. "Sick. As in nauseated. Like when you eat too much green chili. Her eyes were kind of hazy and unfocused. But that woman was not talking about killing herself. She was upset, but she wasn't crazy."

Bailey's memory was vivid, painfully so. In her mind, she heard Kate's fierce whisper. *I don't want to die.*

"What about this?" Bailey suggested. "What if she was cleaning out her system? What if she'd gone off the antidepressants? Cold turkey. Quit."

Salton lifted his feet from the coffee table. His expression was alert. "I hadn't thought of that. Of course, there would be withdrawal. Nausea. Dizziness. But why would she? I hadn't told her to stop her medication."

"Kate might have made that decision for herself," Bailey informed him. "After she found out she was pregnant."

"Pregnant? My God, I didn't know." Salton was no longer glib and superior. When he turned to Joe, his expression was sincere. "I'm sorry. You lost your wife and your baby."

"It wasn't mine," Joe said. "She was six weeks pregnant. Except for the night before the accident, we hadn't made love in over two months."

Obviously agitated, the psychiatrist rose to his feet. He paced the length of his spacious office. "This changes things."

"But you knew she was having an affair," Joe said.

"Yes."

"Who? Who was my wife's lover?"

Salton paused. The air in the office swirled with turbulence. It was like the gathering of a storm when the atmosphere crackled with ominous portent. Where, Bailey wondered, would the lightning bolts strike? Who was Kate's lover?

When Salton returned to the sofa, his attitude was wholly different. Lacking sarcasm, his voice was crisp and professional. "I need time to consider, but I will have an answer for you within twenty-four hours." He checked his wristwatch. "That's all the time I have right now."

As Joe gave his home phone number and promised to check for messages from Salton, Bailey considered the transformation of Dr. Salton. Until he'd heard about Kate's pregnancy, he'd been snotty and smug. Then, all of a sudden, he was serious as could be. Why?

As he ushered them toward the door, Joe asked one more question. "When we first came in, I asked about why Emily was so sure the crash was not an accident. You said you'd think about telling us. Have you thought about it?"

"I see no reason why I can't tell you," he said. "Emily is superstitious. She was scheduled to be on that plane. At the last minute, something came up. She was running late and couldn't make the flight. Therefore, she thinks the crash wasn't an accident, it was fate. Add to that her paranoia."

"Explain," Joe said.

"She blames everyone but herself." He turned to Bailey. "You've had a taste of her anger, haven't you?"

"Who does she think was really responsible for the crash?"

"Claude Whistler."

Maybe, Joe thought, Emily wasn't as crazy as everyone thought.

Chapter Twelve

"We have to talk with Claude," Joe said as he leaned against the front fender of the Mustang and turned his face to the sun, enjoying the warmth. "We need to ask about Emily."

"The woman is a fruitcake. And Greta told me this morning that Claude is in a foul mood because of a loan he needs to pay off. I will not jeopardize my job because of a fruitcake."

"Then who?" he asked. "Grambling or O'Shea?"

"Yuck and double yuck. Isn't there a more precise way to conduct an investigation?"

"There would be if we were working with machines," he said. Joe missed that precision. Usually, when he was investigating a crash, he got the in-flight performance details from a pilot who discussed mechanical data. The rest of his time was spent with the equipment, determining cause. On a big job, like the airliner crash he'd worked in Alaska, there was a read-out from the black box to decipher.

With people, the most fallible of creations, there was no direct cause and effect. There were theories, motives and a ton of second-guessing.

"Let's talk about blackmail," he said.

"And Kate?"

He nodded. "Somehow, the stuff Salton said didn't surprise me. About Kate being a user, thinking there was nothing wrong with blackmail. When she wanted something, she was single-minded in going after it."

"But who would she blackmail?"

Distastefully, Joe considered the possibilities. If his wife had been blackmailing someone, she had to have something on them. "Her lover?"

"That brings us back to square one," Bailey said. "Who was Kate's lover?"

Joe groaned. Ever since his trip to Florida, he'd been rolling that question around in his head. Though he should have cared desperately, he was tired of speculating, of rehashing his failed marriage. He wanted to move on. "Is it too early for lunch?"

"Eleven o'clock. Let's call it brunch and eat."

"Good. I'm starving."

They popped into the Mustang, and Joe aimed back toward the airfields, choosing a breakfast-specialty restaurant called the Chicken or the Egg. The name was appropriate, he thought. Which came first? Kate's lover or the man she was blackmailing? Were they one and the same?

In the parking lot, Bailey slammed her car door. "What about Salton? Do you think he was her lover?"

"Why would you think that?"

"His reaction when he heard she was pregnant. He was pretty intense. He's childless, you know. Could have been his kid."

"Though I would like nothing better than to nail his smug, superior hide to the wall, I doubt it."

They strolled into the cutesy restaurant with its gingham tablecloths and adorable table decorations. Their conversation seemed morbid in comparison with the beaming waitress who introduced herself as Marilou.

Joe glanced up and down a menu that was decorated with grinning chickens who were obviously unaware that they were about to be axed, plucked and fricasseed. "It seems more likely to me that Salton had an attack of professional ethics when he realized that Kate's lover might have played a part in the crash. Maybe she threatened to expose him, and he retaliated by sabotaging the plane."

"Hard to believe," Bailey said. "I mean, an extramarital affair is nothing to brag about, but sabotaging an aircraft seems a bit extreme."

"Maybe not for the husband of a congresswoman, like Grambling."

"Or Ross O'Shea, the lover of a congresswoman, who hoped she would divorce that husband and marry him."

"Or if you were Claude Whistler, the owner of an airline and charter service who was happily married with children."

Since Bailey didn't want to suspect Claude she rushed forward with another scenario. "Or a psychiatrist like Salton who was breaching his professional ethics by messing around."

Joe looked up from the menu. "You might be on to something, Bailey. If Salton was messing around with Kate, one of his patients, it would be more than an embarrassment. He could lose his entire practice."

They both ordered Denver omelets and settled back to sip their coffee.

There was a thought forming in Bailey's mind, a connection with Salton that she couldn't quite fathom.

She glanced over at Joe, who seemed similarly preoccupied as he toyed with his spoon and fork.

She liked the way he looked today, in his Levi's and an oxford cloth blue shirt that was open at the collar, showing a bit of crisp, black chest hair.

Her mind flashed back to the morning when he was lying on her bed with his chest bared. That was a mental picture she would savor in her fantasies for a long time to come. Joe, half-naked, was her idea of the perfectly sexy male.

Her grandpa Mac used to say, "When you see what you're looking for, don't shop around."

But that didn't apply to Joe. He was very close to the man she'd been seeking all her life. Unfortunately, she couldn't plunk down thirty-nine dollars and thirty-nine cents on the counter, throw him in a sack and take him home. There were too many strings attached.

He looked up suddenly. "The necklace!"

Dragging her mind back to the topic at hand, Bailey nodded. "The gold airplane with a diamond propeller?"

"Do you remember Salton's office?"

"Sure, he had all that cute airplane stuff. Photos and models. Snoopy flying his doghouse."

"That necklace is his taste," Joe said. "Not Kate's."

"But if that's a real diamond, the pendant is worth a pretty penny, and you said Kate loved expensive things."

"What if—" Joe sipped his coffee "—what if that necklace was the first blackmail payment?"

"Perfect!" she said.

"Then the guy who called you last night had to be Salton. He saw you wearing the necklace, and he thought you knew something, that you were hinting about blackmail.''

''Perfect again!''

He reached across the table and took her hand.

To the rest of the world, they probably appeared to be lovers sharing a moment of deep intimacy, and there was nothing in the world she wanted more. Bailey laughed to herself. Nobody would guess, looking at them, that they were more like Sherlock Holmes and Watson than Romeo and Juliet.

There was a sudden beeping noise. Bailey started. She sat up straight in her seat.

''That's you,'' Joe said. ''You're on call, aren't you?''

''You bet I am.''

She dug in her purse, snatched up the plastic beeper and turned off the sound. Her grin stretched wide. She was going flying! Claude was calling her to the airfield.

Stamping her feet on the floor under the table in a victory dance, she squinted her eyes, clenched her fists and whispered exultantly, ''Oh, yes! I'm going to fly!''

She pressed the beeper to her lips and kissed it.

''I assume you're pleased?''

''This makes me so happy. Oh, Joe, I was afraid Claude was going to lay me off.''

''Why would he do that? Not even Claude is dumb enough to fire the best darn stunt pilot west of the Mississippi.''

''Let's go.'' She was already up and out of her chair.

''What about my food?''

''When I get back from this flight, I'll buy you a four-course dinner. Heck, Joe, I might even cook.''

"That's a deal." He rose from the table, pulled a twenty from his wallet and dropped it beside his half-finished coffee.

They were close to the airfield, and it took less than fifteen minutes before the Mustang was parked in the lot.

Bailey felt fantastic. A warmth flowed through her as she watched a Saberjet slice into the air. She was going to be flying again. Everything was going to be okay.

Her excitement carried her out of the car, past the hangar and into the offices. She whisked past Greta's vacant desk and entered Claude's offices.

Grinning from ear to ear, she said, "You beeped. And here I am."

Claude didn't look up from the paperwork on his desk. "Close the door, Bailey."

She wondered why. It wasn't as if they flew secret missions at Sky Air. But she obeyed her boss.

"Sit down, Bailey."

Something was wrong with this picture. He should have just handed her the assignment and wished her luck. Instead, his mouth was drawn, and his eyebrows furrowed. Claude looked old. He appeared to have aged twenty years overnight.

"It has come to my attention, Bailey, that you failed to report a possible sabotage on the Cessna. The brakes on the landing gear were cut."

She almost cried out. Her enthusiasm withered like a dead rose on the vine, leaving only the thorns. "There was no danger at all. Of course, I caught the problem in my preflight procedures, and I did not take off. Really, Claude. It was more like a prank than an actual attempt at sabotage."

"That prank cost me a charter flight. I'm in business here, Bailey. I need paying customers."

"Yes, sir."

"It's your job to report these things." He raked his hand through his silver-streaked hair. "Especially in light of the other crash. With all your racing around and stirring things up with Joe, I don't suppose it's occurred to you that if there was sabotage, I might be the target. Somebody might be trying to put Sky Air out of business."

"Why would they want to do that, sir?"

He slammed his fist down on the desk top. "This is a cutthroat, competitive business. There's more call for charters than ever before. I've got to stay on my toes."

"I'm sorry, sir. I wasn't thinking. I'll be more careful in the future about filing the proper reports."

"In the future?" His gaze pierced her fragile hopes. "I can't ignore this, Bailey. I can't just pat you on the head and tell you not to screw up next time. I'm afraid I will have to dismiss you."

Her hand flew to her mouth, holding back a scream of protest. Her career was over. She was grounded. The likelihood of finding another job as a pilot was slim to none.

Trembling, she lowered her hand. "Please, Claude. Don't do this. I'll do anything to keep my job. I'll work for free for two months. I'll pay you."

"This business runs on safety. We can't take chances."

"I didn't. I could have taken off, but I didn't."

"You're a liability. Right now, everyone thinks of you as that girl pilot who crashed and killed five people, including a congresswoman."

Though she felt like bursting into tears, Bailey reined herself in. Now was not the time to behave like a little girl. She needed to be cool. "That's not altogether true, Claude. Some people refer to me as the girl pilot who performed an incredible landing and saved the lives of nine people."

"I'm being sued by that actor, Ross O'Shea. He's been tromping around on talk shows, blabbing about the horror of surviving a plane crash. On Sky Air."

"We can fight him, Claude. Two days ago, he stalked me to my apartment and attacked me. He came after Joe with a knife."

Claude's eyes widened. "My God. Is he insane?"

"I probably shouldn't tell you this, sir. But he was having an affair with Congresswoman Grambling."

"Are you certain about this?"

"Yes, sir. That's why he showed up at that fund-raiser last night. I would have to guess that he was looking for blackmail money from Ted Grambling."

"Blackmail, huh?"

Claude tilted back in his desk chair. His hand rose to shield his eyes, but Bailey could see that he gazed inward, speculating and calculating. For the first time, she realized the most obvious characteristic about her boss. He was a schemer. His success depended upon more than simply delivering passengers from one destination to another. He played politics. He figured the percentages, then played his hand with the ruthless finesse of a riverboat gambler.

He focused directly on her. "I'm sorry to hear somebody might try to blackmail Ted. He's a good friend. We go way back."

But wasn't Grambling calling his debt, threatening the growth of Sky Air?

"Like all good friends," Claude said, "I owe him, and he owes me. Do you understand what I'm saying, Bailey?"

"I think so. If I scratch your back, you'll scratch mine." Claude wanted something from her. Bailey had no idea what it was, but she'd do anything, almost anything to keep her job. "How can I help you, sir?"

"It's about the investigation. Joe's investigation for the FAA." His fingertips rubbed hard at his temples, as if he were trying to reach inside and massage his brain. "Whatever he discovers, whether it was sabotage or equipment failure, the publicity is bad for us. I want people to forget. Not to look at the Sky Air logo and think of the crash."

"What can I do, sir? I'll do anything to help."

"I have a feeling that Joe is the only person at the FAA who's interested in pursuing this investigation. Am I right?"

She nodded. Bailey had the distinct impression that she was a trout with the hook in her mouth, and Claude was reeling her in. She felt totally outmatched.

"Of course," Claude said, "I wouldn't ask you to interfere with an FAA investigation. I wouldn't ask you to use your influence to convince Joe to drop this case."

"No, sir. You couldn't ask me to do that."

He lowered his hands, folded them across his chest and regarded her for a moment in silence. "Who is Joe reporting to at the FAA? Who's his supervisor?"

"I don't know."

"He's not reporting to anyone, is he?" Claude pressed forward. "Joe's obsessed with his wife's death and he can't let go. This is a renegade investigation, isn't it?"

She said nothing. Though her job hung in the balance, Bailey would not betray Joe.

"You don't have to answer me, Bailey. I can see the truth on your face."

He opened his top desk drawer and reached inside. A set of keys dangled from his fingertips. "Mac left these for you. And this map. There's a Piper Tomahawk on the south runway. I think Mac wanted you to meet him in Aspen."

"That's right."

"Did you know that I used to fly for Mac?"

"In the airshow?"

"That's right. About twelve years ago. I met you. You were a skinny teenager who couldn't get enough of airplanes."

"I don't recall." But that wasn't odd. She'd met dozens of Grandpa Mac's flying buddies. They were all so much older than Bailey that they were a blur. "Which plane?"

"I loved the Spitfires, but I kept getting stuck in the replica of a Japanese Zero. Those were the good old days. Ask him sometime. Ask him about Claude Whistler and Jimmy Cannon."

"Jimmy Cannon?" She seemed to have a vague recollection of a man named Jimmy. Uncle Jimmy.

"Does the name mean anything to you?"

She shook her head as memories faded. "Can't say as it does."

He slid the keys and map across his desk top. "Here's the only favor I'm going to ask of you, Bailey. Go today. Take Joe with you to Aspen. Take a few days off and put things in perspective. If Joe still wants to investigate after that, more power to him." He focused again on the paperwork that spread across the top of his desk. "That's all."

So, she was still fired. "May I ask you a question?"

"Sure."

"In the course of our investigating . . ."

He looked up, interested again.

". . . we learned that Emily doesn't believe the crash was an accident. She said somebody prevented her from taking that flight."

"If somebody did," Claude said, "it was Ted Grambling. She's a heavy contributor to his campaign."

"She said it was you, sir."

"Me?" He frowned, then nodded. "I know why. Do you remember before takeoff I had a phone call? That was Emily. She was on her way to the airport, stuck in traffic. I told her that we wouldn't hold the plane for her. Does that set your mind at ease, Bailey?"

"Yes, sir, it does."

"You and Joe don't really believe I had anything to do with the crash, do you?"

Bailey wasn't sure what she believed. "Am I still fired, sir?"

"I'm willing to reconsider. As a favor to Mac and the good old days. Let's make that two weeks' suspension. Two weeks. No pay."

She started to protest but caught herself. At least she was being given a chance. "Yes, sir. Two weeks."

"Consider yourself damn lucky," he said. "And keep in mind that I won't stand for your stunt-pilot attitude. You can't ignore a cut brake line because it's not a big deal to you. This is a business, not an airshow."

Stiffly, she rose from her chair. "Yes, sir."

"Have a good time in Aspen, Bailey."

She stepped into the reception area of Sky Air and closed the office door behind her. Joe was waiting. His expression changed from a smile to concern when he looked into her eyes. "What happened?"

"I'm suspended. Two weeks."

When he approached her, she pulled away. This was his fault. He'd told her not to report the cut line, the possible sabotage. She'd been protecting him and his renegade investigation. Now her career was on the line.

If she was smart, she would tell him off and erase him from her mind. But she couldn't. She and Joe had been through too much together.

"Damn you," she said as she charged out of the office. Joe was the only man she'd ever really wanted, and he was the one man she could never have. "Damn you a thousand times, Joe Rivers."

"Tell me what happened."

"Claude found out about the cut brake line and he suspended me."

"How did Claude know?"

"Didn't say. Maybe Greta overheard more than we'd thought. Maybe Mac threw the cut cable in the trash when he repaired it, and somebody else found it."

"But why would Mac do—?"

She whirled and faced him. "It doesn't matter. Claude found out, and I got caught in a big, fat, juicy, shameful lie."

"It's not right for you to be blamed," Joe said. He hadn't meant for things to turn out this way. If he had thought for one minute that they'd be found out, he never would have asked her to lie. "I'm sorry."

"Forget it."

"I can't let you risk your career for me. I'm going back to the office to talk with Claude. I'll explain to him that I coerced you."

"Leave it, Joe. Please, leave this alone."

"I can't do that."

He didn't know what kind of men she was accustomed to dealing with, but he wasn't going to let her take the blame for something that was his fault. Joe wasn't a coward. He wanted to protect her, not the other way around.

He pivoted and headed back toward the Sky Air office.

"Where are you going?" she demanded.

"I'm going to do what's right."

She ran up in front of him, halting his progress. "Don't you dare talk to Claude. You'll only make it worse."

"I shouldn't have asked you to lie, Bailey."

"And I shouldn't have agreed. But it was my choice. Now it's over and done with. Really, no big deal. I can live with being suspended for two weeks."

"I can't," he said.

"Well, you have to," she said. "You're going to have to swallow your macho pride and let me take care of this."

"My macho pride?" He didn't get it.

"That's right, Mr. Test Pilot. You don't like the idea of hiding behind my skirts."

He glanced down at her shorts. They were cut full enough to almost qualify as a skirt, but they were mid-thigh. "I can't hide behind that skirt. There's not enough material to cover a squirrel." He eyed her long, tanned legs with sincere appreciation. "Not that I'm criticizing."

"Don't you get off the subject," she said sternly. "What we're talking about here is your arrogant attitude. And this time, you're just going to have to back off and let me take care of things."

He didn't feel arrogant. The opposite, in fact. Joe felt like a weasel for allowing her to jeopardize her lifework. "It's not right. This was my stupid idea, to pursue the investigation without FAA sanction. And I got you sucked in. What kind of man would I be if I let you protect me?"

"What kind of man," she said slyly, "would act against my wishes?"

She had him. He was hoist on his own chivalrous petard. Damned if he did, damned if he didn't. Joe didn't much like the situation, but her grin went a long way toward convincing him that everything would be all right. "Somehow, Bailey, I'll make this up to you."

"Glad you see it my way." She took a set of keys from her purse, tossed them in the air and caught them. "I'm going to Aspen this afternoon. Mac got me a Piper Tomahawk. It's fueled and ready to go. Want to come?"

"There's this small matter of an investigation."

"What else can we do today? Talk to Grambling? He hates you. Talk to Emily? She hates me. Or Ross O'Shea? Talking to him would be a total waste of time and breath."

"True," Joe said. "I guess the only thing is to wait until we hear from Salton and he tells us the identity of Kate's lover."

"We can wait in Aspen."

"Okay," he said. "I'll drop you at your place, then I'll go home, make a couple of calls. And we're off."

"Roger dodger. Over and out."

Chapter Thirteen

Everything would be better when she was in the air. The world would be a brighter, cleaner, kinder place. Her hopes and dreams would once again be put in proper perspective. In spite of a niggling doubt that she should have told Joe that Claude had practically ordered her to take him to Aspen, Bailey was perfectly delighted with the prospect of an afternoon spent stunt flying and an evening with Mac and Greta in Aspen.

It was two o'clock in the afternoon when she and Joe finally strapped themselves into the cockpit of the Piper Tomahawk. Mac had said it was souped up, and he had not lied. Not only did the Tomahawk feature a custom paint job in yellow and black, but the standard power had been doubled with a Lycoming engine, 230 horses, plenty of shove for stunts. The only problem would be looping so hard that the wings were torn off.

They hadn't needed to file a flight plan for this pleasure trip, and Bailey was absolutely pleased to be sitting in the left seat for takeoff. She spoke into the headset microphone that was necessary to communicate over the whine of the engine. "Ready, Joe?"

He gave her a thumbs-up sign.

Bailey felt that old, familiar flutter in the pit of her stomach. Anticipation. She wondered if the condor shared that instant of thrill before spreading wing and soaring. What would it be like to be a bird? Free as a bird, she thought. Did the winged species know how they were truly blessed among creatures? Not weighted down by worries and guilt, they could fly. In moments, she would be like them.

She taxied into position, running through the pre-flight checks with thorough efficiency.

When she was a little girl, she remembered, after her parents had died, she'd stood on a verdant hillside outside Atlanta and watched Grandpa Mac in his flying machine. Little Bailey had spread her arms, wishing the air currents could lift her away from all the mess and debris on the earth. She'd longed to leave her tragedies behind, to live on the wind, to float on the pure, clear air.

"Bailey?" Joe's deep voice resonated through the headset. "You love this, don't you?"

"More than anything."

She turned her head toward him. In the mysterious, deep blue of his eyes, she saw a reflection of her own anticipation. They were kindred spirits. He shared her deepest feelings, the emotion she could not express in words or gestures, the swelling of her heart, the tremble that coursed through her blood when she knew she was about to take flight.

When he grasped her hand, she squeezed his with the fierce intensity of her unfettered excitement. Finally, she thought, here was a man who could understand. They were mated on the most profound level. Not as lovers, but as soul mates.

And if they ever could make love? If she could indulge herself in a long, slow exploration of his lips, if they could discover the intimate secrets of each other's bodies, Bailey knew that she would finally achieve perfect fulfillment.

She revved the powerful single-prop engine. All systems were okay. A-okay.

Bailey accelerated, throttled back and the wheels left the earth. She had to suppress the urge to shout "Yippee!"

They leveled off at sufficient altitude for Aspen, and she glanced at Joe. He had leaned back in his seat. Totally relaxed, his arms rested loosely at his sides. And he was smiling, drinking in the sky. Lazily, with utter contentment, he rolled his head toward her.

His lips moved.

She couldn't hear him over the whirring of the engine. "What?"

He formed the words carefully.

"Love? Did you say love?"

Did he? He was making some kind of declaration, and she couldn't imagine what it was. Love? She could hope. She could dream that he was telling her that he loved her, that the past was gone, Kate no longer mattered, no one mattered except for Bailey. Together, in the limitless horizons of her mind, they would soar to magnificent altitudes.

"Joe, what are you saying? What do you love?"

He put on his headset and spoke into the mike that communicated with her headset. "I said, Bailey, that I'd love to take the controls. Whenever you're ready."

Bailey grinned. Maybe he hadn't professed his undying affection, but she was literally too high to let that drag her down. For a change, she felt in control of the situation. "I don't know if I should let you fly. Have you had any experience in this kind of plane, Jet Man?"

"If I can handle a Stealth bomber, I think I can probably do okay in something with a motor the size of a lawn mower."

"Two hundred and thirty horses?"

"Nothing to it."

Her eyebrows lifted. Such unbridled arrogance could not go unanswered.

When they passed the first foothills, well beyond the range of circling passenger planes and well below the altitude of any others, she swooped low, diving into a deserted, barren canyon with palisades rising on either side. She skimmed a mere fifty feet above a dry riverbed. "Ever try this, Jet Man?"

"Same altitude," he said with a shrug. "Of course, I was moving at Mach 2."

She nosed upward. The maneuverability in this little plane was outstanding—better than Grandpa Mac's Spitfire. Though she shouldn't have been goofing around, Bailey couldn't resist. She was riding low in the sky, nearly a thousand feet below any commercial flight, and their plane was highly visible in the nearly cloudless sky.

She decided to indulge herself.

Bailey soared upward, arcing steadily to keep the engine from stalling out at the pinnacle of the stunt maneuver. They made a slow, upside-down circle in the air. The blood rushed to her head. Seat belts kept them from falling.

Joe raised his hands above his head and braced them against the window ceiling until Bailey had completed her arc and they were once again right side up. Then he merely grinned. "Cute."

"Is that all you've got to say for yourself?" Most people were screaming their heads off before the circle was complete. Of course, she hadn't expected Joe to be that jumpy. But she wanted some kind of reaction. "Cute?"

"Like a quaint, old-time barnstormer."

"Yeah? I'll show you quaint, Jet Man."

She executed a spiral dive, pulling up only seventy feet from a nose-first crash landing. Her desire to astound Joe warred with her sheer exhilaration at once again performing these aerial acrobatics. Like a bird, a crazy bird—a loon or a long-beaked cormorant. She was in her element.

Below them, the waters of a small reservoir glittered in the afternoon sun. Balancing the rudder and flaps, Bailey performed a barrel roll, then pulled out and shot straight up.

She leveled off. "Okay, Jet Man. Your turn."

"I'm just going to start out by returning to standard altitude and going straight, maybe even trying to get back on course. Do you mind?"

"I'm fine." With a contented purr, she leaned back in the pilot's seat. "Whatever you want to do. I'm great."

"Your eyes are all dreamy and unfocused."

"Are they?" she murmured.

Over her headset, she heard him chuckle. "I'll tell you, Bailey, you look like a woman who should be stretched out on satin sheets, asking if it was good for me."

"This is better," she said definitely. Making love had never given her the kind of thrill she got from flying.

Gazing out the window, she enjoyed the day, the puffs of passing clouds, the unfolding panorama of spreading foothills marked with ribbons of streams and distant snowcapped peaks. On their route to Aspen, they would climb over Vail Pass and the Continental Divide.

Joe was a good pilot. He was careful about the unpredictable downdrafts that made mountain flying dangerous, and he kept their course steady.

Bailey felt safe with him. She'd never been so calm when flying with Kate. Not even when Kate was at her best. Though she hadn't intended to mention the investigation, she asked, "Did you ever fly with Kate?"

"A couple of times." He adjusted the altitude, making the steady climb. "I usually took over. It makes me nervous to have anyone else at the controls."

"Typical male," she muttered into her headset.

"What?" he asked over the engine noise.

She rested her hands on the wheel. "I'll take it from here, Joe."

Without the slightest argument, he allowed her to once again pilot the plane. He settled back in his seat, giving the impression that he was content to simply sit back and enjoy the ride. But she knew better.

Joe liked being the boss. He hadn't felt right when she took the responsibility for dealing with Claude. And it was probably bothering him that she was a more experienced pilot on this type of aircraft. And yet, she realized, he was able to compromise. Grandpa Mac would have said that he was trainable. Like a puppy? Or a horse?

No way, Bailey thought. There was one thing for doggoned sure. Joe Rivers was one hundred percent all man. Fascinating and unpredictable and so handsome that she couldn't help wanting to touch the line of his jaw, to measure the breadth of his shoulders with an embrace. When he'd kissed her, she'd felt as if Joe was the most remarkable creature on the planet.

She looked over at him, sitting so close in the copilot's chair. He had taken off his headset and was simply relaxed, soaking in the view, lulled by the steady whir of the engines. What would it be like to have him make love to her? Better than flying?

Bailey chased those thoughts from her head and concentrated on the route to Aspen. With apprehension, she realized that they were nearing the point where the crash had happened. Bailey didn't want to think about it. But the voices replayed in her head. Kate, being nasty, had sneered and told her that she wasn't Joe's type.

But Joe had said differently. He'd told her that if he had a type, it would be Bailey.

Oh, my gracious heavens, she wanted him so badly. Just for a day. Just for one night. If she could forget everything and love him for one night, a matter of hours, she'd be happy. If he would make love to her just once...

But wouldn't that be worse? Then she would know what she was missing. Once she felt his caresses, she would regret the loss of sensation. Now she could only feel sorry that she wouldn't have the dream. She would never know what she was missing.

Over the headset, she heard a burst of static. Another plane signaling her? An airfield?

The last time she'd looked down on this view, disaster had been moments away.

A fuzzy voice on the headset whispered, "Bailey. Do you remember? Bailey."

She tapped the headset. Obviously, she was imagining this strange signal. She spoke into her mouthpiece. "Please identify."

The voice continued. "Listen hard, Bailey. You can still hear the screams of your passengers when the plane went down."

Was she going crazy? This wasn't possible.

And yet the voice whispered in her ear, "Listen to them, Bailey. You and Kate killed them. You shared in it. You shared everything. Even Joe."

"No!" She tuned the headset to another frequency, and made a call to the ground, repeating the identification numbers on the Tomahawk. "Airfield, this is Tango Charlie One Five Five. Do you read me?"

"What did she tell you, Bailey? What did Kate say?"

"This is Tango Charlie One—"

"They can't hear you, Bailey. You're going to die. Like Kate died."

"Who is this? What do you want?"

"Five people died because of you. Your friend Kate died. She burned. You killed her."

"No! I tried my best."

"You failed."

A horror spread through her, paralyzing her limbs, tamping her breathing. Vivid pictures flashed across the surface of her mind. Fire! Spreading fire consumed the flesh, burned to the bone.

"You should have died, too," the voice said. "Take it down, Bailey. Erase their deaths with your own."

"Who is this?"

Joe touched her arm, and she turned to him. Unable to speak, she gaped and touched the earphones.

Quickly, he put on his headset. "What's wrong?"

"I don't know," she said. "Somebody is on my frequency."

"I'm listening," he said.

But there was silence.

A sob crawled up her throat. Had she imagined the voice? Was it her conscience?

She'd failed. Those people had died because of her. Pain tightened in a band around her skull. "You take it, Joe. I can't. I can't fly anymore."

She yanked off her headset, leaned back in the pilot's seat and squeezed her eyes closed. The voice had been right. She shouldn't be flying. Those five deaths, horrible deaths, had been her fault. Kate had died, strapped into her seat and unconscious. It was all Bailey's fault. She should have rescued her, should have climbed back in the passenger section and told Joe that his wife needed to be moved.

He could have saved Kate and her unborn baby. Instead, he'd been struggling with O'Shea, helping that shoddy actor from the plane instead of taking care of his own beautiful wife.

Guilt and sorrow consumed her. Behind her eyelids, she saw the crash, the flames. Her ears rang with the explosion.

Joe held her shoulder. He shook hard, and she turned toward him. Forcefully, he gestured to her headset. She held the equipment in her hands. If she put it on, would she hear the voice again? Accusing her? *Five people had died because she'd failed.*

Joe reached over and put the headset on her.

"What happened?" he demanded.

"I thought somebody was talking to me." Her fingers trembled uncontrollably, and she laced them together on her lap. "There was a voice."

"A voice? From the ground?"

"I don't know. There's no airfield around here. Usually, up here, if I can't see them, I can't hear them, either."

"Must have been another plane." Joe leaned forward and scanned the clear blue skies. He couldn't see another aircraft. Slowly, he banked and turned, trying to glimpse the view from a different angle. If she'd heard a voice, the other plane had dropped back, far enough behind them that he couldn't tell if they were being followed or not.

Nothing. There was nothing in sight.

"Bailey? What did the voice say to you?"

"We're near where the Otter crashed," she said.

Even over the headset, he could hear the tremble in the back of her throat.

"I know where we are," Joe said. He was very well aware of the topography. Not only had he flown this route himself, but he had also studied the maps endlessly, trying to determine if there had been any other landing site for the Otter, trying to understand why the plane had gone so far off course.

Now, of course, he knew why. It had been Kate's fault. She hadn't properly weaned herself from her medication, and her ego wouldn't allow her to admit that she needed Bailey to take the controls. "Don't blame yourself," he said.

She leaned forward as far as the seat belt would allow and buried her face in her hands. A fierce shudder shook her shoulders. Abruptly, she lowered her hands. Her eyes were dry. "I'm okay," she said. "Sorry."

Touching her shoulder, he felt the tension in her body. This tall, beautiful woman had been through the worst hell a pilot could imagine, and she'd not only survived, but had also been strong and admirably game.

He wasn't sure if he could have coped with the guilt as well as she had. Five deaths. Innocent people killed in a crash. He knew that, at some point, logic faded and the ghosts of those people would rise and haunt you.

Trying to say the right thing, the comforting thing, he spoke into his headset. "If anyone is to blame, it was Kate. She was screwing around with medication, flying impaired and drifting off course."

"I know that."

She looked directly at him. Even in grief, she was lovely. Her dark eyes held a wealth of sorrow, and he wanted to soothe the pain away.

"Tell me about it," he said. "Talk it out."

"Five people died on my watch. They died when I was at the wheel. I'll never forget."

"You don't need to forget. But you've got to go on with living. Now, tell me about the voice on the headset."

"It was probably in my head. I was hearing things."

"But if you weren't," he said, "it means somebody's there. Maybe they're listening to us right now, monitoring every word." He glanced through the skies, seeing no sign of another aircraft. "Maybe there's some coward on our frequency who's afraid to show himself."

Joe waited, hoping that he could goad the voice into speaking again.

But there was no response.

Joe turned back to her. "Who knew where we were headed?"

"Nobody. I didn't file a flight plan. And I just have this map from Grandpa Mac."

"Claude gave you the map," he argued. "He knows our frequency. And he knew you were headed to Aspen."

"Why would he talk to me on the headset? Why would he say those things?" She shook her head. "All I was hearing was the voice of my own conscience."

Though Joe hadn't been planning to put forth any new information on the investigation, he realized that Bailey was even more involved than he was. She stood to lose her reputation as a pilot. Worse than that, she might lose her nerve.

Being a pilot, he knew, required equal parts of determination, motor skills and sheer lunacy. Mechanical logic balanced with the completely unreasonable suspension of gravity. No matter how many aerodynamic principles were involved, there was the underlying miracle of flight. Tons of metal had no business rising from the ground.

He knew Bailey's tolerance for miracles was wearing thin.

Into the headset, he said, "I heard from Salton."

"Who?"

"Salton. Kate's shrink. I called him when I stopped back at my house to pack." Worriedly, Joe glanced toward her. "Are you okay?"

She held up her hand. With an almost detached gaze, she watched her own fingers jumping and trembling more than the steady vibration of the plane would cause. "I don't know what's wrong with me."

"Should I take it down at the next chance?"

"No," she said firmly. "I want to live in the skies, Joe. I don't ever want to return to earth. Up here, I'm safe. Even when I hear voices on the headset."

Her hand flopped loosely to her lap.

"Bailey, talk to me."

"I sure as heck wish I could explain it all to you, Joe. But I'm not real good with feelings. I guess this is despair."

He ached inside when he heard her speak. He longed to erase the sorrow and guilt that she felt.

She continued, "My parents died when I was just a kid, and I thought I'd come to grips with the whole idea of death and dying. I don't know when I figured it out. Grandpa Mac wasn't one to be taking me to a psychiatrist, and I never asked to go. But somewhere in my early years, I faced the fact that my mother and father weren't coming back. They were gone. And I decided that wasn't so bad. To be just vanished, invisible and gone, sucked up into the air like an evaporating cloud."

He reached over and touched her forearm. Gently, he glided his hand down and linked his fingers with hers. She was cold.

"I'm not scared of dying," she said. "Before the crash, I never thought of dying in an aircraft. Even now, I don't think about myself dying. But those other people..." She turned her head toward him.

"It's okay to talk about it, Bailey. Having feelings is natural."

"And flying a plane is not." She managed a slight grin. "Or maybe it is. Grandpa Mac always used to say that if the good Lord intended for man to walk, he wouldn't have invented wings."

He liked the way she thought, admired her innate courage. She was, perhaps, the most remarkable woman he'd ever known. Her strength intrigued him as much as the sweet vulnerability that lurked beneath the surface. She appealed to him—more than the physical attraction he felt for a beautiful lady with long legs and deep brown eyes.

He liked her as a friend, a companion, somebody he enjoyed knowing and learning more about. She might very well be the other half of his soul.

"All right," she said. "Let's talk about Salton. Did he tell you about Kate's lover?"

"He wouldn't reveal his privileged information," Joe said, recalling the brief telephone conversation. "He claimed that the identity of Kate's lover has no relevance to the crash, and he won't open his files without a court order."

"Of course he'd protect the lover," Bailey said. "Especially if the lover was Salton himself."

"True. He's trying to say that if the crash wasn't caused by mechanical failure, Kate was to blame because she was screwing around with her medication." He shrugged. "Maybe he's right. That would explain why she'd allowed the plane to drift so far off course."

Bailey disentangled her fingers from his. In a way, it seemed that she was pulling back into herself. "Being off course is one thing, but the machinery was defective. Kate didn't cause the plane to stall."

"Okay, Bailey." She was riled, vehement.

"That voice... the voice I thought I heard over the crash site..." She was breathing hard. "The voice talked about Kate. Said that Kate was my friend, that she'd told me everything."

"If we're talking about blackmail," Joe said, "that voice could have been Salton."

"He told me I should crash this plane, erase the deaths of the others with my own."

"Mind games." That sounded like Salton. "It's all a lie, Bailey. You know that, don't you?"

"I do, but it still hurts. Oh gracious, it hurts." She sighed heavily. "Did you mention to Salton that we were flying to Aspen?"

"No."

"But I guess he could have followed us."

"And he's still worried about blackmail," Joe said.

She settled back in her seat. "You know what's the worst thing? If he doesn't admit it, we've got no proof. Seems to me like we're a couple of hound dogs chasing our tails, Joe. We've got lots of speculation and no solid evidence."

When they neared Aspen, the map indicated that they should veer southwest. With Bailey navigating, Joe followed the coordinates Mac had given along with simple instructions. Though secluded, the cabin was simple to find. There was a four-hundred-foot runway out in front with a barnlike hangar.

Bailey glanced down. "Look at the size of that place! It's huge! I wouldn't call it a cabin."

"By Aspen standards, it's a cabin."

"Let me take over now," she said. "I'll land it."

He didn't hesitate for an instant, but lifted his hands from the yoke and pulled back his feet from the rudder pedals. "All yours."

"Thanks, Joe." Even over the headset, he could hear the warmth in her voice. "I'm glad that you trust me."

With all his heart, he believed in her. More than he had ever trusted another person, he had faith in Bailey.

Her descent was perfect. The touchdown was as neat as a feather gliding across silk.

The puzzles came on the ground.

"No other plane," Bailey noted. "That's weird. I'm sure Greta said they were taking the Spitfire."

After securing the Tomahawk against the unpredictable wind and weather of the high Rockies, they approached the cabin, which was larger than most
multifamily dwellings. Joe could have put the entire
block of town houses in this cedarwood structure with
its soaring roof and vast display of windows and encir-
cling porch.

No one responded to the doorbell, but the front door
was unlocked. "I guess we should just walk in," Bailey
said.

The interior of the cabin was as opulent as the outside. The front room had a huge fireplace, surrounded
by attractive leather sofas.

Bailey regarded their surroundings with a frown. "I
feel like Goldilocks walking into the home of the three
bears. Maybe we should go looking for three bowls of
porridge in the kitchen."

Joe lifted his eyebrows. "Why?"

"Don't you remember the fairy tale? Goldilocks
tastes the Papa Bear porridge and says it's too hot, then
Mama Bear's, and that's too cold. But Baby Bear's
porridge is just right."

There was no porridge in the kitchen. Only a bottle
of chilled champagne and a note.

Joe read it aloud. "'We're spending the night in town
so I can get a fresh start in the morning. There's drink
and food in the fridge. Make yourselves at home.
Greta.'"

"Did she leave a phone number?"

"No."

"This is very strange, Joe. I'm sure Greta told me this
place didn't have a phone, but it looks fully equipped to
me."

She lifted the kitchen wall phone off the receiver. "It's dead."

"No problem, lady." Joe unzipped the gym bag he'd packed with one change of clothes. Wrapped in his sweatshirt was a modern marvel. "Cell phone."

"But we still don't have her number." She eyed the champagne. "Oh, well, let's make ourselves at home. Like the note says."

"Is that what Goldilocks would do?"

"Actually, Goldilocks tried three chairs until she found the one that was just right. Then she tried the beds."

Joe smiled. He was looking forward to finding the bed that was just right.

Chapter Fourteen

They snacked on pâté and crackers, washed down with champagne. Champagne? Bailey thought that was a particularly odd gift from her grandfather. Though Grandpa Mac was no stranger to strong libation, he did not necessarily encourage his granddaughter to drink, except for special occasions. And leaving her alone in a glamorous, secluded cabin with Joe seemed to invite only one sort of celebration.

"Apparently," she said, "Grandpa Mac and Greta aren't above a little matchmaking." She pushed back her chair from the kitchen table and stood. "Champagne? 'Make yourself at home'?"

"I like the suggestions," Joe said. "I would have added roses and chocolate. Soft jazz. Dimmed lights. The scent of musk in the air."

His gaze locked in on hers, sure and steady as a radar beacon, drawing her closer. Rising, he closed the distance between them. As he stood before her, she was aware of his superior height. It was good to be with a man who was taller. Happily, her head tilted up, and she gazed into the blue of his eyes. He had to be the most handsome man in the world with his tousled black hair and those eyes that penetrated to the very core of her being.

His hand lightly caressed her shoulders, and she suppressed a trembling response. "This seems too planned," she said.

"Not by you or me," he said. "I don't think we had placed lovemaking on our agenda."

"No, sir." She took a step backward. "That was not scheduled."

"I'm willing to be spontaneous."

He caught her arm before she could dart behind a flurry of objections. Joe dragged her close against him. His mouth claimed hers for a long, melting, sensuous kiss.

It was the kind of kiss that caused her heartbeat to accelerate and her toes to curl. And Bailey wanted more. For days, weeks, months, she had fought this attraction. All of her resistance was spent.

Languidly, she said, "This is a mistake, Joe."

She leaned back in his arms, reveling in sensation. His lips demanded her response.

"Joe." She sighed. "We shouldn't be thinking about lovemaking."

"Too late, Bailey. I'm already thinking."

"So am I," she whispered. "Lord help me, so am I."

"Let me make love to you." His voice lowered seductively. She felt the heat of his breath on her cheeks. "Say the word, Bailey. I'll take you on a flight you won't forget."

She wanted him more than she'd ever wanted anything in her whole life. But the word she said was "No."

Though the light in his eyes dimmed, the flame was not extinguished.

She swallowed hard. She couldn't just stand there, staring at him with her heart twirling in her chest like a kite on a string. In order to put an end to these dangerous thoughts, she needed a diversion. "I say we need to make an exploration of this house. We'd better locate the important facilities," she said, "before it's dark."

"Right," Joe said, without much enthusiasm.

"In a place this size, we might get lost."

Determined not to succumb to her desire, Bailey set out, putting one foot in front of the other, exploring the home of one of Grandpa Mac's old buddies. The lower floor was actually three levels—a sitting room with a fireplace, a dining area and kitchen and a couple of smaller rooms. The opulent cabin spread before her in a kind of blur, a haze of suppressed passion. Her rebellious mind concentrated only upon Joe. All she wanted was to melt into his arms and feel his body against hers.

But that was wrong. There could never be anything between them until she told him the truth about what happened in the cockpit. And then...he would hate her.

Bailey could barely stand to think about it.

On the first floor of the cabin, there were two spacious offices. His and hers. In the "his" office, Bailey noticed a framed black-and-white photograph of a rag-tag group of aviators standing around a single-prop airplane.

"I've seen this picture before," she said delightedly. "This is from the show, Mac Augustine's World War II Airshow."

Joe studied the photo and pointed. "That looks like Claude Whistler."

"So it is. He mentioned that he had flown for Grandpa Mac, and I felt kind of bad that I didn't remember him or his friend, Jimmy Cannon." She shrugged. "I never paid too much attention to Grandpa Mac's buddies."

She went to the desk and found another framed photo. "How about this one, Joe. It's Claude and some other guy. He must be the one who owns the cabin." She leaned close and squinted. "I wonder why Claude didn't say anything when he gave me the map."

"Good old Claude," Joe said jokingly. "No ego there. Have you ever noticed the wall of photos in his office with Claude in almost every single one?"

"You don't like him, do you?"

"There's something rotten under that perfect veneer." He leaned against the desk. "By the way, I still want to know how he found out about the cut brake cable."

"Greta must have told him."

"Are we talking about the same Greta who is so besotted with Mac that she can't see straight? Why would she worry about you and your brake cable?"

"It's her job. She was probably trying to do the right thing, and I can't hold that against her."

Still, she thought, Joe was right. It didn't seem characteristic for Greta to go running to the boss with information. At least, she would have talked to Bailey first.

Joe suggested, "Let's call her and find out."

"No number," Bailey said.

"What about this race she's in?" He checked his wristwatch. "It's after six, but we might be able to reach somebody. Let's get her a message to call here."

"Is it really that important?"

"We'll want to hook up with them in Aspen tomorrow, anyway."

Joe strode into the living-room area, grabbed his cel-
lular phone and the Aspen phone book. He settled
down at the kitchen table with a glass of champagne. "I
need to check my home messages, anyway."

Bailey went to the living area and settled on the
leather sofa. Nursing her champagne, she positioned
herself so she could watch Joe. The view of him was far
more satisfying than the vista of snowcapped peaks
outside the picture window. He was exactly the way a
man should be.

He glanced over at her. "Amazing. Ted Grambling
actually called me back and left a message with his
home phone number."

"Why did you want to talk to him?"

"To push a few buttons about blackmail."

"We know why Ross O'Shea was trying to blackmail
him."

"But he mentioned another time. Something about
a mess that Jillian had gotten him into."

Joe turned his attention back to the telephone. Again,
she indulged herself in the sheer pleasure of observing
him.

After a half a dozen calls, he set the phone down.
"I've left messages for Greta."

"That's nice." What would it be like to make love to
him?

——————— allowed to ponder because Joe came
second floor. Up there, she knew, were the bedrooms.

There were three rooms, all decorated in a similar
rustic style with incredible handmade quilts and pine
furniture. The fourth bedroom, at the end of the second-floor hallway, was huge. The king-size mattress

nestled in a four-poster wooden bed frame. The south-facing wall was all windows and a French door that opened onto a balcony.

Bailey opened it and stepped outside, where the last vestiges of dusk were fading and the stars began to light the skies. The clean air in the mountains was different than anyplace in the world. It wasn't heavy with moisture, like in Florida. The breeze was light and caressing, redolent with pine.

When Joe came up behind her, he didn't touch her. But she felt his masculine presence, his tempting nearness.

"It's beautiful up here," he said. "So quiet."

"Like there's nobody else in the world."

"Just you and me," he concurred.

Her resolve not to make love to him began to slip. Her guilt would never allow her to have a lasting relationship with Joe. But she could have one night. If only for tonight, she could find pleasure in his arms. Then she would tell him. Then she would divulge the secret that would drive him away from her forever.

When she glanced toward him, Joe was watching her intently.

"This light becomes you," he said. "There's a little bit of red in your hair. And your skin..." closer to him.

"It's true," he asserted. "You're a lovely woman."

She couldn't hold off any longer. Her willpower shattered, and she breached the distance between them with one determined stride. In his arms, she looked up into his cool blue eyes. "Make love to me, Joe."

He held her tightly, crushing her body against his. "Don't say that if you don't mean it."

"I want you to take me into that big wooden bed and give me a night I won't ever forget. I want the memory."

He kissed her. His mouth was hard and fierce against hers. His arms, so strong, pinned her to him, and when she moved, the friction between them aroused all her senses.

Abandoning all reservations, she hurled herself into wanton desire. As she rubbed herself against his muscular chest, her nipples tightened. Electricity shot through her.

Bailey wasn't sure how they got into the bed. Driven by unbearable need, she wasn't even sure of how they got out of their clothes. But they were naked, lying together on the cool cotton sheets, when Joe paused.

He caught her wrist and firmly placed her hand on the pillow. "I want to go slow, Bailey. Let me look at you."

Breathing hard, she endured his intense scrutiny. Then, delicately, he leaned over her. His tongue flicked at the hard peaks of her breasts.

Groaning with intense pleasure, she flung her arm across his back. "Make love to me, Joe. Make love to me now."

"Not yet." He remembered what she'd said in the plane. She'd told him that making love was nowhere as good as flying a plane, and Joe intended to show her how wrong she could be.

If he could hold back, if he could wait until she was as aroused as he was, he could tease her to the brink of ecstasy. Only then would he complete their lovemaking.

But she moved so sinuously beneath his touch. He didn't know how long he could control himself.

She whispered, "Please, Joe. Make love to me. Now."

His arousal could no longer be contained. He needed her. Now. This moment. He separated her thighs. She was slick and hot. She felt like heaven. Transported, he thrust hard.

Her gasps encouraged him. Again and again, holding back until he couldn't wait another second. He exploded within her.

Then he held her, cradled her against him. Belatedly, all the important thoughts raced through his brain. He hadn't asked about birth control. He hadn't worn a condom. What if she turned up pregnant in a month? His heart stopped for a second as a deep realization spread through him. He would love to make babies with this woman. To have children.

He wanted to tell her, to declare this feeling that must be love. Gazing down into her rich, brown eyes, his heart was full. He felt as if he'd come to the end of a very long journey, and his destination, his goal, was Bailey.

Lazily, she smiled up at him. Her long legs rubbed against his. He could feel her relaxation.

"Don't fall asleep, Bailey."

"Why not?"

"I'm not done with you yet."

Startled, her eyes snapped open. "What do you mean?"

"This." He kissed her gently. The time wasn't right to declare his feelings, but he could show how he felt.

With far less urgency than the first time, he skillfully manipulated the tender buds at the tips of her high, firm breasts.

"Joe, what are you doing?"

"Making love to you again."

"Not necessary." She wriggled beneath his touch. "The first time was absolutely wonderful."

He kissed the hollow of her throat, tasted the sweet nectar of her lips. "Doesn't that feel good?"

"Oh, yes."

"You don't want me to stop, do you?"

"Oh, no."

Bailey felt positively decadent. Still awash in the ultimate pleasure of their lovemaking, her flesh was tender and moist. His delicate caresses trembled on her skin. Exquisite sensations raced through her. This was more physical pleasure than she could stand. "Maybe we shouldn't—"

"Yes. We should."

He directed her hand to feel the hardness of his arousal, and she shivered with anticipation. Again? So soon? She couldn't imagine what it would be like to build on the pleasure she'd already felt. Never before had she been with a man who was so concerned about her pleasure. Never before had she experienced the need that surged inside her, blanking her mind.

Her gaze feasted on his body—his broad shoulders and powerful chest, sprinkled with crisp, curling black hair. She loved the way his torso tapered. She adored the heaviness of his muscularity.

Tenderly, he prepared her for lovemaking, and when he again entered her, Bailey moaned with pleasure. Every thrust drove her higher. She was flying. Defying gravity, she soared to a realm beyond the bluest sky.

Together, they rode to the heights, and she heard herself crying out at the final thrust.

Slowly, magically, she floated back to earth, riding the air currents, subsiding into ecstasy.

BAILEY WAKENED EARLY. Through the uncurtained windows, she saw the morning lighten the cloudless skies. She propped herself on one elbow and gazed down at the sleeping man beside her. And she remembered. Last night had been more wonderful than anything she'd ever experienced.

Maybe she didn't really need to tell him about her fight with Kate in the cockpit. Maybe she could let that slide, and accept the pleasure he gave her. One little secret? It shouldn't make a difference.

She wanted to wake him and have him make love to her again. At the same time, his complete relaxation made her hesitate. He needed rest.

But if she stayed here in bed, she couldn't leave him alone. She'd want to tickle his ear and squeeze the hard muscles in his arms.

She crept from the bed. Her suitcase was all the way downstairs, so she took the liberty of peeking in the closet, looking for a robe. These were all men's things.

Still shivering and naked, she went into the next-door bedroom and turned on the overhead light. Mama Bear's room, she thought. The closet held a few women's shirts on hangers, a fancy dress in a dry-cleaner's plastic bag and a long terry-cloth robe, which Bailey slipped into.

This really was a lovely house. There were windows everywhere. She looked out and saw the Piper Tomahawk on the runway near the hangar. Who lived here?

When she found out, she'd have to send them a thank-you note and a dozen red roses.

On the top of the long dresser, there was a framed five-by-seven photograph of a woman who looked familiar. Bailey picked up the frame. A blond woman, her head thrown back, laughing. It must have been enlarged from a snapshot because she was unposed, wearing a casual halter top. With a shock, Bailey recognized Claude's wife.

She'd only met the woman once, but she'd seen her picture in his office dozens of times.

Was this Claude's cabin?

With growing apprehension, Bailey studied the picture. His wife was wearing a necklace. A tiny golden airplane with a diamond for the propeller. The same necklace that they had found in Kate's drawer.

She hurried back into the other bedroom. "Joe, wake up!"

He was startled. His blue eyes opened wide. Then he saw her and relaxed. "Morning, darlin'."

She thrust the photograph in front of him. "Look at this."

He winced and rubbed his eyelids. "Are you always like this in the morning?"

"Look!"

He glanced at the picture. "Nice. Who is she?"

"Claude's wife. Look at her necklace."

He stared at the picture, now fully awake. "I'll be damned."

"I found the photo in the other bedroom. This must be Claude's cabin. The necklace must have been what Kate was using to blackmail him. You were right all along, Joe. Claude must have been Kate's lover. Not Salton. Claude."

"Guess so," he said. "The necklace is too much of a coincidence."

Bailey hated the suspicions that ran through her mind. "Let's not jump to conclusions. Just because he was having an affair with Kate, it doesn't necessarily mean that..."

"The necklace," Joe said. "The fund-raiser."

"Oh, dear." She didn't want to believe that Claude had sabotaged his own plane, but he certainly had the expertise and the opportunity. "When he saw me wearing the necklace at the fund-raiser, he must have thought I was hinting about blackmail. He must have thought that Kate told me."

"And he called you in the middle of the night. The bastard!"

"This is his cabin," she said. "Why would he want us to stay here?"

"I can't think of any good reason," Joe said. "What time is it?"

"Almost eight."

"Let's get out of here."

They were dressed and downstairs when the cell phone rang, and Joe answered. "Greta," he said.

"Where are you two? We were expecting you last night."

"Must have gotten our signals crossed," he said. Claude had wanted them there, at his place.

"Well, I'm doing my stretches and getting warmed up. The race starts at nine and I've—"

"Greta, did you tell Claude about the cut brake line on the Cessna?"

She sounded huffy. "Of course not. I told the mechanics in the morning that it was frayed, they logged it and commented on the perfect repair job. Mac does good work.''

"Is he with you?'' Joe asked. "Put him on the phone.''

Mac Augustine's voice was typically gruff. "What have you done with my little girl?''

"Mac, I need to ask you about the repair you did on the Cessna. What did you do with the cut brake line?''

"I might be old, but I'm not senile. I took it with me so nobody would stumble over it by accident. The only ones who knew the brake line was cut were you, Kate, me and Greta.''

"And the guy who cut it.'' Claude. As a warning? As a reason to fire Bailey?

"What's going on?'' Mac demanded. "Put Bailey on the phone.''

She cleared her throat before speaking, not wanting to sound too tense or nervous. "Hi.''

"Where the hell are you?''

"Claude's cabin.'' She rattled off the coordinates from the map Claude had given her. "But we're leaving. Grandpa Mac, do you remember a pilot named Jimmy Cannon?''

"Yes.''

"Tell me about him. Quick.''

"An incredible stunt pilot. But he wasn't a full-time aviator. Jimmy got himself involved in some environmentalist group.'' He paused. "He died ten years ago. In a crash. I could never believe that such a good pilot was so dang careless.''

Maybe he wasn't, Bailey thought. Maybe Jimmy Cannon was the first time Claude arranged a sabotage. "We're taking off. We'll meet you in Aspen, Grandpa Mac.''

"What's going on, Bailey? Are you in trouble?"

"Not anymore." She forced herself to sound calm. "We'll see you later, Grandpa. I love you."

She disconnected the call and looked at Joe. "Let's get the hell out of here."

On the runway, she approached the Piper Tomahawk with some trepidation. Claude had sabotaged three planes before this. The Otter. The Cessna. And Jimmy Cannon's plane. And he'd arranged for them to be here. He'd even provided champagne to ensure they would be too wrapped up in each other to pay attention to what was happening outside the cabin.

"I'd better take a look at the engine," Bailey said.

To a less experienced eye, the innards of the plane wouldn't have looked as if they'd been tampered with. But Bailey had grown up at her grandpa's side. She felt along the hoses, discovering pinprick holes. Some of the electrical wires were crossed.

"We would have gotten off the ground," she said. "But the fuel pressure wouldn't have held. This is a powerhouse engine. If it didn't explode, it would have stalled on the climb we need to get over these peaks."

"Okay," Joe said. "We can hike out of here."

"Not a chance. I can fix this." She grinned at him. "Remember? I'm the one who's accustomed to flying any old machine, held together with duct tape and a prayer."

Joe opened the plane's belly and fetched the tool kit. "Go for it, Bailey. Much as it assaults my masculine pride, I bow to your superior knowledge."

"Thanks, Jet Man."

While she worked, he watched the heavens. Claude wouldn't have left the crash to chance. He'd arranged everything too carefully. He'd be here. And Joe was sure he'd be armed.

On his cell phone, he dialed the home number for Ted Grambling. The congressman himself answered.

"This is Joe Rivers." Taking a breath, hoping he was right, he said, "I know about Jimmy Cannon."

"Damn." Then Grambling recovered. "I don't know what you're talking about."

"You remember, Congressman. About ten years ago. An environmentalist group. There was a plane crash."

"I don't know anything about it. You can't prove that I do."

But he sounded guilty as hell. Joe pressed on. "That would have been just about the time you loaned Claude Whistler a lot of money to start his business, wouldn't it?"

The phone went dead.

Joe drew the conclusions that would end his investigation. "I think we've got our answer. Claude sabotaged his friend. Grambling paid him off. Kate must have found out about it, and Claude had to get rid of her, too. It was a bonus that Jillian Grambling was on the plane."

"I hate this," Bailey said.

"Old secrets never die. They fester and grow."

"Secrets?" She turned to him. Her wide brown eyes seemed frightened. "There's something I've got to tell you, Joe."

"Can it wait?"

"I can't hold it back any longer. After last night, I can't keep this secret. Even if it means I'm going to lose you."

"Lose me? Bailey, you won't lose me."

Panic chased through her. She had to tell him now. "Before the crash, Kate was crazy. She kept trying to fly the plane, but she was too sick to know what she was doing."

"I don't need to know any more about Kate."

"This isn't about Kate. It's about us. You and me. It's the reason I've been holding back, not letting myself get involved with you."

"Whatever it is, Bailey, it's all right." He reached for her, but she dodged away.

"Joe, let me finish." She forced herself to meet his gaze. "I couldn't let her fly the Otter, she was going to put us in a tailspin. But she wouldn't give up the controls. She wouldn't let me take over."

"I understand," he said.

"No, you can't understand this. I hit her. I punched Kate and knocked her unconscious before I landed the plane. That was why she couldn't leave the cockpit."

The distant whir of an approaching aircraft distracted her, and Bailey peered skyward. Only a small black dot against the blue. Her gaze dropped, and she searched Joe's face for forgiveness.

"I tried to rouse her," Bailey said. "But she was out. When I came back into the cabin, I should have told you. Right away, I should have told you. You could have rescued Kate instead of Ross O'Shea."

She stopped talking. All her words were gone, except for two. "I'm sorry."

"Poor Kate," he said. "She never had a chance."

The dot in the sky grew larger. A Piper Cub. Claude's private plane.

Bailey closed the cowling and refastened the snap screws that held the engine cover in place. "We've got to get out of here. I think those repairs will hold us to Aspen.''

They leapt into the cockpit seats. There was so much more to be said, but she couldn't talk about it now. She couldn't think about anything except getting away safely, surviving. Bailey took the pilot's side. Holding her breath and praying that her repairs were good, she fired up the engine on the Piper Tomahawk. No explosion.

"So far so good."

Out of habit, she stuck on her headset. Joe did the same.

The Piper Cub was making an approach on the runway.

"I can't let Claude land," she said. "He's probably armed, and I don't think he means to let us get out of here alive."

"Take off," Joe said. "Do it now."

She wheeled around. The Cub was coming in low, preparing to touch down at the end of the runway.

Bailey revved the powerful engine, holding with all her strength on the brake. Then she jammed the throttle forward to the firewall for a rapid ascent.

They were heading right toward the Cub. Head-on collision was imminent.

A hop, a bounce, and the Tomahawk was airborne, leapfrogging over the little Piper Cub and soaring into the sky.

"We made it!" Joe shouted. "Good work, Bailey."

But Claude wasn't one to give up easily. The Piper Cub swept up and tailed them.

Over the headset, she heard Claude's voice. "Figured it out, did you?"

Her rage was such that she could not reply.

"Doesn't matter," he said. "You'll never make it to Aspen."

"Like heck we won't," she said.

"Check your fuel gauge, Bailey."

Empty! They were riding on fumes.

Claude laughed. "What do you think, Joe? You're the investigator. They'll call it pilot error, won't they? Not enough fuel. Happens all the time."

"Better slow down," Joe cautioned her. "If you keep pouring on the coals, you're going to run dry."

"We can make it," Bailey said. "Aspen is only over a couple of ridges."

"Wrong," Claude said. "You won't make it. You've got to watch out for me."

The Piper Cub zipped up in front of them, and Bailey automatically executed a hard left, wasting fuel. The engine coughed.

"What are you doing?" she yelled into the headset. "You could have killed us all."

"That was the idea. I'm willing to play kamikaze. If you two get out of here alive, my life won't be worth much."

He was in front of them now, flying straight toward them, propeller to propeller. Bailey held firm. She couldn't waste fuel. At the last second, she performed an aileron roll, escaping the Piper Cub.

Bailey pulled off her headset so Claude couldn't hear and shouted to Joe, "I'm taking the Tomahawk back to the landing strip. We're not going to make it over the next rise."

"You're right," he yelled back. "We can't risk a crash landing."

"On the ground, we might have a chance."

Or else, she thought, Claude could shoot both of them and explode the Tomahawk with them aboard. Another chance for him to publicly grieve when laughing in private.

She banked around, heading back toward the cabin. Claude's cabin.

Over the headset, she heard Claude say, "Just where I want you. That's just where I want you both."

Bailey was almost set to make her approach when the engine cut out completely. She'd have to glide it down, hoping that her repairs held.

Over the headset, Claude said, "What the hell is that?"

Joe craned around in the copilot seat. "I don't believe it," he said. "The Spitfire."

Grandpa Mac was coming to their rescue.

Bailey touched down in the Tomahawk and braked to a stop. Both she and Joe leapt from the plane to watch as Grandpa Mac in his World War II Spitfire danced maneuvers around the Piper Cub. There was no direction Claude could turn without encountering the other plane. He was caught.

Foolishly, he tried a dive, swooping lower and lower.

"He's not going to make it," Bailey said.

She and Joe watched in horrified fascination. The engine on Claude's little plane wasn't powerful enough to come out of the maneuver. He stalled. Though he tried to pull up, the left wing tipped, slicing into the top of a tree.

A fiery crash exploded the serene mountain scenery, spewing rock and tree. Claude Whistler went down in flames.

"He's on the way," Joe said. "Straight to hell."

He draped his arm around her shoulder, and she clung to him.

Grandpa Mac in his Spitfire flew over the crash and dipped his wings. A salute to a downed pilot. Then he performed an inverted loop and a roll.

"I can't tell if he's happy or sad," Joe said.

"What about you?" she asked. "Happy or sad?"

"About Kate?"

She nodded. This was the moment she'd been dreading, the moment when she expected him to say goodbye. Might as well get it all over with at once, she thought. The end of the investigation. And the end of the relationship.

With all the feeling of her heart in her eyes, she looked up at him. "I should have told you sooner."

"Maybe you were right to wait. Earlier, I wasn't ready to listen."

"And now?"

"It hurts." His gaze trained skyward, watching the Spitfire. "Kate's death will always hurt. Don't you think I've cursed myself a thousand times for not going forward and checking on her? But she's gone."

He placed a tender kiss on her forehead. "I don't blame you, Bailey. You did what you had to do."

She couldn't quite believe what he was saying.

"We were lucky, Bailey. We're still here. You and me."

She faced the greatest risk she'd ever undertaken in her life. There was more danger in these words than in flying on empty. "I love you, Joe."

"That's a fortunate thing, Bailey. Because I love you, too."

He kissed her hard and passionately. The pressure of his body against hers incited arousal and complete happiness. She loved him, loved him more than anything.

He nuzzled her ear and whispered gently. "I want you. I want you to be with me forever."

"I can't think of anyplace else I'd rather be. Forever."

"Not in a cockpit?" He pulled back to look into her eyes.

She purred. "Not anymore. I finally found something I love better than flying."

SILHOUETTE

Intrigue™

COMING NEXT MONTH

SPENCER'S BRIDE Laura Gordon

The Spencer Brothers

Joanna Caldwell should have been Drew Spencer's bride, but she'd chosen another man. Now that man had gone missing and Joanna was receiving death threats. She had nowhere to turn except to Drew. Would he help her unravel the tangled threads of her life, after all she'd done to him?

TOUCH ME IN THE DARK Patricia Rosemoor

The McKenna Legacy

Chase Brody still made her pulse thrum, but all the evidence pointed to his being involved in Kate Farrell's old friend's death. Something—*or someone*—had set the deadly stampede in motion and Kate was going to find out what or who it had been!

EXTREME HEAT Joanna Wayne

Lawman

Ex-cop Cagan Hall was the kind of man Merissa Thomas should stay away from. But with a killer and the police hard on her heels, Cagan was her only protection. He would protect her from the others, but no one could protect her from him! What would he claim as his reward—if they survived?

THE TALL, DARK ALIBI Kelsey Roberts

Jonas Revell didn't know who Kendall Butler was or why she tempted him so much. He was already suspected of murder so he couldn't afford any gossip. If he made Kendall his wife, his secrets would be safe and there would be excellent fringe benefits!

COMING NEXT MONTH FROM

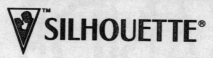 **SILHOUETTE**®

Sensation

A thrilling mix of passion, adventure and drama

WOMAN WITHOUT A NAME Emilie Richards
THE MARRYING KIND Beverly Bird
WANTED: MUM AND ME Kayla Daniels
TO SAVE HIS CHILD Margaret Watson

Special Edition

Satisfying romances packed with emotion

ALMOST TO THE ALTAR Neesa Hart
MISTAKEN BRIDE Brittany Young
MR FIX-IT Jo Ann Algermissen
THE LONE RANGER Sharon De Vita
LIVE-IN MUM Laurie Paige
MONTANA PASSION Jackie Merritt

Desire

Provocative, sensual love stories for the woman of today

THE COFFEEPOT INN Lass Small
BACHELOR MUM Jennifer Greene
THE LONELIEST COWBOY Pamela Macaluso
THE TENDER TRAP Beverly Barton
THE BRIDE WORE TIE-DYE Pamela Ingrahm
ON WINGS OF LOVE Ashley Summers

FOUR FREE
specially selected
Intrigue™ novels
PLUS a Mystery Gift
when you return this page...

Return this coupon and we'll send you 4 Silhouette Intrigue® novels and a mystery gift absolutely FREE! We'll even pay the postage and packing for you.

We're making you this offer to introduce you to the benefits of the Reader Service™– FREE home delivery of brand-new Silhouette novels, at least a month before they are available in the shops, FREE gifts and a monthly Newsletter packed with information, competitions, author pages and lots more...

Accepting these FREE books and gift places you under no obligation to buy, you may cancel at any time, even after receiving just your free shipment. Simply complete the coupon below and send it to:

THE READER SERVICE, FREEPOST, CROYDON, SURREY, CR9 3WZ.

EIRE READERS PLEASE SEND COUPON TO: P.O. BOX 4546, DUBLIN 24.

NO STAMP NEEDED

Yes, please send me 4 free Intrigue novels and a mystery gift. I understand that unless you hear from me, I will receive 4 superb new titles every month for just £2.40* each, postage and packing free. I am under no obligation to purchase any books and I may cancel or suspend my subscription at any time, but the free books and gift will be mine to keep in any case. (I am over 18 years of age)

I7XE

Ms/Mrs/Miss/Mr _____
BLOCK CAPS PLEASE

Address _____

_____

_____

_____ Postcode _____